meltdowns
and
moscato

Cover Art by Teshia Saunders

Book design by Ivica Jandrijević

Edited by Shannan Saunders

Published by Talk+Tell at http://talkplustell.com/

LIBRARY AND ARCHIVES CANADA CATALOGUING IN PUBLICATION
Title: Meltdowns and Moscato / Jaci Wheeler.
Names: Wheeler, Jaci - author.
Description: First Edition. 2020 ISBN 978-1-7770505-2-8
(hardcover) PDF/EBOOK 978-1-7770505-3-5

Distributed by Ingram Spark

meltdowns
and
moscato

By Jaci Wheeler

To my fellow warrior moms.
I see you.
You're not alone!

Contents

CHAPTER

This Could Be Water...
But It's Probably Not

Bang, bang! Taryn pries one eye open and looks at the clock, 2:03 a.m. *Lord above, just one more hour please,* she pleads silently.

Bang, bang, crash. It's always at the crash when she jumps out of bed. Most people would assume they were being robbed. Actually, being robbed would be preferred. They could take whatever they want as long as they leave Taryn to her slumber.

She runs out of her room and pauses in the hallway to see which room the noise is coming from. A crash to the left tells her it's Gavin, this time.

Taking off toward Gavin's room with her eyes still half shut, she of course trips over the freaking therapy dog sleeping in the hallway.

1

"For the love of all things good and holy, Tacoma! You are supposed to calm these kids down…what on earth did we buy you for?" As if the world revolves only around him, he flops over on his back, expecting a belly rub.

"You've got to be kidding me. Move it or lose it pal." Taryn nudges him out of her way, making it to Gavin's room just as a block is hurled directly where her head would have been, if Taryn hadn't ducked.

"Hey, little man. Someone woke up in a mood, huh?" She greets her son, then runs to the medicine cabinet to grab the essential oil used to help calm him.

Gavin comes tearing out of his room and jumps on the couch in the living room. Taryn quickly follows behind, making it to him just in time to get a foot to the face. She chuckles softly as she puts the calming oil on one foot and then the other. He loves the oil and since it seems to help, so does Taryn.

"What should we watch, buddy?" Taryn asks as Gavin leans over and bites her shoulder.

"*Beat Bugs* it is." Taryn decides. It looks like she's going to have to bust out the big guns tonight. Sometimes he just can't turn his brain off and he has too much energy.

On those nights, Taryn pretty much lets him run around in circles until he wears himself out. He wants *The Wiggles* while he, well, gets his wiggles out. The sad nights, those are the worst. Sometimes he wakes up crying for no reason at all. Taryn hates those nights. Nothing seems to soothe him. Taryn would rather take a physical night over the sad ones any day of the week. On the sad nights she puts on *Thomas The Train* and holds him while they both cry.

Tonight is a physical night, so its *Beat Bugs* to the rescue. As soon as it's on, she can feel him visibly relax. She rubs his feet from as far away as she can get while still in reach. Too close and he will swipe at her. He doesn't do it in anger, it's almost like breathing to him. He doesn't really realize it hurts, it's just his way of getting stimulation.

If he can get the stimulation he craves in a positive way, like rubbing his feet and back, or scratching and brushing his arms, it's better for everyone.

Most of the time it's just Gavin during the night, but sometimes he wakes his sister. Jessie is also on the spectrum, but she's able to communicate and comprehend a bit more than her brother. Taryn would never admit it, but some nights she secretly hopes he wakes Jessie, because then Taryn's husband gets up and helps. Sometimes it's just nice to know there's someone in the trenches, fighting the war with you.

Around 5:12 a.m., Gavin finally starts to settle as Taryn goes from rubbing his foot, slowly making her way up to his back. She treasures these moments, the ones where he lets her touch him.

It's about as close to a cuddle as she's allowed to get. Ever so slowly Taryn rubs up his body until she gets to his back, where she slowly leans down until she's laying right up against his back. Bringing him to her chest, she cradles him softly while she watches his eyes grow heavy.

Watching his sweet face finally relax, as his brow no longer hold so much worry, uncoils the knot in her stomach.

Sure, her life is hard... but whose isn't? Taryn would happily take all the hard moments for these few sweet ones. Maybe these moments are so perfect because they are so well earned. She looks down at her perfect little boy and can't imagine him any other way. For all his aggressive moments, Gavin is actually very tender hearted. He hates to see anyone hurt or in pain. Yes, the irony that her aggressive child hates to cause pain isn't lost on Taryn.

Her eyes grow heavy and she contemplates sneaking off the couch to grab a cup of coffee, for some quiet time before Jessie wakes, or if it's worth it to catch a few minutes of sleep. What the heck, quiet time is overrated anyway. Slowly, she runs her fingers through her son's mop of blond curls as her eyes start to flutter shut.

"Good morning, Jessie says hello."

Taryn chuckles as she forces her eyes open to see the little angelic face peering down at her. You can't let that sweet face fool you for a second though. Jessie is one hundred percent trouble. She's smiling so sweetly directly above Taryn's face, that Taryn smiles back... until she sees the light shining off of something in Jessie's hand, just as Taryn feels the slightest pull of her bangs. She jumps up just as Jessie makes a second swipe at her mom's hair with the scissors.

"Dammit, Jessie!" Taryn yells as she grasps at the now short lock in her hand.

"Jessie make mommy beautiful princess."

"All the princesses have long hair Jessie." Taryn's first mistake is trying to negotiate with a terrorist.

"Well, technically Rapunzel gets her hair chopped off in the end." Taryn's second mistake was marrying a man who doesn't recognize when there's murder in her eyes. Although, once shot in his direction, Kevin quickly

4

grabs his daughter's hand and ushers her into the kitchen. Jessie claps and cheers the entire way.

"I make mommy Rapunzel, beautiful princess."

Taryn groans and lays back down on the couch, clutching a curly red lock in her hand. *She couldn't have cut the back?* Taryn wonders as she sighs, then chuckles. She can't help it. Sometimes if you don't laugh, you will cry, and Lord knows that tears in this house won't get you anywhere but dehydrated and puffy.

Taryn's manic laughter wakes Gavin who sends a quick jab to his mom's ribs.

"Sorry baby, but getting woken in laughter is better than with scissors."

Apparently, he doesn't agree because he huffs and flips over. Taryn tries to ease out from under him slowly. Once successful, she makes her way to the kitchen, making sure to bypass the mirror in the hall and walking directly to the coffeepot. She sees not only has it been made, but a steaming cup is ready and waiting for her.

Taryn takes a deep drink and smiles when she tastes the hazelnut creamer. Kevin knows he's in trouble. Taryn loves hazelnut but Kevin hates it, so she buys the vanilla one. However, she knows he has a secret sMia of her favorite somewhere. Every now and then, mostly when he's in trouble, he makes her a cup with it.

"Hard night, huh?"

Taryn's response is just a bunch of noises in between gulps.

"What time did he wake?"

"Two. He went down just after five." She finally finds her words after a few gulps of caffeine.

5

"Sorry doll."

Taryn holds her mug up in a cheers, offering a sleepy smile. "You're forgiven. However, that evil daughter of yours…"

"I thought we were going with spirited?" Kevin chuckles. They both love that girl more than life itself. Taryn probably wouldn't admit it out loud, but she loves how full of vinegar and fire Jessie is. However, every single gray hair on both of their heads has the name Jessica written all over them.

"Shouldn't higher functioning mean easier?" Taryn asks. Kevin just chuckles at her silly question as he draws her into his strong arms. Taryn is a tall woman, coming in at around five-foot-nine, but he's still almost a head taller than her. Even when life seems hard, he always makes it feel just a little easier.

"No, it just means she's able to figure out a way to get out of trouble faster," Kevin answers as he holds her tight.

"I blame you, the intelligence obviously comes from you."

Kevin has always been smart. He was the valedictorian in high school, and graduated top of his class with double majors, a semester early in college, going on to become a brilliant architect.

He kisses his wife's forehead and squeezes her one last time. "I'm off to go be brilliant then. It's Wednesday night, so I'll pick up dinner on my way home so you can get to group on time."

Taryn has to hold back her groan at the thought of having to go to the support group. "Thanks love. You taking the fairy godmother with you? I'm going to let Gav sleep a little more and then I'll take him late."

"Fairy godmother, huh? I see what you did there, Rapunzel. Sure, I'll grab her." He turns and grabs his briefcase before swinging Jessie into his arms.

"Come on princess maker, let's grab your backpack and hit the road. Kiss momma and say bye to Tacoma."

Jessie kisses the dog instead of her mother and waves her little fingers in Taryn's direction.

"Buh bye momma. Wuv you." No matter what, she just can't stay mad at that precious face. Jessie looks like a sweet little cherub, with her blonde curls and big blue eyes. Taryn is pretty sure it's why God gave Jessie that sweet face, He knew she'd need it.

"Bye baby, I love you, too. Be good today and make good choices please." All Taryn gets is a smirk in return. She makes a mental note to e-mail Jessie's teacher a warning. I didn't think she would stress me out this much until high school...and she's only in third grade.

Taryn dreads Wednesdays. To be honest, she and Kevin aren't support group people. They are the type who sit back and mock the support group people. So how'd they find themselves stuck with this bunch? Their kids. Obviously they would do anything for them, and since both lack essential social skills, especially Gavin, Kevin and Taryn took the school counselor's advice and joined a local autism support group. The counselor thought it'd be a great way for the kids to interact with their peers, and for Taryn and Kevin to be around people *who get it*.

It totally makes sense in theory. Jessie actually really likes it, which is the only reason Taryn continues to go. Gavin would always meltdown in the corner, so Kevin stays at home with him, the lucky SOB.

In all those depressing autism help books Taryn read, they all say how important it is to find a good support network, so here she is. The only problem is her support network is a bunch of wackos.

People think it's hard to deal with kids on the spectrum, but they have no clue that the real crazy lies within the parents. Taryn should know. She's not sure if it's the lack of sleep, or the fact that they have to figure out riddles and types of screams all day for communication, but autism parents are their own brand of crazy.

Taryn walks in and heads straight for the food table, where she sets down the gluten, dairy free cupcakes she spent two hours making.

"Well, hi there, Taryn."

Taryn takes a deep internal breath and places the most sincere smile she can manage on her face as she turns to greet the most annoying woman alive. "Tiffany, hi."

"Are those gluten free? You know Adam only eats gluten free."

"Yes Tiff, I know that, and they most certainly are gluten free."

"And dairy free? You know it makes zero sense to give up gluten and not dairy, since they both wreak havoc on the brain."

"Heaven forbid we wreak any havoc, Tiff. Yes, they are dairy free as well."

"And is that red dye?" Tiffany looks at the frosting that is clearly red and gives Taryn a smug look.

"Nope, it's sure not."

"You know red dye sends half these kids into a tailspin."

"Good thing it's not red dye then."

"Then what makes them red if it isn't dye?"

"Uh, beets."

"Beets?" Tiffany eyes Taryn skeptically, so Taryn channels Jessie, giving Tiffany her most innocent smile.

"Yup, you juice them and use the juice as dye. Natural and super healthy, just like eating a salad." The woman gives Taryn one last skeptical look and turns to greet the next sucker, so Taryn takes this as her chance to slip past her.

"Beet juice, huh?" Liz chuckles as she comes up from behind to stand next to Taryn.

"It totally could be."

"Yeah, if you weren't you," Liz chuckles, taking a sip of her drink as Taryn shoots her a look.

"Like you are any better."

Liz throws her hand up in the air in mock surrender. "We are one and the same sister. The only way I can get through these meetings is with my handy-dandy sippy cup." Liz raises said cup in salute.

"What's in there?" Taryn wonders out loud, totally jealous she hadn't thought to bring something to take the edge off these horrible meetings.

"This could be water, but since I have two autistic children… it's probably not," Liz says with a big toothy grin, as she lifts her cup to take another large sip.

Liz and Taryn are both cut from the same cloth. In fact, she's one of the only mothers here that Taryn hasn't felt judgment from. It started on the first day they walked in the doors over two years ago.

Kevin had Gavin swung over his shoulder while he screamed and bit him.

"That's Kevin holding our son Gavin, and I'm Taryn," she introduced.

"And who is this adorable little girl?" Tiffany asked, kneeling in front of Jessie.

"What's your name, princess?"

"My name, dammit Jessie."

Taryn wanted to die right then and there. Everyone looked taken back, and Tiffany looked like she swallowed her tongue. You could hear a pin drop and Taryn was so red she was sure she looked like a tomato. All of a sudden, someone burst out laughing. She laughed so hard she started snorting. When she finally got herself under control, she motioned the family over.

"Come on over here hun, I don't bite. The name is Liz, and my little one over there is Mason. He doesn't say much, but I'm sure he'd love a friend, Jessie." That's all Jessie needed to take off toward the toy area.

"I could just die." Taryn admitted.

"That one's a troublemaker, huh?" Liz asked pointing to where Jessie ran off.

"Now that I think about it, the last few weeks every time we've said her name… she might have been causing trouble. Oh Lord, I hope she doesn't tell everyone that's her name!" Taryn dropped her face in her hands and groaned.

"Don't sweat it hon. I have an older son, Marcus who is an Aspie. He told some lady at the mall the other day that she wouldn't be so fat if she ate only one corn dog and not four," Liz shared, making Taryn instantly feel a connection to her.

From then on, they were best friends. Liz is the only reason Taryn was able to come back to the group.

That's the beauty of autism, each person is different. So even though there are twenty people in a room, all of their kids might as well be on different planets.

Each parent is an expert on their own kid and therefore thinks they are an expert on how to handle everyone else's. Those are the kind of parents Taryn hates the most, the expert parents. They are right up there with the Pinterest moms. You know the ones; their kids always look amazing, without a hair out of place, they bring the cutesy themed snacks and the fabulous teacher gifts for every holiday.

Hell, half the time Jessie's hair is in a bun because it's hiding about five knots, and Taryn is lucky if she can get her kids to not strip down buck naked in public. Taryn is what she likes to call, the flying by the seat of her pants, kind of mom.

Anyway, support groups are really for the Pinterest and expert types of parents. Those flying by the seat of their pants type are the kind that sit in the back and have to sneak in the *mommy juice,* just to be able to stomach the others.

Taryn is now thinking about having cups made that say, *this could be water, but I have autistic kids, so it's probably not.* She could sell them and make a killing. She's been so lost in thought, that she doesn't know what's happening. Oh, wait another fight over who's kid is harder... yay.

"I'm just saying, you have no clue how hard it is to have a low functioning child. I wish my Jeremy could talk, but I never know what he wants or needs, it's so horrible. It's so much easier that yours can tell you those things."

Oh Lord, and it starts. The debate between *frizzy hair* and *wants to die*. At least that's what Liz and Taryn dubbed them a while back. *Frizzy hair's* son is a high functioning kid with Asperger's, which comes with its own set of challenges. *Mrs. wants to die* doesn't understand this fact, and they get into a fight about it at almost every single meeting.

"How dare you Lindsey!"

Oh, *wants to die's* real name is Lindsey, Taryn figures out once she starts listening.

"You have no idea the kind of struggle I deal with on a daily basis. At least people look at Jeremy and can tell he has special needs. At least you don't have to constantly hear every day how he was picked on and called names. Because he looks so-called *normal* that people just think he's weird because he spouts off facts when he's nervous, or has to walk the same path and sit in the same chair every day. We might not have the same struggles, but we all struggle just the same!" *Frizzy hair* ends her rant and then bursts into tears and runs to the bathroom.

"She has no clue how much I would wish for that life. Every time my son starts screaming and I can't help him or calm him down, I just want to die!"

"Now, now. Let's calm down for a minute. This is a safe place everyone." Maya, the leader of the group, tries to bring everyone back from the edge.

"Autism is all about perspective. You can have five moms with kids on the spectrum, and they all feel and view it differently," Maya adds.

"It's true, our life is like one big *Lost* episode. I'm on an island, you're in a government experiment, she's dead and in purgatory," Liz pipes up.

"Nope, that's me. My life is for sure purgatory," someone else shouts out, causing a round of laughter.

"That's a really good point, even though *Lost* ruined me forever." Rarely does Taryn speak up in group, but *Lost* is a topic she can get behind.

"You didn't like it?" Liz asks with a shocked look on her face.

"Of course, I liked it. But now, every time I get on a plane, I spend my entire flight judging each and every passenger. If we were to crash and land on a deserted island who will be most helpful? Who do we let get eaten first? I go through each and every person, and by the time I land I'm so exhausted and burnt out. Plus, it's all for nothing; we didn't crash, so that man with the survival training that just screams military doesn't even matter now. And that's when you know you've hit an all-time low, when you are disappointed that you didn't crash and land on a deserted island." Taryn finishes by throwing her hands up in the air.

"Freaking *Lost!*"

"Cheers to that." Liz raises her drink and Taryn mock cheers her with her empty hand.

"I swear you guys, this is an autism support group for God's sake, not an ADD group. You totally missed the point!" Tiffany huffs and brings everyone back to topic. But Liz and Taryn are already off in their own worlds.

13

"Hey," Taryn whispers to Liz.

"What?"

"That's what we need."

"An ADD support group?"

"No, a group where we can just sit around and talk about whatever we want."

"And drink wine out in the open?" Liz asks while loudly slurping the last of her wine in her sippy cup.

"As long as it's sweet, yes," Taryn whispers back.

"Well, sign me up then."

Wine & Whine, Then Beer & Bare it

"Well, what do you think?" Taryn asks her husband, as he gives her a blank, unblinking stare.

"You want to start a support group? But you hate support groups."

"Yeah, I hate regular support groups. But this is going to be a real support group. Not where people sit around and attack each other or bore people with their problems. But one where you can be honest and talk about whatever you want."

"And how can you guarantee it won't turn into the other kind?" Kevin asks skeptically.

"Because, we will have alcohol and hugs," Taryn replies with a wide grin.

"What?"

"It's going to be a safe place where we can relax, have a glass of wine and just listen to each other. It's brilliant!"

"And where are the dads going to be?"

"Watching the kids with Emily?" She asks sheepishly.

"Think again."

"Um, having your own group?" She questions, confused about what answer he is looking for.

"I can just see it now. The women wine and whine, while the men beer and bare it."

"Hey, that's pretty catchy. Are you sure you are an engineer? You might have missed your calling in advertising."

"Taryn, are you serious about this?"

"I mean, I haven't gotten it all ironed out yet, but I need this Kev. I never get to talk to adults, let alone other moms who actually get it. We have a heavy load, what better way to unwind than with a glass of wine, and someone who gets why we might just need to hide in the basement for an hour."

Taryn knows he's going to cave. He always does, but especially if he thinks she needs it. And because her husband knows her better than anyone else, he knows she really does need this.

"Okay, but no men's group. I'll watch our kids and Liz's once a week for two hours. But if any more people start to come, then you have to talk to the nanny about helping out." She throws herself at him, wrapping herself around him in a full body hug.

"Thank you, thank you, thank you babe. I love you so much."

"Yeah, I know. I mean it Tar, I can't handle a ton of kids every week after work. You'll have to figure out how to pay extra hours for Emily or someone else if she can't do it."

"That's easy, we can charge dues for the sitter and wine. It'll be amazing!"

Liz eyes the clock for the third time in the last fifteen minutes. The hours from four to six p.m. are always the longest for her. The boys are getting restless and she's trying to make dinner while keeping an eye on them, the dinner, and her sanity. By the time five o'clock rolls around, Liz is totally exhausted and ready to call it a night.

Liz honestly has no clue how Taryn does it, because her kids don't even sleep. Liz's boys might wake up early, but they are great sleepers, thank God. She drains the noodles in the sink and then opens the oven and slides the garlic bread in, just as the front door opens.

"Hey love, I'm in the kitchen." Liz yells out as she shuts the oven door and makes her way to the front of the house to greet her husband, Tom.

"How was your day?"

"Oh, you know, different day, same problems." Tom is the foreman for a pretty big construction company, and most days he says he's just a glorified babysitter. Liz knows his job is hard and exhausting so she tries to make home as easy as she can for him.

"How about you?" He asks as he takes off his jacket and places his wallet and keys on the table by the door. Liz takes a moment to look over his big frame. He's built like a Viking, but working on constructions sites can be dangerous. He's come home banged up a time or two. Seeing that he isn't worse for wear, she smiles and answer his question.

"Yeah, a few meltdowns at school and then some head banging at home. Luckily, I've finally got Mase calm now. Marcus has a test tomorrow, so he's been in his room freaking out over it, of course."

"That kid is probably smarter than the teacher," Tom says with a chuckle and Liz laughs because he isn't wrong.

Marcus is afraid of failure, and for a test on only one chapter he feels like he needs to memorize every fact ever written about the subject.

Tom kisses his wife's forehead before heading to the back room to shower before dinner. She makes her way back to the kitchen, in time to pull the bread out of the oven and turn the sauce to simmer.

She walks to the table with a stack of plates and silverware in her hand. Just as she places the last fork on the table, Liz hears a loud wail coming from the living room. Taking off at a sprint toward the sound, she slams her hip on the edge of the counter in her hurry to get there.

"Son of a monkey's uncle." She fake curses, limping into the living room where she finds Mason in a full-blown meltdown. He's wailing and hitting himself repeatedly in the head as he rocks back and forth. Her husband has the remote in his hand, the baseball game on the television with a frustrated look in his eyes.

"Knock it off, Mase, I mean it." Tom admonishes him and then throws a look of annoyance to his wife.

"Liz, get him to stop, please. My head is splitting, I've had a hard day and I just want to relax for ten damn minutes before dinner. Is that too much to ask?"

Liz wants to say yes, yes it is too much to ask. When does she ever get ten minutes to herself after a long day or have someone to cook her dinner? Never, that's when. But the last thing that Mason needs right now is for them to start fighting. So she takes her son into her arms and hugs him, gently whispering soothing words into his ear. Mason keeps pointing at the television and wailing.

"Tom, he was in the middle of a show. He doesn't understand why you just turned it off. You know you have to give him a five-minute warning to prepare him for any transition. Dinner is ready anyway, let's just all come sit down and eat." Tom glares at his wife but turns off the television and storms into the kitchen.

"Come on Mase, Momma made your favorite for dinner. Want some spaghetti?" Liz asks in a soothing tone. Luckily, it's his favorite meal and he calms down upon hearing the word. She brings him a plate in the living room. Not wanting to start another fight, Liz turns on some music and not the television. She then stops in to bring a plate to Marcus in his room, so she can have some much needed adult time with her husband.

Liz barely sits down with her own plate of food, when Tom gives her a look of disapproval. "You spoil the boy, Liz."

"It's been a long day, and I just want to have a peaceful dinner, that's all."

"Everyone bows down to what Mason wants, and that's not how the real world works and you know it."

"No, the real world is cruel and unkind and Mason knows that more than anyone. He gets teased on a daily basis, he is in meltdown mode practically from the time he wakes until he gets home because the world doesn't bow down to the way he wants. I want his house to be a haven for him, and if you see that as spoiling, then I'm sorry."

"And what about me? What about my haven? I work hard too Liz, and I think I earn the right to relax after work for a few minutes in my own home."

"Of course you do. I'm not asking you not to, I'm just asking that you give him a five-minute warning before you do."

Tom stands abruptly and takes his untouched plate to the sink.

"I've lost my appetite. I'm going to go catch the end of the game."

With that he turns and walks right back out the door he entered less than thirty minutes prior, while his wife falls apart over her plate of spaghetti.

Liz pulls herself together and gets the boys to bed, pouring herself an *it's been a bad day* glass of wine, which is basically just wine up to the rim and calls Taryn.

"Hey, what's up?" Taryn answers, as chipper as ever.

"Is now a bad time?"

"Nope, I just put one kid in the bath and one in the shower. Everything okay?" Taryn asks, picking up the melancholy in her friend's voice.

"It's kind of been a bad night."

"Okay, give me a sec to get Kevin to take over while I hide in the closet."

Liz laughs because she knows Taryn's not kidding.

She's hidden in some pretty weird places herself, trying to find a moment of privacy. She hears a door shut and then Taryn's back on the phone.

"What's up, chica?"

Liz relays the events of the night, having to stop a few times to wipe her nose and compose herself. Taryn listens quietly until Liz finally finishes and then she sighs faintly.

"Okay what do you need from me? Pity party, voice of reason, or ass kicker?" Taryn asks. Liz can't help but chuckle, this is exactly why she called her.

Liz's mother would tell her to be patient and more understanding. Her sister would tell her that Tom is an asshole and that Liz should leave him. Neither of which Liz needs at the moment. Taryn has always asked what she needs before she offers up any advice.

"How about all of the above?"

"Well, first then, that really sucks. You work just as hard every day and deserve a partner who can under-stand and support you."

"I agree." Liz feels validated, even though she knows the voice of reason is about to follow.

"But?" Liz asks knowing there is a follow up, since she did ask for all three, after all.

"But, like it or not, you understand the boys and their needs better than Tom, because you are with them more. That doesn't make the situation any less sucky for you, but it's the reality of it. He's a hard worker, and you know he loves you and those boys more than life itself. Maybe him leaving was so that he didn't take those frustrations out on you."

"Do you agree with him?" Liz holds her breath, not really wanting to know the answer.

"No, I don't. But I do understand it. Men are fixers, where women tend to be nurturers. He just wants to be able to fix the situation, and with autism there is no quick fix. Just re-learning how to handle each situation as it comes. In order to make it work as a couple, I think you both need to try and see it from the other person's perspective. Wait until you are no longer upset and then let him know how you are feeling."

"That's good advice I guess. I'm just still so mad."

"That's because he was being a basta... uh, bullfrog. Hi honey, why aren't you in your pjs? Go tell daddy to brush your teeth and I'll be right there." Liz chuckles at Taryn's quick redirection.

"Yes, he certainly was a bullfrog. So now what do I do?"

"Well, the way I see it, there's only two ways to handle frogs."

"And what might those be?" Liz inquires.

"Either hire an exterminator or kiss it and see if it turns into a prince."

Liz can't stop the laughter that explodes from deep in her chest, as she quickly looks around to make sure that she didn't wake the boys.

"Since an exterminator costs too much, I'm guessing the only thing left to do is kiss, huh?"

"It couldn't hurt. Okay love, sorry to run, but I gotta do bedtime."

"Oh, no worries, thank you so much for talking me off the ledge. Hopefully, the kids sleep for you tonight."

"Anytime, that's what friends are for. And from your mouth to God's ear. Goodnight."

Target, the Happiest Place on Earth

While Liz and Taryn are out for coffee, they try to iron out all the logistics of their new support group. Right now, all they have is wine and whining in Taryn's bonus room.

"So should we have food?" Liz asks while looking down at the very short list of ideas they have so far.

"And risk angering the Allergy Gods? No way! Wine is perfect for everyone. It's gluten free, dairy free and even red dye free if it's Moscato."

"I'm pretty sure red wine is naturally red, Taryn."

"You are missing the point entirely. Our group is going to be laid back and chill. Eat at home and come ready to drink and dump."

Liz scrunches up her nose and gives Taryn her, *what the hell are you talking about,* look.

"I mean *emotionally* dump. Kevin is so much better at this than I am," Taryn sighs, resting her chin on her propped up hand.

"Works for me." Liz frantically writes everything down. That's one of the endearing things about Liz, she tries to be one of the slackers, but it's just not in her.

"Okay, so how do you want to handle the childcare?" Liz asks, all business.

"Since we will be in your basement, that leaves the backyard free, and the living room with the television when it's too cold outside. All we need now is someone to watch all our crazy kids."

"Obviously it can't just be our husbands, not if we want to avoid being part of the dreaded eighty percent autism parent divorce rate," Taryn remarks, and they both shudder.

"I can talk to our nanny, Emily. She only works for us part time, but with extra incentive she might be willing to take on the other kiddos just once a week," Taryn says as she sends a quick text to Emily while it's on her mind.

"Oh, that's a great idea," Liz remarks, as she writes Emily's name with a question mark next to it under childcare.

"Are we going to allow siblings?" Liz brings up since they are on the topic of kids.

"Oh, I didn't think of that. As much as I would love for siblings to come, especially since it's so good for our kiddos to be around typically developing kids, I just don't think Emily and Kevin could handle any more kids," Taryn

24

says with a nervous look, knowing some moms would be offended if they are told to leave some of their kids at home.

"I think that's totally understandable. Maybe we can do an outing or BBQ or something once every few months so the siblings and everyone can participate," Liz offers in solution.

"That's a great idea."

"So, what day should we have it?" Taryn asks mischievously.

"You aren't thinking about keeping it on Wednesdays, are you?" Liz asks with mock shock, but she can't hide the twinkle in her eye at the idea.

"I mean, it's already in our weekly schedule. Can you imagine having to make our kids changed to a different day?" They both grimace at the thought. Kids anywhere on the spectrum tend to hate change of any kind. Taryn's kids don't understand any kind of change, and even though Liz's kids are higher functioning, they still hate when change is made. It takes months for them to adapt to the simplest changes.

"Good point. Okay, Wednesday nights it is then," Liz says, writing the day down in her notebook.

"Perfect. What's the next item on your handy little list?" Taryn asks, pointing to where Liz is frantically writing.

"Hmm, people. Where are we going to find all the crazy cool moms, and not just the crazy ones?"

"That's a tough one. Do you know of any?"

"I don't really talk to any of the parents from my kids' schools since they ride the bus," Liz says trying to wrack her brain of any other moms she might know with kids on the spectrum.

"Same here. Hmm. Oh, I've got it. Target!" Taryn yells in excitement.

"What?" Liz asks, keeping her voice down since Taryn already caused a scene with her excitement.

"What is the one store you do all of your shopping at?" Taryn asks with a smirk. "Clothes, food, video games… Target has them all. Name one mom with kids on the spectrum who doesn't shop at Target. It's literally our happiest place on earth." She had Liz there, and Taryn knows it.

"So we are just supposed to stalk moms at Target?" Liz doesn't bother keeping the skepticism out of her voice, or off her face.

"Don't look at me like I'm a creeper, Liz."

"Then don't act like one, Taryn."

"You know it's a brilliant plan. For the next few weeks I say we talk Kev into watching the kids and we go shopping."

At the idea of a kidless shopping trip, Liz's eyes light up and she laughs. "Oh, my God, I think you might be a genius."

Oh, my God, Taryn is an idiot. Liz wonders why she lets Taryn talk her into these things. They've had Target security called on them three times this week, and Liz's husband is moments away from cutting up her Target card.

"I think that could be one over there." Taryn perks up.

"Over where?"

"Between the Disney dolls and the Troll Lego."

"I'm pretty sure that's just a kid who needs a nap, Taryn," Liz replies, not bothering to hide her eye roll.

"How will we know unless we ask?" Taryn asks, throwing her hands up in frustration.

"What are you going to say? *Excuse me ma'am, I noticed your child throwing a fit. Is she having an autistic meltdown, or is she just a brat?* Yeah, that'll go over real well. Forget Target security, they are gonna call the boys in blue on your ass."

"Okay negative nelly, what do you suggest then? We've come every day this week, and nothing."

"Maybe we should go back to the drawing boar... ooh, ooh, ooh... noise canceling headphones, three o'clock," Liz half shouts, half whispers as Taryn turns to her nine o'clock. Liz has to physically turn Taryn's head to three.

"See, right there. The Gabrielle Union look alike."

Taryn squints her eyes to see better. "She's way too put together for an autism mom. She looks like a runway model."

"Wow, thanks Taryn. What does that say about us? Never mind, don't answer that. Look, that's a chewy."

"Jackpot! Now you go talk to her." Taryn starts shooing Liz with her hand in the woman's direction.

"Me? Why me? This is your stupid idea, you do it."

"Because you are better at peopling... and you have a trusting face," Taryn points out.

"That's not even a thing," Liz comes back.

"Which one?"

"Both!"

"They so are, and while we are standing here arguing, she's getting away." Taryn points as the woman rounds the corner, and Liz figures it's now or never. She prays she won't sound like a rambling idiot. Or that Taryn will get hit by that old lady with the cart. Really she'd take either.

They speed walk like its double coupon day, trying to catch up with this poor unsuspecting woman and her kid. Just as they round the corner, they see an old lady approach the woman and her kid.

"He's a bit old for a pacifier isn't he? It's not good for their teeth, you know." The rude old woman points out. The mom just smiles but takes a step in front of the cart, partly shielding her son.

"Yes, he is, but that isn't a pacifier, it's a chewy."

"No difference, still bad for a kid that age." The old woman is clearly looking down her nose at the mom. Taryn practically growls and Liz puts a hand on her arm, telling her to wait. There's an intelligence and wit in this mom's eyes, Liz can tell she can handle herself.

"Actually, there is a big difference. A pacifier is to keep babies from crying. A chewy is to keep kids with sensory issues from biting strangers in the store. But you are right, maybe we should take it away and take our chances. You're not a bleeder, are you?"

Taryn snorts out a laugh at the woman's comeback, and Liz chuckles under her breath.

The little boy starts screeching, just as the old woman makes her exit, scowling in retreat. Taryn pulls Liz in the mom's direction just as the boy throws his chewy, smacking Taryn right in the eye.

Liz does a mental happy dance. That's way better than the old lady hitting her with the cart.

Liz picks the chewy up off the floor, as Taryn rubs her eye.

"Oops, can't drop this," Liz says, as she pulls a disinfectant wipe from her purse and cleans the chewy off, before handing it back to the little boy.

"I'm so sorry about that. Thank you so much though for cleaning it off, that's so thoughtful of you."

"Oh, no worries, I have two kids on the spectrum and with the amount of things that go into their mouths, I always keep them handy."

"You have kids on the spectrum? Ashton is as well." She points to the little boy who is about five or six years old.

"Really? Taryn, did you hear that? Another autism mom, what a coincidence."

"Hi, I'm Taryn, this is Liz. I have two kiddos on the spectrum too, Jessie is eight and Gavin is nine. It's so nice to meet you."

"I'm Mia. It's nice to meet you too. Ashton is six, and I'm so sorry about your eye. It's been a rough trip."

Taryn waves her hand in the air, like it's no big deal.

"It's fine, I have a spare. We saw that woman, what a jerk. You sure put her in her place though." Liz discreetly elbows her in the rib to stay on topic and not be so weird. Picking up on her nonverbal hint, Taryn finally starts acting normal.

"So, I know this is totally random, but Liz and I were just talking about this new support group we are starting for autism moms."

At the mention of support groups Mia takes a step back, almost knocking into the Honey Nut Cheerios. The stigma is real.

"Not the usual type of support group." Taryn jumps in. "Mostly it's just getting together so the kids can play, while the moms drink wine in the basement." Jesus, Liz wonders why she even lets Taryn talk.

"The basement?" The poor stranger is one step away from crawling into a box of Lucky Charms, so Liz decides to step in.

"We've had some issues with the traditional support group settings, and we thought of doing something a little more chill so the kids can socialize, while the moms have a few hours to just unwind and have a glass of wine or two. It's in Taryn's bonus room, I'd hardly call it a basement, this is California after all."

"Oh, well, that actually sounds refreshing."

"It's completely low key, and very small. Here is my phone number, think it over and let me know if you are interested." Liz gives Mia her million watt, you can trust me smile, as she hands her a paper with Liz's number. Mia smiles and tells Liz she will think about it as she walks away with her child.

"See, I told you that you were a better peopler than I am," Taryn chides.

"That's still not a thing, but next time you want to seem less creepy, maybe don't mention the basement."

"What? It's not like I said next to the freezer where we store the dead bodies," Taryn says as she dramatically rolls her eyes.

"That was kind of implied."

And Then There Were Four

The ladies totally lucked out when not only Mia showed up, but she also brought her friend, Corina. Corina has four kids, three are her adopted niece and nephews and her six-year-old son, who is on the spectrum, like Ashton.

Taryn has never been the type to care what people think of her. Even before her kids, she's always been the type who marches to the beat of her own drum. But being judged for being weird is very different from being judged for being a bad parent. You develop very thick skin when people are constantly judging you on the way you parent. But for some unknown reason, she really wants these ladies to like her.

"Hello ladies, welcome to my home. Our kids are already playing in the backyard with Emily, the nanny. Feel free to take them back and stay until they are comfortable, then we can sneak out and have some adult time."

"Oh, that sounds amazing!" Corina is all smiles, and one of the warmest people Taryn has ever met.

"This is so nice of you to open your home like this." Mia seems a little more at ease this time. Then again, they aren't stalking her in the middle of a Target either.

"Ashton, why don't you take Max outside and play?" He doesn't acknowledge his mom, but he grabs the shy little boy's hand and takes him outside, where Max instantly pulls away and goes off to the side yard to jump on the trampoline.

The moms all stand at the window and watch as the kids play.

"It's so funny when a group of autistic kids get together to play." Liz points out exactly what Taryn was thinking.

"It's like their own little antisocial support group," Corina adds.

Jessie is off playing with Tacoma on the side yard, Gavin is hiding in his treehouse, while Marcus reads a book on the hammock.

"Max and Mason are kinda playing together." Liz points to the boys on the swings.

"They are in two separate swings ignoring each other Liz," Taryn laughs.

"Yes, but they are next to each other and nobody has been bitten, pinched or spit on. It's a total win," Liz points out, and nobody argues because that is quite the feat.

"How old are your boys, Liz?" Mia asks.

"Mason just turned ten, and Marcus is already fourteen."

Ashton is running circles in the backyard, and Taryn keeps envisioning him falling in one of Jessie's blasted holes and breaking an ankle. When she can't take it anymore, she opens the door and yells out to him.

"Be careful around the holes, Ashton. I don't want you to fall or hurt yourself sweetie."

"Jessie dug them again? Didn't Kev just fill them all in?" Liz asks, knowing full well he did.

"Yup, he sure did, less than two days ago," Taryn says shaking her head at her daughter's antics.

"Is Jessie your dog?" Mia asks, causing both Liz and Taryn burst into a fit of laughter.

"No, Jessie is my daughter. She taught her therapy dog, Tacoma, how to dig."

"And chase squirrels," Liz adds.

"Yup. We paid $27,000 for a trained therapy dog, and my daughter broke him in a record amount of time."

The other ladies bite their lips, fighting smiles.

"It's okay to laugh, I do. It's either that, or cry," Taryn points out.

"I mean, it's kinda cute." Corina smiles as she watches Jessie point out squirrels for Tacoma to bark at.

"Yesterday I told her that if she and Tacoma dig another hole in the grass, she's grounded from going outside for a week," Taryn states, then sighs.

"Did she listen?" Sweet, naïve Corina has so much to learn about Taryn's little spawn.

"Yes, she did not dig another hole… in the grass."

"Where *did* she dig the holes?" Yup, Liz knows the child well.

33

"I caught her pointing to the stepping-stones on the side of the yard and commanding Tacoma to *pick up*. He picked the stone up with his teeth, while Jessie dug underneath."

"I went out and scolded her for digging after I clearly told her not to. She just looked up at me with those angelic little blue eyes and declared, *not in grass, Mama. Jessie dig in dirt*."

"That girl, I just love her," Liz manages between chuckles.

"Yeah, until you try and step on one of those stones. I might have forgotten to warn Kev. Poor guy got the shock of his life when he went to water the grass last night."

The women all start laughing. It's so refreshing to just talk life with those who get it.

"I think this needs some wine. Shall we, ladies?" Taryn offers.

Everyone makes their way down to the *basement,* although in California they are more bonus rooms, not classic basements. Taryn's house is two stories and built up, so the basement is actually above ground.

Taryn and Liz converted it from a junk room into a cozy little den, just for this group. It took them nearly a week, but they did an amazing job. It's a beautiful shade of robin's egg blue with off-white trim. They added all the things that they can't have around the kids, basically nice things. Candles, picture frames, and positive quotes on the wall.

Kevin even built a nice little wine bar off to the side, fully stocked and ready to be consumed by a bunch of overwhelmed mothers.

The focal point is a little sitting circle with a gray circular sofa. A sign on the wall declares, Wine & Whine.

"Everyone takes a seat and get comfy while we get the wine." Liz announces as she walks toward the bar, when Taryn stops her.

"I'll grab that, why don't you go ahead and start Liz."

Liz knew she was going to do that. She shoots her a look that says so, and Taryn tries to pull the Jessie, *I'm so innocent* look on her, but Liz knows better than to fall for that.

For someone who is so spunky, Taryn tends to dislike speaking in groups, or really being social at all. She's what Liz calls an extroverted introvert. Taryn says her kids' social skills have rubbed off on her. While Liz entertains the virtual strangers, Taryn starts passing out glasses of Moscato, handing Liz two extra bottles. She opens one, placing it on the table, while holding onto the other.

"First, we want to say thank you for joining us this evening. I know it might seem a little weird, but we just had such a good feeling about this." Liz starts the group after a few sips of courage.

"Thank you, it's so nice to have some adult time, and not have to worry about meltdowns," Corina replies, lifting her glass in salute.

"Wednesday nights Emily deals with the meltdowns, while we deal with the Moscato," Taryn adds between sips.

"We thought it might be fun to start with our high points for the week. A child hitting a goal, or mastering a new skill, fewer meltdowns, maybe sleeping through the night." Liz looks over at Taryn who smiles her thanks for taking over.

"Once we all do our highs, we can talk about our lows. We want to make sure it's a good balance."

"Don't forget the winner," Taryn chimes in.

Liz rolls her eyes. She can't believe Taryn was serious about having a winner. One thing about Taryn is she's super competitive, everything has to be a game. Personally, Liz hates games, but as usual, she goes along with it.

"I don't want you to see this as a competition, because it's not. But Taryn thought it might be nice to give the person who had the hardest week a bottle of Moscato to take home with them."

"So even when you lose, you win!" Taryn pipes up.

"Best support group ever!" Mia cheers Taryn's glass and everyone has a good laugh.

"I'll start. My high for the week was getting Mason to eat a kiwi."

"Oh, I'm always trying to get Ash to try new foods, it's close to impossible. How did you do it?"

Liz can feel her cheeks start to heat up. She looks down at her lap.

"Oh, this is gonna be good." Taryn fills up Liz's glass and she takes a healthy sip.

"Um, I might have told him it was a green strawberry."

"You lied?" Taryn said at the same time Mia proclaimed it to be, "genius!"

"Hey, you do whatcha gotta do, sister!" Corina pumps her fist in the air as she takes a sip of her wine.

"Until he asks someone for a green strawberry, and it's like Santa died all over again." Taryn deadpans.

"Isn't this group supposed to be about positivity?" Liz reminds her.

"Yes, it is! Great job duping your kid!" Taryn says with fake enthusiasm.

"Thank you." Liz ignores her sarcasm and turns to Corina. "What about you Corina?"

"Max started ABA last week, and it's been rough. He goes to school all day, and then right to the center for two hours after. Yesterday was the first day he didn't throw a fit when I dropped him off."

"That can be so hard. Ashton had a hard time at first too, but now he loves it. Max will get the hang of it in no time." Mia comforts her.

"I felt like a fish out of water. I mean I don't even know what it stands for and didn't want to sound stupid so I never asked." She says looking sheepish.

"Never feel stupid, I can't ever keep up with all the crazy acronyms in the autism world. ABA technically stands for applied behavior analysis. In lay terms, it's basically the study of behavior and how it works. What they do is study the child's behavior and see how it is affected by the environment. Which is why most places start off in a controlled environment, or small room. Then as the child progresses they move to bigger areas with more distractions," Mia explains.

"I know when Marcus first started, I hated the idea of him being in a little room. But his behaviors decreased, and they slowly moved him to a less restrictive environment. In the end, he was in a full classroom setting and mainstreaming without many behaviors," Liz encourages.

"That would be amazing. Thank you so much for explaining. I knew they worked on behavior and speech and such, but it all gets a little overwhelming."

"It's great for the kids that need a little extra help for sure. And it's nice that they help work on their school goals as well. I have seen a huge improvement in Ashton," Mia adds.

"ABA really helped Marcus's social skills for a while, but I think it really depends on the kid. It was a good fit for Marcus, but not at all for Mason. He found it much too restrictive, and his behaviors actually got worse," Liz says, filling her glass and passing the bottle to Taryn.

"It's not for everyone. There are so many different types of therapy for our kiddos. I've been wanting to put Jessie into equestrian therapy. Since she loves animals so much, and ABA wasn't a good fit for her either," Taryn says as she turns to Mia.

"How about you Mia? What was your high of the week?"

"Honestly? Meeting you guys. Corina has been a godsend to me, but it's so nice meeting other moms who just get it. I'm so sick of the usual judgment I see in people's eyes. Like when Ash threw his chewy and hit you, Taryn. Do you know how many times I've been scolded in the store for my child's bad behavior?"

Taryn quickly grabs mia's hand and gives it a squeeze. "That's something you never have to do with us. In fact, I'm making that a rule right now. We don't apologize for our kids, ever. We just get it, and we salute each other for making it through another day."

"Here, here!" Liz raises her wine glass.

"To a judgment free friendship."

"To a judgment free friendship." Everyone echoes and clinks their glasses.

"And to more Moscato than meltdowns!" Mia adds.

"Here, here!" The women all chant as one.

It's Better Than the Sex Closet

Max lets out a small snore from the back seat, and Corina smiles at his peaceful face. Max doesn't have friends. Sure, they try to get him and Ashton together often, but the boys usually go to their separate corners and play independently.

The ladies couldn't believe it when they came upstairs to get the kids ready to go and saw them all playing together. They all decided that Nanny Emily is a wizard. She had a cardboard teepee, that the kids were coloring on. It was pretty genius. They were all participating but they each had their own side, so it wasn't too overwhelming.

Corina needed this tonight. Lately, things have just seemed... overwhelming. Her and her husband, Michael have been trying to get pregnant again, but it's been a year and nothing. They haven't told anyone because they don't want to hear all of the negative comments. Yes, they have four kids, who they love very much. But only one of those she carried and loved every single moment of it. Corina wants nothing more than to have that experience again.

Every single month when she gets her period, it feels like her heart is bleeding as well. They have also been getting more painful each month and she hates how depressed she feels for almost a full week afterwards. Then there's the week before her period where she feels hopeful. The false hope is almost worse than the despair. It was so nice to not have to think about that tonight. Even though it was just a few hours.

Corina wipes the tear that falls of its own accord. Geez, she needs to get herself together before she pulls into the driveway. She takes the back way to allow herself a few extra minutes. She looks at the clock on her dash and gives herself exactly one minute to cry. Only sixty-seconds, for her empty womb. Once the clock changes, she swipes a hand under both eyes, wiping away evidence of her pain. She cranks up her favorite playlist, and sings a happy song all the way home.

Corina looks in the mirror and sings her heart out to Max, who is still blissfully asleep in the back seat, determined to change her mood.

She had a fantastic night and refuses to let any dark thoughts to rob her of it. Pulling into the garage, she takes a quick look in the rearview mirror. Quickly dabbing at the smeared makeup under her eyes, she places a bright smile on her face.

40

It's not hard to do when she looks in the backseat at her sweet boy, sound asleep. She sends off a fast text to Michael to come help get Max to bed. Seconds later, the door to the house opens and out comes her handsome husband.

She takes in his shirtless form and the worn jeans that hang low on his hips. It's so unfair how age has only added to his beauty. She still has yet to see a single gray hair in his beautiful thick jet-black hair.

He goes straight to the back seat and lifts Max in that magical way that never seems to wake him. As he starts towards the boy's room, Corina taps his shoulder and points to their room. Michael narrows his eyes at his wife and nods his head back to the boy's room.

"He is just going to end up in ours anyway when he wakes up with a night terror," she whispers, trying not to wake Max.

"But at least we will have a few hours to ourselves… without having to hide in the sex closet. You want a baby, don't you?"

He's got her there and his slow smile tells her he knows it. He continues to walk Max to his room as Corina sighs and makes her way to theirs. She knows she should be happy Max is sleeping in his own room. She should take advantage of it and try to sleep when he is, but she also knows she won't. Instead, she'll end up staying awake, worried that he will wake up in a fright.

Michael comes in and shuts the door behind him. "Don't shut it all the way, what if he wakes?"

"I'll open it after…" He lets the rest of the sentence hang, and Corina quickly fills it in; after they finally have sex

41

in their own bed. Since Max sleeps with them most nights and they have three other kids in the house, it leaves them with very little room for each other.

As a joke, when Corina was ovulating one night, she mentioned the walk-in closet in their bedroom, since it had a door. Well, it was actually a pretty brilliant idea, and has been dubbed the *sex closet* ever since.

Michael can see where her thoughts have strayed as she eyes the closet. He walks slowly toward her like she's his prey, his eyes narrowing and his smile spreading. He reaches her ear and slowly nips the lobe as he whispers, "it's been years in that closet, just think of what I could do with a bed."

And just like that, Corina's ovaries explode.

Mia pulls up to the house and feels a sinking feeling in the pit of her stomach when she sees that her husband's car isn't in the drive. This is the third night this week he's been gone, and it's only Wednesday.

She sighs and then takes a deep breath, swallowing her disappointment. She just needs to get Ashton to bed, then she can fall apart.

"Come on sweetie, let's get you inside, it's late." Ashton has a hard time going down most nights. Once he does, he sleeps pretty well, but it's like pulling teeth every single night to get him to sleep.

The bitter woman in Mia says that's why Ty works so late every night, so he doesn't have to deal with it. But it is what it is. First, she needs to tackle bedtime, then she'll worry about her marriage.

Ash walks into the house and heads straight for the couch. "Movie."

"No baby, it's bedtime."

"Movie." He demands again, this time pointing at the television, like she doesn't understand what he wants. Mia knows what he wants, she just doesn't want him to have it.

"Come on love, it's time to brush your teeth."

Walking over to the couch, she leans down and touches his shoulder, as he swipes at her arm.

"Movie!"

"I know you want a movie, but it's very late and time for bed. We are going to brush your teeth, and I'll read you a story."

Ashton starts to wail, and Mia knows she's in for a hard night. Even though he had fun at Taryn's house, it was a change. Sometimes even good changes are over-stimulating, and the comedown can almost not seem worth it for him.

But being with those women made her feel normal for the first time in a while, so it's worth it for her. She keeps chanting those words over and over as she drags her screaming child up the stairs and to the bathroom. She continues to chant them while he bites her when she brushes his teeth and as he spits the toothpaste back in her face.

Mia puts him in bed and holds him tight. Her heart breaks, along with the skin on her forearm, but she just keeps rocking him as she softly sings. Her silent tears fall, but they are ignored.

Mia hurts when Ashton hurts. She cries for his lack of understanding. She lets the tears fall for his lack of communication. And she sobs for her lack of support. His rocking starts to slow, as she rubs his back twice before he points at the door, for her to leave. He's ready to sleep.

"Goodnight sweet boy." Mia bends down to kiss his forehead, before getting up to make her way to the door. As she walks out, she turns on his nightlight then quietly shuts the door behind her.

Like he planned it, her husband's car pulls into the drive at the same moment. Mia can't stop the bitter laugh that tears from her throat as she softly makes her way to the landing, but she won't go down the stairs just yet.

Tyson walks in the house and makes a beeline for the laundry room, where he takes off his clothes and puts them in the washer. He moves from the laundry room straight into the downstairs bathroom. As soon as the shower starts up, Mia falls apart.

CHAPTER

Bacon Solves Everything

Taryn wakes up to the ringing of her internal mom alarm. It's not the danger alarm, it's the something isn't quite right alarm... which usually only means one thing.

"Where is Jessie?" Taryn whispers to Kevin as she pokes him in the side.

"Sleeping, where she should be."

Taryn strains her ears to listen. No sound... but the feeling doesn't go away. "I think she's up."

"She's not crying."

"That just means she's getting into trouble." Kevin looks at the clock on the nightstand and sees its only 2 a.m. Groaning, he rolls back over, putting his pillow over his head. "A lot of help you are. Fine, go back to sleep," Taryn says with a huff.

"You and your feelings, I swear I'm married to a witch," He mumbles, as she jumps out of bed and tiptoes across the hall to Jessie's room. Taryn opens the door as slowly as she can, making sure it doesn't make a sound. She sprays it daily with WD-40, but one still can't be too careful. Taryn pokes her head in, and sure enough… no Jessie, or Tacoma. That can only mean one thing, trouble.

She takes off running through her room to look under the bed and in her closet. One can't be too thorough. On her way back through Jessie's room on the way to the door, Taryn steps on one of those stupid little spiky toys from hell, and damn are they sharp. Half limp, half running down the hall, she looks in the bathroom, living room, dining room, office, laundry room, and kitchen. No Jessie.

The panic has set in full force now, Jessie is gone. Taryn takes off running back down the hall as fast as her injured foot will allow. She reaches her room where she turns the light on and whisper yells at Kevin, "she's gone, Kev she's gone!"

That has him flying out of bed, as Taryn frantically holds her boobs and scrambles around the room. "I need a bra, I need to call 911, but I can't find my bra. For God's sake, get some pants on and find our kid! Should we wake Gav? Drive around the neighborhood?"

"Did you check the locks?" Leave it to her husband to ask the logical question while she's in a full five alarm panic.

Of course I checked the locks, she wants to scream in his smug, calm face. But she can't, because she didn't check them. So instead of answering, she limp/runs back down the hall to the front door. All three locks are engaged. The back door and garage are the same. Taryn's heart rate slows just a bit at the sight.

"Well, what the hell. Where is she then?" Taryn asks out loud to herself.

She jumps out of her skin when Kev answers from behind her. "Is the dog missing too? I don't see sign of either."

"Yes, they're both gone. Jessie? Jessica Kathryn Leighton, you come out right now! Jessica!"

Kevin calmly walks into the kitchen and grabs a frying pan, then proceeds to the fridge where he grabs a pound of bacon and walks to the stove like it's just a lazy Sunday.

"Kevin, are you kidding me?! You are making breakfast? At two in the morning when our daughter is missing?"

Taryn knows she sounds like a hysterical shrew. However, in this moment she feels like one, and thinks it's completely valid. Kevin stops what he's doing and faces his wife. Placing both hands on her shoulders, he looks down into her eyes.

"Love, I get that you're scared. The locks are engaged and I am helping. You get to be scared but don't get to take out your worry on me." He repeats himself like she's a few crayons short of a full box. "The locks are all engaged."

"Yes, but what if she was stolen through her window?"

"The locks are engaged on those too."

"You checked?" Taryn doesn't know why she's even asking, of course he checked. He's mister cool, calm and

47

collected. Kevin smiles, kisses her forehead then turns back to the stove, as he puts the bacon to sizzle in the hot pan.

"Jessie! Tacoma! Come out right now. Jessie?" Taryn goes back to her search, and she once again looks everywhere, still no sign of either. A little girl isn't always easy to find, but a sixty-five-pound dog usually is.

The smell of bacon starts to fill up the kitchen, just as Kev grabs a piece and holds it up in the air.

"Tacoma, Bacon."

"Like that's gonna—"

Arf! Arf! Arf!

Taryn's head shoots up at Kev in surprise, wanting nothing more than to smack that proud smirk right off his infuriating face.

"Shut up."

"I didn't say a word."

"You didn't have to. Where is that barking coming from?"

Arf! Arf!

"Laundry room," Kevin answers as he takes off his apron and tosses it on the counter. Yes, the infuriating man took the time to put on an apron while their daughter was missing.

The words are hardly out of his mouth before Taryn rounds the kitchen corner, running into the room she's already checked twice.

Arf! Arf! Scratch. Scratch.

She can clearly hear him, but still sees no sign of hound or hair. Taryn follows the scratching to the washer and dryer and throws open both doors. Tacoma comes flying out of one, covered in… dirt? He jumps out and goes tearing off towards the kitchen, leaving a trail behind him.

Taryn leans in and takes a sniff. It's not dirt after all, its coffee. She turns to peer into the washer and is met with an angelic little face, covered from head to toe in coffee grounds. Taryn looks at the floor, and sees five empty bags of very expensive coffee from Brazil.

"Dammit Jessie! What on earth are you doing?"

"Hi Mommy. Jessie dig for treasure in cave."

Taryn takes in the grounds all over her new, very expensive washer and dryer, her daughter, and every item of clothing in the room all covered in fancy coffee. But with Jessie looking up at her with those big blue eyes and innocent smile, so full of joy, Taryn can't find it in herself to be angry.

She looks at this sweet innocent little girl, who is nothing but trouble and can't help but burst out in laughter. She laughs so hard she has big fat tears rolling down her face. Jessie just shrugs her shoulders and looks at her mom like she's lost her mind.

"Okay my little Indiana Jones, out you come."

Kevin plucks Jessie from the washer and shakes her a bit, so all the coffee spills onto Taryn's feet, causing Taryn to go into another fit of giggles.

"Well, Jessie girl, it looks like you finally broke mommy." He shakes her a few more times and then grabs his keys from the hook on the wall.

"Where we go daddy?"

"We are going to buy mommy some more coffee, and hopefully some sanity. Come on, you too Tacoma. I don't trust that you won't be sent to the glue factory for this."

"Seriously, didn't we pay all that money so he'd wake us up when she was off causing crazy shenanigans? I'm writing that company right now and giving them a piece of my mind," Taryn says, finally snapping out of her hysteria.

"Let's make that coffee and chocolate for Mommy, shall we? Come on nugget."

Kev whisks her away and once they are out of the house, Taryn looks around the room again and laughs so hard the fat tears are back and running down her face. Let's be honest, this shit is funny. And if she doesn't laugh, she'll cry.

However, an hour later it's no longer even remotely funny. Taryn still hasn't gotten to the actual mess yet. Instead, she's stuck trying to clean this nasty vacuum/ mop thing. She always forgets to clean it when she's done, because there is usually one crisis or another to see to before she can get to the cleaning part of the machine she just used to clean. Go figure.

Taryn finally gets the freaking thing cleaned and goes over the area about seven times before Kev and Jessie get back. She's surprised Gavin hasn't come out of his room yet, but chances are the sound of the vacuum has him staying in there.

"Still at it?"

Taryn looks up and sends her husband one of her best glares. "I hate this stupid vacuum. It takes me an hour to clean it before I can actually clean. I want a Kirby." She stops for a second and wipes the sweat out of her eyes. "Didn't you say when we weren't poor anymore, you'd buy me a Kirby?"

Even though it's phrased as a question, they both know that it isn't one. Taryn's been eying that particular vacuum for years. Every time she brought it up, Kevin said that would be his first purchase once they could afford it. They passed that bracket years ago, but then they had kids and they are expensive. Even the ones who don't need thousands of dollars worth of expensive therapy.

"Maybe for Christmas." Kevin tries to placate his wife.

"That's forever away! I heard Groundhog Day is a wonderful day for gifts," Taryn adds tossing him a cheeky grin.

"Groundhog Day was two months ago," Kevin shoots back in triumph.

"See, you owe me! I didn't even make you feel bad for missing it!" Taryn gives him a triumphant smile of her own for besting him. He laughs, and she takes the silent touché that it is.

Kevin tips his imaginary hat and walks away. She knows this means she'll be getting a Kirby soon, so she smiles as she empties the little canister for the fifth time. Taryn would never admit it, but this latest little escapade of Jessie's might end up paying off after all.

Insanity and Brilliance are Close Cousins

"You want to do what? Liz, are you insane?"

"Probably, but that has nothing to do with my decision, Tom. If you would have been there you would have done the same thing."

"No, I wouldn't, because you baby the boys, Liz. Kids get picked on in school every day."

"That may be true, but these kids didn't even care that his mother was standing right there. They pushed him, Tom. Pushed him, back and forth between them like he was an object and not a human being."

"He hasn't complained before has he? I'm sure he's fine."

"Of course, he doesn't complain, but that doesn't mean it's not bothering him. He's not fine. He was rocking back and forth, hitting his leg and spouting off train facts for three hours after those little jerks harassed him."

"But did you have to pull him out of school? Couldn't you just report it or something?"

This man doesn't listen to a word his wife says. It's the third time they've gone over the situation, after she told him in detail what took place this afternoon. Stating that fact, however, will do nothing but rile him up. Liz takes a deep breath and launches into her third explanation of the evening.

"I did report it. I marched right into the principal's office and explained what I saw. Marcus was minding his own business, walking to class, when those boys just started shoving him back and forth while taunting him. It broke my heart. All of which I related to the principal who told me that boys tease and they were probably just trying to play with Marcus. Play, like they were kids. These are teenage boys who were ridiculing our son!" Liz takes another calming breath, and tries to cool her blood, which is currently at molten lava level at this point.

"When we got home, I made Marcus sit down and write a list of all the ways the other students have interacted with him since school started. Just a list to see what has been going on, nobody will get in trouble because of it. Tom, it killed me. There wasn't a single kind word or gesture on that entire list. Eight months worth, and there was nothing but hate."

"Liz, he's been mainstreamed his whole life and done fine. It's just boys being boys. Homeschooling is not the answer," Tom states with authority.

"Why not? I'm the one who will be doing all the work. And he's so bright anyway, he's been ahead of his class for years. He is doing college prep classes already. It wouldn't be like trying to homeschool Mason or anything."

"You are stressed enough as it is. How are you supposed to teach him and still get everything around the house done?"

What he really means is, *is this going to affect me and my dinner time?* But he knows well enough not to ask that. Their views on parenting have always been different and Liz has never pushed. She's been the calm one who picks up the pieces after the storm… but not today. Today Liz is the storm.

"I'm done."

"Excuse me?"

"You heard me Tom. I'm done. You are usually the one that gets to throw the fit and storm out. But it's my turn tonight! Those assholes have abused our kid for the last time, do you hear me? The last time! I'm taking the boys and I'm going to group. If you can't get yourself right by the time I get home, you can pack your things and be out. At this point I don't care, because he's our son. The world sucks, and people are mean. Out there is the battle Tom. In here should be the safe harbor. If we can't offer our kids safety, what kind of parents are we?"

With that, Liz grabs her purse and ushers the kids out the door.

Men are From Mars

Part of Mia thinks she should stay home tonight and not go out in public. She's never felt so drained in her life. Even the thought of bringing Ash back down after exhausts her. But she knows deep down, this is where she really needs to be tonight. Because she feels empty. She's a shell of a woman and needs to be filled.

Mia refuses to be empty for her son, because he relies on her to fill him up. She needs to have something to give him.

She takes a deep breath and robotically applies her makeup. She took a sick day today and just laid in bed, doing nothing but staring at the ceiling and crying all day.

She is better than this pathetic woman who stays in bed crying over a man. She was the valedictorian, got a full ride to college, and paid her way through law school. She is a strong independent, successful woman who refuses to be brought down by a man. Even if that man is her husband.

"Come on baby, it's time to go to group." Mia grabs her purse and Ashton's bag of toys just as the front door opens. Ty comes in looking as handsome as ever, a large smile on his face and a bouquet of flowers.

For a minute it takes Mia back to college. The tall, dark, handsome guy she met, who had all the confidence in the world. She thought they had so much in common. They were both so determined to prove themselves; him to his parents, and her to the world.

"There's my family. Where are you going? I thought you were sick."

"I'm feeling better now and it's Wednesday night. We have group on Wednesday, remember?" Of course, he doesn't remember, he doesn't even pretend to care.

"Skip tonight, I came home early to spend some time with my family. We can put on a movie for Ash and have a nice dinner."

How is that spending time with his family? Sending his son in the other room so Mia can cook for Tyson? Yeah, sounds great… not!

"I'm sorry Tyson, you should have let me know. We can't miss group tonight. I'm sure you can find something to do in our absence."

Mia winces at her own comment. Now is not the time to get into all of that, she refuses to let the scorned woman take over. They will deal with their marriage another time, when she's not an empty shell. Plus, she's too smart to allow her emotions to rule her. She needs to be methodical about her next plan of action. For Ashton, if nothing else.

So she smiles and stands on her tiptoes to kiss his cheek. "Take the night off and relax. You've been working so hard lately, you deserve some you time, *alone*. We will be back in a few hours." Mia almost winces at the emphasis she put on the word alone. But hides it with a smile instead.

Tyson's smile is genuine and he looks down at her for a moment too long, as he cups her cheek. *Yes, I'm the woman you fell in love with, who sacrificed everything for you. Can you still see her?* He brushes a sweet kiss across her forehead, one that has the tears threatening to take over, and memories threaten to cloud her judgment. That is, until he reaches down to squeeze her butt and whisper in her ear.

"Hurry back tonight. I'll be waiting in bed for you."

Yeah, moment passed. The tears are replaced with bile in her throat as she ushers Aston out the door.

They pull up to Taryn's house, Mia taking a moment to push everything down. After a few beats, she gets Ash out and they walk around back where all the noise is.

Mia can't help the joy she feels as she takes in the scene. There are two small, baby pools full of colorful water beads. Next to each pool is a large bucket. Gavin, Max, and Mason are in one pool and Marcus and Jessie are in the other.

The boys are taking turns running cups of beads to the bucket, but Jessie has a pail that her and Marcus are filling. Once it's full, Tacoma takes it in his mouth and dumps it into the bucket.

Mia full on laughs at the brilliance in that child. At the same time she thanks her lucky stars Jessie belongs to Taryn and not her. Being outsmarted by a small child and animal daily is not on her list of things to do.

"Hi Ashton! Come on over and join the fun. The first team to fill up their buckets gets to pick the flavor of ice cream." Emily smiles at me and takes Ash by the hand leading him over to Jessie's team. Ash smiles and just that one small action seems to release all the grief Mia has been holding inside.

We will be ok. This won't crush us. This group will bring us joy, I just know it, Mia chants to herself.

"You made it!"

Taryn comes running over and gives Mia a warm hug, one that she can feel all the way in her marrow. She can't remember the last time anyone embraced her this way, with so much sincerity. The thought brings tears to her eyes.

Taryn releases her, takes one look at the tears glistening in her eyes and declares it is time for Moscato. They leave the kids to their antics, as the women head downstairs to their own little oasis.

"Hey love, good to see you." Corina gives Mia a hug, taking one look at her and instantly knowing something is wrong. They haven't been close friends for long, but they have known each other long enough to know when something is off. Mia shakes her head no. Corina gives her a soft understanding smile in return.

"Let's sit, shall we?" Taryn declares as she plops down on the couch with a loud sigh. "I don't know who I love more, the person who created the water bead or the person who created Emily."

All the women laugh at that while they take turns filling their wine glasses.

"Is it just me or did this week suck?" Taryn asks, followed by another round of laughter and lots of head nodding. "Okay, I declare tonight's topic is bitching, who wants to start?"

Look Awkwardness Head-On and Give it a High Five

Tonight is going to be heavy. It's in the air, stress and unshed tears lingers like a bad smell.

Most people like to avoid that kind of tension and joke it away. But not Taryn. She likes to look awkwardness head-on and give it a high five.

"Since nobody is volunteering, I will go first. But let's just say, the person with the worst story this week gets the bottle of wine. I just happen to have a few bottles in the reserves, so let's make this good." That does as desired and gets everyone laughing. Taryn looks around, even without words, she can just feel the burden of her poor friends.

This is why she wanted this group. She wanted a safe place where moms can come and feel crappy if they need to. Not having to pretend, even if it's just for an hour.

Taryn starts them off by going into a humorous version on Jessie and Tacoma's little disappearing act story. The girls are laughing so hard, Liz has tears rolling down her face. Maybe Taryn missed her life purpose of doing standup.

"Lord, the things that girl and her dog get up to. How the heck did they fit in there?" Liz asks, drying her face.

"Who freaking knows, but I'm pretty sure they have officially ruined bacon for me."

Another round of laughter, then Corina asks the question of the hour. "So did you get the Kirby?"

Taryn smiles wide, her eyebrows doing a little dance of smugness. "I sure did. It was sitting there with a large bow and a card that said, *Happy belated Groundhog Day.*"

Liz just shakes her head. "I hope you know how lucky you are. That man of yours is a saint."

"I do know. I have no clue how he hasn't figured out he's too good for me yet. I'm pretty sure he knows just how crazy I am and is too afraid to leave."

Corina and Liz laugh at that, while Mia breaks out in a sob. Liz narrows her eyes at Taryn. Taryn can practically hear her thoughts loud and clear. *Dammit Taryn, you broke her.*

Taryn's eyes widen and her shoulders go up like, *oops... now what?* Thank the man above for Corina, who actually does know what to do, which is to grab Mia and bring her into a comforting hug. *Man, I really am awkward,* Taryn thinks.

Liz runs to grab a box of Kleenex, Taryn runs to the wine. Liz shoots Taryn a look like *really?* Taryn shoots her back a look like, *what? Both are helpful in time of crisis. Don't judge me.*

Obviously, they have been hanging around nonverbal children for way too long. Liz hands Mia the Kleenex and Taryn tops off Mia's glass, as well as her own for solidarity.

Mia blows her nose. *That's how you know you're among good friends; she actually blew. None of that ridiculous ladylike tapping junk,* Taryn thinks as she fights a smile.

Mia takes a deep breath and a healthy swallow of wine. "Tyson is having an affair."

"What?" The women all yell in unison.

"Yup, it's been happening for a while now, but I finally realized that our marriage is officially over."

"Oh, love." Corina brings her in for another comforting hug, while Taryn tops off her glass again. If Taryn keeps this up, Kevin will have to drive Mia home at this point.

"So now what?" Taryn asks the question of the hour.

"I have absolutely no clue. And therein lies the problem."

"You aren't going to stay with his cheating ass, are you?"

"Taryn!" Liz yells, shooting Taryn a look that says to behave herself.

"What Liz? It's true. Everyone was thinking it."

"Maybe, but it's not your place to ask."

Mia actually laughs. She throws her head back and laughs, and Liz is back to shooting Taryn the *you broke her* look.

"No really, I needed that. Taryn, you might be my favorite person on the planet, you know that?"

Ha, take that Liz, Taryn thinks.

"Obviously our marriage is over. And If I'm honest, it has been for a while now. When Ashton was diagnosed, it was like Tyson just checked out. He couldn't handle it, he started working more hours. He said it was to pay for the therapy but we both know it was to avoid the real issues." Mia takes a deep sip before continuing. "Somewhere down the line, the late nights working turned into late night screwing and here we are."

"Do you know who it is?" Corina asks gently, as she grabs her friend's hand.

"No. It's not like I can pack up Ash and go follow him," Mia points out.

"The hardest part is he came from money, and I didn't. His parents thought I was a gold digger and made me sign an ironclad prenup. If I file for divorce, he gets everything." As if it was choreographed, all four women take a healthy sip of wine.

"I can care less about the material things. But that home, it's all Ash has ever known. He hardly ever sees his father so I don't think that will change much, but losing his home will rock him. I can't do that to my son," Mia cries, while she grabs another tissue.

"Of course not. It's okay honey, we will think of something." Liz pats her hand as Taryn's devious mind starts working overtime. Jessie obviously got that from her, but Taryn would never admit it.

"So the prenup states you get nothing if you file right?" Taryn asks.

"Not a cent."

"What about if there is infidelity on his part, isn't that usually a clause?"

"*If* I have solid proof of it, then I might be able to contest it. But we have joint accounts. If I hire someone, he will know. If he's tipped off, I'll never be able to prove it. He will divorce me so fast my head spins."

Taryn's head snaps up and she breaks out in a huge smile. "Then you don't hire someone. We will do it, for free."

"Excuse me?" Liz practically chokes.

"I'm an excellent amateur sleuth," Taryn defends.

"Give me a break, you are just a bored housewife with too much time on her hands," Liz shoots back.

"I'll have you know I busted a drug ring just last month."

"Oh, please, you saw your seventeen-year-old neighbor buying pot from the pizza boy. It's California, pot's not even illegal anymore."

"Um, ladies, I think we are getting off topic here."

"You are right Corina, sorry," Liz says with a guilty smile.

"Well, I actually think that might be a good plan, if you ladies really want to help," Mia speaks up.

"You do?" Liz asks shocked.

"I mean, I don't exactly have any other options."

"Ashton losing his home is not an option. We can take shifts. He's never met us," Taryn follows up.

"He's met me," Corina pipes up, "but I don't really have any extra time right now, anyway. Any child-free time I have is saved for doctors' appointments lately."

"Is everything okay?" Mia asks concerned.

"Oh, it's fine. I've just been having a lot of women issues. More pain that normal and weird periods, but I'm sure it's no big deal. They have been doing a bunch of tests, just to be on the safe side."

"Well, he doesn't know Liz and I, so we'd love to help." Taryn brings the subject back to the matter at hand.

Liz grabs the unopened bottle of wine and puts it in her purse.

"You didn't even share your sob story yet." Taryn points out.

"No, I didn't, and Mia would have won anyway, so you owe her one. Consider this bottle payment for whatever ridiculous shenanigans I know you are going to get me involved in." Everyone chuckles at that, while Taryn only shrugs, because Liz isn't wrong.

Try Not to Punch Someone in the Face

Liz gets home much later than usual, since they all had to sober up first. They are going to have to start putting a two-glass limit on these nights so it doesn't turn into everyone having to go to a whole other type of meeting.

"You're home!" The desperation on Tom's face sends guilt through Liz. With all the drama with Mia's marriage, she totally forgot about her own for a few hours. And it felt good.

"Let me get the boys to bed, and then we will talk," Liz replies. Tom nods once and turns to go back to the living room.

"Come on boys, go to the bathroom and then brush your teeth." Liz goes to Mason's room to get his pjs, just as Marcus walks by on his way to his room.

"I love you, baby. Sleep well." Marcus only nods and practically zombie-walks to his room where he shuts the door.

She helps Mason change and then tucks him into bed, giving him a quick kiss. It won't be long before he won't let her do that anymore, so she cherishes these fleeting moments in time.

"Sweet dreams, love bug."

Heading to the bathroom to wash her face buys Liz a few extra minutes. When that's done she goes back out to the living room where Tom is sitting with his head in his hands.

The look of devastation on his face is almost too much for her to bare. Liz places her hand on his knee while taking the seat next to him on the couch. His eyes are rimmed in red when he faces her.

"I thought you left. I thought you took the boys and left me," he admits in a gravelly voice.

Liz feels horrible that it didn't even occur to her that he would have thought that. But at the same time, she's also a bit mad that it takes something so dramatic for him to actually hear her.

"And if I had left?" Liz whispers, refusing to back down.

Tom looks as though her words have stabbed him right through the heart. "Liz, you and the boys are my life. I might not understand them the way you do, but I love them with all that I am."

"I know that Tom, it's clear to see now, but you've got to start showing it. I know it's hard for you, trust me I know. But these boys aren't like you." Liz starts rubbing his back while she continues speaking.

"They are sensitive, they can't always voice their needs. It's our job as their parents to advocate for them and give them a voice." She wipes a lone tear that falls down his cheek.

"Do I want to homeschool Marcus? Of course not. He needs the social interaction that school offers. But at the same time, I don't want him to turn into one of those kids who shoots up a school because his pain was ignored."

Tom winces at the harshness of Liz's honesty. He never thought of that before.

"I get that now. I do. I'll talk to Marcus about it, and if he wants to be homeschooled, we will make it happen. If not, I'll march down to that school myself and give his principal a talking to."

Liz can't help but chuckle at his protectiveness. This is the man she fell in love with. "I know it's hard for you to express your feelings, but blowing up on us, or shutting my ideas down is damaging to not only our marriage, but to our family. The world is hard and this little team might be the only thing we have. We've got to stay united Tom."

"I know, I know we do. I'm sorry Liz, I really am. I just feel like I have no freaking clue how to be a parent to these boys."

"Welcome to my life, babe. You just do what I do, fake it till you make it, and try not to punch someone in the face."

Liz adores Taryn. She's her best friend for a reason, but Liz has never wanted to strangle anyone like she does this particular friend. The number of crazy situations that woman gets her into is just plain ridiculous.

"Liz, will you calm down? We are going to stick out like a sore thumb." Liz turns her glare in Taryn's direction.

"You're kidding, right? We already stick out like a sore thumb. For one, we are at a golf course. For two, we don't know how to golf. And three," Liz nods over to her train-fact obsessed son who has been spouting them off since they arrived.

"It's good for Marcus. You said he needed more socialization now that he's being homeschooled," Taryn points out.

"I meant with kids his own age, not club wielding senior citizens."

Taryn squints her eyes, looks down at her phone and up again. "Ooh, there he is. I think that's him."

Liz takes another look at the picture of Mia's family on her phone and then back at the man standing only a short distance away. "Yeah, it looks like him."

"And look, there's the tramp." Taryn full on points to the young woman hanging off his arm, while Liz quickly slaps her arm down.

"Jesus, Taryn! So much for your sleuth skills."

"Oops. Here, let's get a little closer and then you and Marcus stand right about… perfect. Smile and say cheese."

Being the obedient boy that he is, Marcus does as she asks while Liz glares hard. As much as she hates doing this, Taryn is right. She will be able to get what they need for Mia so Liz goes with it.

"Perfect. Now if we just can get a little closer, I can try and get a few more intimate shots." Liz rolls her eyes and starts to walk in that direction.

"Here, text that picture to Mia, while I get closer and see what I can find."

Taryn hands Liz her phone as she saunters over to where Tyson is now walking to get his ball. She is so close to him now that she could probably tell what kind of cologne he wears. He turns toward her and Taryn looks just like a deer in the headlights. He starts asking her something, and Taryn turns to run, but falls right into the lake.

"Jesus! Come on Marcus." Liz grabs her son's hand and takes off running toward Taryn. She sure hopes Taryn can swim. Liz gets there just as Taryn is being fished out.

"What the hell is wrong with that woman?" Liz hears Tyson ask his companion.

"There was a bee, I'm allergic," Taryn chokes out. She must seriously be on God's good list, because it had barely left her mouth when two bees come flying by. Tyson's companion's eyes go wide as she jumps into the same pond Taryn had fallen into just moments before.

"Jesus Christ Tammy, what on earth are you doing?"

"I'm allergic to bees, too!"

Taryn starts to laugh, and then quickly covers it with a cough.

She walks over and helps the girl out of the pond. "Kindred spirits, I guess. Come on, let's go get cleaned up, shall we?"

The soaking wet women slosh away, arm in arm. Taryn tosses Liz a wink over her shoulder on her way towards the clubhouse with the other woman.

Liz's life may be many things, but it's never boring!

Facebook is For Old People

Falling into the lake wasn't exactly planned, but it ended up being bloody genius. After Taryn's *steam* with Tammy, she is practically giddy.

Taryn's not one of those people who can take a secret to the grave. Nope, she can't even take it five steps without telling someone, so she's bursting to find Liz.

Crap! Taryn just remembered that she handed her phone to Liz. Liz better not have left her here. Taryn frantically scans the golf course, finally finding them in the parking lot.

"For heaven's sake Taryn, it took you long enough! We almost got kicked out. Marcus wouldn't stop spouting out train facts and some asshole called security on us."

"Don't worry, we will never be setting foot in this place again. But it was totally worth it." Taryn puts her hand out for her phone, which Liz happily places in her hand, then puts her key in the ignition.

"Wait, not yet. Look at this, I hit the mother-load." Taryn brings up tons of selfies taken by Tammy, in half of which Tyson plays a starring role.

"The idiot! How on earth could he be dumb enough to take pictures with her?"

"Apparently, only old people are on Facebook these days, and his wife is *too old to even know what Instagram is*," Taryn says using air quotes.

"Hold up, we are both on Facebook." Liz says, not trying to hide the offense in her tone.

"I know! Stupid little twat."

"And what the hell is *Instantgram*?"

"In*stagram," Taryn corrects, "it's just a dumb selfie sight from what I can tell. But it's what the kids are on these days."

"Lord, you sound old," Liz states, while she fights the urge to look in the mirror for wrinkles.

"Well, luckily I don't look old. I was able to convince Tammy that I'm twenty-five, and here with my married lover. You should have heard how fast she started spilling the tea," Taryn brags proudly.

"She spilled what?"

"Never mind. Anyway, once I started dishing about my man, and showing her pictures, she had to one up me, of course."

"Wait what pictures did you show? I had your phone."

"The ones of me and my dad on Facebook. Thus, the comment. But that's how I learned of her Instagram, and where I found all these. Now I just have to screenshot them all for Mia."

Taryn was expecting Liz to be excited, but she only looks sad. "I thought you'd be happy."

"How can we be happy, when we are ruining their marriage?"

"No Liz, he did that. We are just keeping Mia and Ashton from being kicked out of their home."

"I know that, but it's just so sad to me. You know with the extra added stress that our kids bring and everything… that could easily be us, Taryn."

"I know, but it isn't us. All we can do now is be there for her and Ash. We are her family now."

"So, the woman, did she know he was married?"

"Yup. She seemed almost proud of the fact, too. Not at all disillusioned that he would not leave his wife for her. She was perfectly content being his side piece, as long as she got all the benefits, while the wife got all the responsibilities. Another direct quote by the way. Lord, it made me sick."

Liz is very quiet. Taryn knows this is hard on her, so she finishes sending the pictures to Mia and turns around to give Marcus a smile and hopefully a subject change.

"Marcus my man, way to stick it out with us. You'll be a junior sleuth before you know it."

"Aunt Taryn, did you know that a bullet train can top three-hundred miles per hour?"

"You don't say? No, I didn't know that. Did you know that one fourth of the bones in your body are in your feet?"

He looks down at his foot for a minute and then smiles back at her. "No, I didn't know that. You are so smart, Aunt Taryn."

Liz rolls her eyes, and while her friend smiles at her kid she whispers, "what flavor?"

"I haven't a clue what you mean."

"What flavor Snapple did you read that from?" Liz clarifies. Damn, Taryn had a feeling Liz had suspected for a while now.

"Kiwi-Strawberry," Taryn finally admits, causing Liz to laugh.

"I knew it!"

"I have to swing by and pick up Mason from school. Are you coming with, or do you want me to drop you off at home first?"

"Can you drop me off at Starbucks? Mia wants to meet me there."

Liz looks nervous but nods once and takes a right at the corner. "You sure you don't want me to come? I can head over after I get Mase."

"No, it's okay. I have a feeling the fewer people to witness the fall of her marriage, the better."

"You are a good woman Taryn, even if you are slightly nuts."

Taryn laughs and gives her best friend a big hug, then hops out, and prepares to ruin her new friend's marriage. Man, sometimes life sucks.

Time to Stop Believing in the Maybes

They say a woman always knows. Maybe that's true, because deep down Mia has known for months. But even deeper down, she prayed she was wrong.

It was easy to keep lying to herself, maybe it wasn't as it seemed. Maybe it was a mistake, maybe it was just a one-night stand. All those stupid maybes that she kept telling herself in order to get through the day.

Then she got the texts from Taryn and the maybes all came crashing down. All that was left of her marriage was the carnage at her feet. She had to get out of the office before she lost it right there.

Mia knew they would find something. She just didn't think it'd happen on the first day they went looking.

Tyson was stupid enough to take that woman out in the daytime and to a place she, herself, has gone with him for years. That was the moment she knew that her marriage was truly over. Because he stopped caring. And Mia stopped believing the maybes.

There was no freaking way she was going to be sitting in the office when Tyson strolled back through, which is why she's sitting at a table in the corner of Starbucks when Taryn comes walking through the door.

Taryn's smile doesn't reach her eyes and Mia can tell that she feels bad for her. It's awkward, that she has to be the one to reveal Mia's sham of a marriage.

Taryn opens her mouth and Mia waves whatever she's about to say away.

"I know." Taryn looks into Mia's sad eyes, then nods once. "Thank you Taryn, really. I appreciate you guys doing this for me. I sent everything you found over to my lawyer. He's with a different firm so Tyson won't know until we are ready."

"Is it enough?"

"More than enough. We now have proof that he's been in a relationship with someone else for over a year." Mia chokes out the last part, slowly closing her eyes. Willing the tears to stay put. *It's just another divorce case with a cheating client*, she tells herself to try and create emotional distance. It doesn't work.

"How long have you known?"

"I've been suspicious for a few months now, certainly not a year."

"I'm so sorry, Mia."

"Don't be, I'm not. I'm feeling a ton of emotions right now, but that's not one of them. To be honest, everything changed when I got pregnant. Before we found out about Ash, we'd been this dynamic duo for so long. Both career minded, both focused on advancing. A child was never in the cards for us, until it was." She thinks back to the day she knew her life was going to change forever.

"I was just as thrown off by it as he was, but the difference is I learned to adapt. He never could see past what he always saw as our future. I know he loves Ashton, but I can't help but think he blames me for getting pregnant at all."

Mia gives herself a moment by taking a long sip of coffee. This is the most she's ever shared about her marriage. Her real marriage anyway, not just what they showed people.

"Once I started working less, so I could be there more for Ashton, it was like he almost viewed it as me choosing Ash over my career."

"Your child should come first, Mia. You did nothing wrong."

"But in Ty's eyes, my career was directly linked to him."

"He sounds like a selfish jackass to me."

Mia can't help but smile at Taryn's candidness. It's one of the things she instantly liked about the woman. "Yeah, he is... and I loved him, so what does that make me?"

"Too good for him, that's what," Taryn replies, not skipping a beat.

"So what's the time frame look like?"

"My lawyer needs a few days to build the case and go back over the prenup. I'm not going to say anything to Tyson as of now. All I'm asking for is the house. I want nothing else from him, not a cent of alimony. I'm successful in my own right, I don't need him to provide for us."

"Good for you," Taryn says, with pride in her eyes for her friend's strength.

"I told myself I wouldn't ask, I don't really want to know anyway..." Mia trails off, not able to bring herself to ask about the other woman. Taryn doesn't need her to finish the sentence to know what she was asking. A slow smile spreads across her face as she leans in close and grabs Mia's hand and answers her unasked question.

"She's got nothing on you, girl. She's slow as rocks and spreads like peanut butter, that's all."

Mia's eyes widen in surprise and then she bursts out in laughter. Leave it to this crazy new friend to turn a moment as crappy as this one into laughter.

"So, what now?" Taryn asks when they both settle down.

"My plan is to take Ashton on a trip the day Tyson is served. He will need a few days to get his things out of the house, before we get back."

"Well, it looks like we are going on a trip then." Mia's head flies up, her eyes meeting Taryn's.

"You aren't in this alone Mia. We aren't going to let you go through a single moment of this alone. We are your tribe, your people. So how do you feel about camping?"

The only thing Mia could hear was that they weren't alone. Those words broke her almost as much as Tyson had. That's exactly what she's been feeling these last few months, utterly alone.

Four Letter Words

Corina squeezes Michael's hand until her knuckles turn white. She can't take her eyes off of the scan, nor can she get the doctor's words out of her head. Words that should only be four letters, but aren't, swim around in her head.

Uterine cancer, hysterectomy, menopause, full recovery. She's not able to process any of the words. None of the words make any sense to sense. Because she's stuck on her own four-letter word. Baby. As in she still desperately wants one. As in, now she'll never be able to have one again.

"Take a deep breath love, it's okay."

"Is it? Is it okay Michael? Because last time I checked they weren't removing your ability to have children. Last time I checked you weren't diagnosed with cancer. So maybe it's okay if I take shallow breaths for the moment?

Maybe it's okay that I'm freaking out? I love you, and I appreciate you trying to calm me down, but I need to freak out, okay?"

Her dear, sweet man offers her the slightest of sad smiles, then pulls her in close. "Yeah, it's okay to freak out, love."

"I'm sorry," Corina says instantly, when the shame comes for snapping at him.

"You have no reason to be sorry, love. You have every right. I don't know how that feels. I only know how it feels to sit by helplessly, able to do nothing. And that feels pretty shitty."

Corina holds him tight, burying her face in his chest as she cries. For a moment they both completely forget the doctor is still there until he clears his throat.

"I know this is a very hard, emotional time Corina, but we have to act swiftly," the doctor says, pulling them both back to the decision at hand.

"A hysterectomy is the only option?"

"If we want to get all the cancer and ensure it doesn't return. It's not the only option, but it is the best. You are lucky that it hasn't spread anywhere else yet. So, let's get rid of it once and for all while it's contained, yeah?"

Corina looks up into her husband's eyes, seeing the resignation there. "Yeah?" she asks him. One lone tear makes its way down his check and he nods.

"We have four beautiful children, and only one of you. We need you, babe."

Corina blows out a harsh breath, and with it the desires of her heart. "Okay then."

"I'm going to have Shelly book the OR for as soon

as we can get you in, and then she will call you with the date for your pre-op."

"How long will I be out of commission Doctor Havison?" Corina can already tell by his face, that she's not going to like his answer one bit.

"The average healing time is around six to eight weeks for most women, however that's without any complications."

"So, I'll be back to normal in six weeks?"

"Corina."

"Yes?"

"You are a very rare case. Your allergy to opioids and narcotics, changes things a bit."

Corina looks over at Michael trying to gage what this means. Michael pulls the hair at the back of his nape, telling her this is going to be bad. Corina had to have an emergency c-section with Max, during which, they discovered she's deathly allergic to every pain med they tried.

"What does that mean doc?" Michael puts into words what his wife was just wondering.

"It means Corina is going to have to undergo a major surgery without any narcotics. Motrin will help with the swelling, and might help some with the pain, but it's going to be a hard recovery."

Corina swallows hard.

"You have small children at home, one who can be aggressive, right?"

"Yes..." *What's his point?*

"So you will have to be out of the home for at least two weeks while you heal, possibly longer."

81

"Two weeks!" Both Corina and Michael practically shout together.

"No, no way, that's not even possible. You know I have four kids right? Max, he's very low on the spectrum, he won't understand."

"Which is exactly why you can't be there. We have to make sure your body is healed enough before we send you home. All it could take is one well-placed punch, and it could mess up the entire surgery. We can't risk it."

"There's no way I can leave my kids that long."

"Can you promise me that the kids won't climb on you, or hit your incision?" Corina looks over at Michael who looks just as defeated as she feels.

"I can promise the older two won't. But Max and Jasper still climb on me daily and wouldn't understand. Max also hits when he gets frustrated or overexcited."

"Exactly. I send most women home directly, but I'm sorry, we can't risk that with your unique situation."

Cancer, no more babies, menopause… these things Corina can take if she has to. But being away from her family for two weeks? That breaks her. Right in the middle of her doctor's office, in an ugly green hard chair, Corina falls to pieces.

———————

Somehow, they make it home and Corina cooks dinner, does bath time, reads a story, and gets four little ones down for bed. She does it all without thought or feeling. Numbness, she can do numbness.

"Babe, you're scaring me. Come sit down and talk to me for a minute." She ignores Michael's request and finishes washing the dishes. Dishes she can do. Emotions, nope, she can't handle those right now.

She feels so close to breaking that she needs to keep doing this mundane task so she doesn't have to feel, doesn't have to think or process. Michael doesn't ask again, instead he picks up the dishrag and stands next to her, drying each dish she washes.

Neither of them say a word. Neither mentions the fact that they have a perfectly good dishwasher that can wash and dry the dishes. They both just stand there and robotically wash and dry everything in the sink. When the task is done, Corina remains standing still, staring helplessly into the sink like it holds the answers. It doesn't.

Michael grabs a beer from the fridge, then pours her a glass of wine, ushering his wife out to the porch swing. They swing, then sip, repeat. After about thirty minutes of this, Michael is the first to speak.

"Biggest fear?"

"Too many to name. I guess I just can't wrap my head around them all."

"Fair enough. Can you list them, and then maybe we can put them in order?"

Corina thinks about it for a while, it's a fair question and one she hasn't given a lot of thought to. After a few minutes she speaks out her fears in order.

"Not making it through surgery, leaving the kids for two weeks and having something happen to one of them while I'm gone, not getting all of the cancer and going through all of this for nothing, never being able to have kids again, menopause." She ticks each point off on her fingers.

"So, we take them as they come. First, we get you through this surgery. I'll handle the kids, I'm not sure how yet, but I will. I can take time off from the garage if need be."

"You can't, we won't be able to afford the bills if you do. Plus, I won't be able to work my side jobs for a few weeks, depending on how bad the pain is."

"Then we table that one for now and come back to it later. As for the cancer, the doctor seemed pretty confident he could get it all with a full hysterectomy, so I think that doesn't need to be a concern for this moment."

"Fair enough."

"I know not having any more kids is a huge blow. It is for me too. But I can't help but look at my beautiful wife and my fantastic kids and just feel lucky. You are here with me, and breathing. That is a blessing I'll never take for granted, ever again." He reaches for her hand and gently rubs the back.

"You gave me such an amazing kid in Max. He has your eyes, my devilishly good looks, and your amazing laugh. We are truly blessed Cor. Our other three, I feel like they are our most precious gifts. Would I love another baby with you? Of course, but that can still come later. You, of all people, know you don't have to birth a child to be their mother."

Corina no longer feels numb, she now feels… everything. All the things, rolled into one. This man, this beautiful man broke down all her worries in one go. He is a gift, and she knows that they will get through this together, no matter what happens. Then something occurs to her and she dries her eyes and looks up at him.

"You forgot the menopause."

Michael's eyes widen while he rubs the back of his neck. "No, I didn't. I purposely left it out, because babe… that shit freaks me out."

That was all it took, and Corina is now in a fit of laughter. She laughs so hard she has to hold her stomach. "You afraid I'm going to go banana bonkers?"

"You have met my mother, right?" Michael asks, eyes wide in terror at the thought. Corina has met her, she's totally nuts.

"Before menopause she was the sweetest, most mellow person ever… then *BAM*! Crazy eights!"

Again, Corina breaks into a fit of giggles. "We are going to be okay, right?"

"Yes, we will." He kisses her forehead, and deep down, passed all the fear, grief, and worry Corina knows that he is right.

Sounds Like the Start of a Lame Joke

"You want to do what? Are you out of your bloody mind?"

"Why do I feel like that is the start of all of our conversations lately?" Taryn pouts.

"Probably because you are out of your bloody mind!" Liz yells again.

"Even Kevin didn't say that."

"Oh, yeah, what did *mister perfect* say then?"

"Well, not very much through the laughter," Taryn replies sheepishly.

"You want to take six autistic kids out in the woods? That sounds like the start of a lame joke. Half the time I wonder what's in that head of yours." Liz shakes her head.

"Most of the time? Dr. Dre and DMX lyrics," Taryn replies with a wide grin, while Liz just rolls her eyes. Taryn grabs Liz's hand and pleads.

"Come on Liz, I think it's a great idea. Everyone's in a funk lately, and I think it's just what we need. Obviously, Mia needs to get her and Ashton out of the house for a few days so Tyson can move out. Marcus is probably bored to death being homeschooled, just think of all the science he can be learning."

"And what about you? What are you getting out of this?"

"A break from the mundane. Plus, Jessie is running out of ways to drive me insane at home, she needs some new material."

"You joke, but you'll be lucky if she doesn't kill you and have Tacoma hide your body out there."

"Geez, Liz! I think this is a great time to teach the kids the beauty and dangers of nature."

"I have a feeling poison oak is in our future."

"Liz, where's your sense of adventure, huh? Although, it wouldn't be a bad idea to pack the calamine lotion, just to be safe." Taryn makes a mental note to pick some up.

"What about Corina? Is she on board?"

"That's the weird thing, nobody can get ahold of her. I tried, Mia tried, it's been a ghost town."

"That is weird. It doesn't seem like her at all."

"I know, which is why we are going to just show up at her house today."

"What? Taryn, do you not have any boundaries?"

"Only in the bedroom." Taryn winks, causing Liz to cringe. *Score.*

"Come on, I'm worried about her. Let's just go check in. We can bring a casserole. It's hard to shut the door in someone's face, while they are holding a casserole."

"I really need to grow a backbone."

"What was that? All I heard was, Taryn wins." Taryn grabs her purse as she yells up the stairs.

"Marcus, come on, it's field trip time."

"Aunt Taryn? What are you doing here?"

"Kidnapping us," Liz states under her breath. Taryn shoots her a look and then plasters a smile on her face for Marcus.

"I'm here to take you for some socializing."

"With who?" Lord, this kid is as skeptical as his mother.

"Corina's little boy, Jasper."

"Isn't he a baby?"

"He's almost two, so he's old enough to play trains," Taryn baits. Marcus thinks about it a moment and then his eyes light up.

"Did you know America's first steam locomotive lost a race to a horse?"

"No, I didn't know that. Did you know that a honeybee can fly at a speed of fifteen miles per hour?"

"No, I didn't. That's very useful to know. I wonder how fast I can run?"

"Hopefully at least sixteen miles per hour," Taryn says, winking at Liz.

"That, or you can teach him how to jump into a pond, you're pretty good at that," Liz quips back.

"Oh, hush, negative nelly. Last one to the car is a rotten egg!" Marcus and Taryn take off running toward the door, while Liz just sighs and follows her friend's crazy antics as usual. Everyone needs a Liz.

They pull up to Corina's house and park in the driveway. Taryn hands Marcus the frozen lasagna that she had in the freezer, and they pile out making their way to the door. They can hear Jasper crying, so at least they know she's home.

Taryn rings the bell, then knock a few seconds later.

"Corina? It's us!" Taryn yells through the door, while Liz rolls her eyes but stays silent. A few minutes later the door opens. Corina is standing there with tears rolling down her face, matching the little boy in her arms.

"Oh, dear." Liz jumps to right away, taking the baby from her arms and ushering Marcus into the house. "Go put that lasagna on the counter Marcus and then take Jasper upstairs to play trains okay?"

Marcus doesn't look too sure of this plan, but one more look at Corina and it appears he figures a crying baby is better than a crying woman so he takes Jasper and runs off.

"Come on now love, Taryn is going to make us some tea while we go sit on the couch," Liz says, wrapping an arm around Corina, and taking her to sit down.

While Liz guides Corina to the living room, Taryn rummages around the kitchen for some tea. Tea sucks anyway, so she stops her search when she sees beer in the fridge. Taryn grabs two bottles of water and a beer for Corina.

"Here you go, I figured you could use something a little stronger than tea."

"Tea is calming," Liz scolds.

"It also sucks," Taryn counters, handing over the bottles.

"Thanks you guys. I'm sorry you have to see me like this, I'm just a bit overwhelmed is all." Corina manages to get out between sniffles.

"It's fine, everyone has bad days, what's going on?" Liz asks as she puts her arm around Corina.

Corina takes a deep breath, it's the first time she's admitted it out loud. "Apparently, I have cancer and have to have a full hysterectomy. The doctor's office just called to let me know that they can fit me in Monday, as in three days from now." Corina rambles it all out in a rush, not bothering to stop for a breath. "Also, I have to be out of the house for two weeks, and have no clue what I'm going to do with the kids, let alone Max. Michael can't get off work with this short of notice and it just feels like too much right now. I'm falling apart."

Corina starts to sob again and Taryn's eyes go wide. Taryn tends to be awkward in most situations and has absolutely no clue what to do in this situation. Although, apparently neither does Liz, because she takes the untouched beer sitting in front of Corina and downs it one go. Liz wipes her mouth and then claps her hands.

"It's not great news, but we will figure it out, don't you worry. Taryn and I were just coming over to ask if we could take Max on a camping trip."

"We were?" Taryn asks as she shoots daggers at Liz, after the rant Liz went on earlier about how dumb the trip was.

"We were. We will be gone a week, so that is a full week you won't have to worry about Max. He will have so much fun camping, he won't have any time to worry about you," Liz says as she eyes the empty beer bottle, probably wondering if it'd be tacky to grab a second.

"Can Michael find someone for the other three?" Taryn asks.

"I'm sure the older two can stay with friends, it'd just be the baby..." Corina starts to tear up again and that's all it takes to get Liz to turn into a motor mouth.

"Marcus loves Jasper, we will take him too!" Liz declares much too cheerfully.

"We will?" Taryn asks with her eyes the size of saucers.

"We will." *Again with the daggers.*

"You guys can't take them alone. It'd be far too much for you. Although it would be such a blessing to us for sure. But way too much for you." Corina's voice of reason kicks in, although her eyes remain hopeful.

"Oh, nonsense. It's not that many kids." Liz tries to sound convincing, but she's not fooling anyone.

"It's seven kids, six of whom are on the spectrum." Taryn reminds her, shocked that she is the voice of reason for once.

"And three whole adults," Liz declares like that's not suicide.

Taryn is the one who got them into this whole camping mess, although, to her credit, she thought they were only adding one more child, and another adult. But one look at their sobbing friend has made up her mind.

"Yup, piece of cake," Taryn says, also eyeing the empty beer bottle, wishing she wouldn't have taken a water.

The ladies leave an hour later, with a very relieved Corina waving to them from the doorway. They both smile all the way until they get into the car where Taryn tries to incinerate Liz with her eyes.

"Well, what did you want me to do? You saw her! That could have been either of us." Liz tries to defend herself.

"You are worse than my husband! A few tears and you turn into a rambling fool. What's a few more kids? Throw in a baby," Taryn mocks.

"You are forgetting this was your stupid idea to begin with. What the heck do I know about camping?"

"Hey Marcus?" Taryn yells into the back seat.

"If you do some research on camping for us, you know, how to prepare food, set up a tent, etcetera, I'll buy you an encyclopedia on trains and locomotives."

"The one from C.J. Riley?" The excitement takes over and his voice cracks.

"Sure buddy."

"Yes!" He screams from the back seat while Taryn throws a triumphant smile at Liz in the passenger seat.

"See, no worries, we will have ourselves an expert in no time."

"Why am I even friends with you?" Liz groans.

"Because everyone needs a Taryn."

CHAPTER

The Quickest Way to Lose Your Mind

Mia makes sure to pack their bags while Ashton is still in school. She goes down the check list: ice chest, tent, sleeping bags, pillows, noise canceling headphones, chewies, five bags of neutral-colored foods, since that's all Ashton will eat.

"Mia." The strangled word comes from behind her and she freezes on the spot. *No Ty, don't do this. Not now.*

"Tyson, I can't."

"Don't go, please. Let's talk this out. You haven't even given me the courtesy of hearing my side."

"Your side? Your side!" Any pity she felt for him fled, only anger remains.

"I don't need to hear your side Tyson, I've seen it. Loud and clear on Instagram, along with Tammy's 5,983 followers."

"Mia, it was a mistake."

"A mistake is one time, not an entire year. An entire year is a choice, Tyson. For three hundred and sixty-five days you chose to lie to me. You chose to leave me and your son behind, while you spent your time, and gave your body, to someone else without giving us a second thought." Mia is terrified that she'll crumble if she looks at him, but she slowly finds the courage to turn and face him.

"You are a very intelligent man, one that knows the consequences of your actions, yet you chose them again and again. You chose her." She take a deep, calming breath and look him straight in the eye.

"And now I'm choosing. Every day for twelve years I have chosen you. When times were easy, hard, things were good, and bad. I chose you when you were sick, or stressed. I chose you when you were grumpy or lost a case. I chose you when you continually put work ahead of our son I..." Mia wipes the single tear that falls down her check. "I chose you each and every day. Four thousand, three-hundred and eighty days I chose you. Now, I'm choosing me."

She grabs her list and the last of the bags on the counter, making her way to the door without giving him a second look.

"Leave your key on the counter on your way out. Everything else that needs to be said, you can say to my attorney. You may have supervised visits with your son and keep all your money. All I'm taking is the house,

Ashton, and my clients. Say another word and I'll take half of everything." She waits a beat with her hand on the door, almost daring him to say another word.

Even with her threat, she wants to see if he will fight for her, for them. She waits and all she gets is silence. She should have known as much. Mia swallow's down the angry tears, and quietly shut the door behind her. He made his choice. She loads the rest of the bags into the car, and dries her eyes, then retouches her makeup the best she can.

Mia still has an hour before she has to get Ashton, so she drives to a nearby park and sits in the parking lot. She calls the one person who she's always trying to shield from her pain, yet the only one who can manage to heal her, her father.

"Hey sweetie, how's it going? This is a surprise."

Of course, just hearing his voice sends her back to childhood and she bursts into tears. Mia relays the whole sob story to him, all of it. He's quiet for a moment and then she can hear him sigh, long and deep.

"First of all, I hate that you waited so long to come to me with this. Why don't you come stay with us for a few days?"

"You know how Ashton's screaming wears on mom's nerves." He sighs again, because he does know, visits are always bittersweet.

"Plus, I'm taking him on a camping trip with my friends and their kids, I just needed someone to put things into perspective and help calm me down before I go."

"Alright then, let's do that." She can almost hear the smile in his voice as he gets into full-on dad mode.

"Mia, you are a strong, intelligent, beautiful, black woman. You've always forged your own path and worked harder than anyone I've ever known to get there. Anytime you had a bump in the road, you didn't go around it, you climbed a mountain." Mia swipes at the tears that pour down her face, yet somehow she manages to find her smile at his fierce belief in her.

"You deserve to be treated with the respect you have earned. You know your value Mia, that's why you left. Now you dry your eyes and have an amazing week with that beautiful boy you created."

"Thanks, Daddy."

"I'm so proud of the woman you are Mia, don't let anyone make you feel inferior."

"I won't." Mia looks down at the clock and starts the car again after one more swipe at her makeup.

"That young man and I are going to have a serious talk."

"Dad, I've already handled it."

"You've handled your business, as you should. Now, we have our own." Mia can't help but laugh at the thought of her dad chewing out Tyson.

"I love you, old man."

"I love you more. Now don't touch anything that makes you scratch."

"Are you talking about poison oak?" He's quiet a moment and then chuckles. "Uh, sure. Love you sweet pea."

Mia had to take a whole week of paid vacation, so the crying stops now. She might be going on the most insane vacation ever, but it's with the family of her choice. And dammit, they will have fun!

An hour later Mia is questioning her sanity as Jasper cries in the back seat. She calls the other two ladies on conference call on her cars Bluetooth.

"How did I end up with the crying baby?"

"Because Jessie and Gavin can't ride in a car together, and Liz refused to take Jessie, so I had to take Marcus plus Jessie and the big ass dog, leaving no room for the baby."

"Yes, well I have Gavin and Mason, who are stimming out of their minds at the moment, and my car only holds two in the back, so there was no room for the baby either. I can pull over and we can switch out one of the boys for Jasper if you want… but I think the crying will send one of these two over the moon to be honest."

Mia sighs and looks in the mirror as Max and Ash hold hands over their ears.

"No, that's okay, I'll figure it out."

"Did you try giving him milk?"

"Cheerios?"

"A stuffed animal?"

"Music?"

They trade off listing all the things she has tried and failed. "Yes, I've tried it all, but I think he just misses his m-o-m."

"Why did Corina spell out mom and not just say it?" Marcus asks in the background.

Of course, Jasper hears this and then starts chanting, *"momma, mooommmaaaaaa, mommmmmmmmmmaaaaaaaa."*

"The boys have gone from just holding their ears to rocking back and forth.

"Lord help me, okay I gotta go." Mia hangs up to try and shush Jasper.

"It's okay hunny, we are going to go camping, it'll be so much fun. You can see birds, and squirrels, and a lake."

"*Mooooommmmmmmmaaaaaaa.*"

"I know baby, I know."

She has two hours left of screaming children, because now the other two have started up. It gives her plenty of time to hatch the most evil plan she can to get revenge on Tyson. Starting with recording this insanity and playing it on speaker all night long, over the intercom of wherever he lives next.

Best $30 I've Ever Spent

They finally get to the campsite and Taryn hops out of the car in a great mood. Jessie, thank the dear Lord above, fell asleep about fifteen minutes into the trip. She gave Marcus his train encyclopedia, so she had a nice peaceful drive.

Judging by the haggard look on poor Mia's face, and the bright red eyes and noses of her three traveling companions, I'd say that wasn't the case for her.

"I don't care if I have the biggest vehicle or not. The return trip home we are trading cars... and kids!"

Taryn takes a still crying Jasper out of her hands and nods, if nothing else, to calm the crazy.

"Of course, not a problem. I'm sorry Mia."

Liz comes running over with that *you broke her* look again, Taryn waves it off and passes her the baby.

"Here Liz, you take Jasper and the boys, and Marcus and I will set up the tents okay?" Taryn turns back to Mia who looks to be close to a mental breakdown by this point.

"Mia, why don't you go scout out the nearby bathrooms for us okay? Take five, come back nice and refreshed?"

She looks ashamed for a moment, but then nods and wipes her eyes as she goes.

Taryn looks around at their motley crew trying to figure out how they are going to corral the kids while they set up camp.

She looks around at the three campsites they purchased next to each other. With a little finagling she thinks they can manage.

Taryn pulls the long tables all over to the middle camp site. She angles them so that they are all touching, creating a weird triangle in the middle.

"Okay guys, we are going to play farm, okay? Everyone in the pen, you are all animals, and Mason, you are the farmer. You sit on top of this table, okay?" She places each child in the middle of the triangle, then tosses as many toys as she can find to them. Taryn grabs a small blanket from the car places it on the ground, then plucks Jasper from Liz and plops him on it, along with some snacks and books.

"There, isn't that fun? Okay, you play farm until we get these tents set up. Mase, if one of the animals escapes, as the farmer you need to put them back."

"Or tell a shepherd, which is an adult," Liz yells over her shoulder. Mason nods, looking proud to have such responsibility.

100

The tent, however, is easier said than done. "Have you ever set up a tent before?" Liz asks skeptically.

"Of course I have. I'm just not sure the best way to do it with three, did we figure out which way we should face?" Taryn asks, trying to figure out the weird configuration on the campsites. Too bad they didn't just purchase a large group site.

Mia makes her way back, looking much better than before, laughing when she sees their little makeshift farm.

"Not bad, not bad at all. Sorry for my little meltdown earlier, I promise I'm fine now."

Taryn pulls her aside, where she can still keep an eye on all the *farm animals.*

"Look Mia, I was a jerk, I'm so sorry. We got caught up in the packing of it all and who had more room. We didn't even consider the fact that you probably had the harder kids. I'm so sorry. As my punishment I'll take Jasper, Jessie, Max and Ashton on the way home. But I'll need your car… and probably a fifth of Jack once I get home." Taryn teases and it does the trick, making Mia laugh.

"We can talk about the ride home later, I'm just happy to be here. I ran into Tyson before I left and, well… let's just say it didn't make the trip any easier."

"Oh, crap, now I really feel bad."

"No worries, Let's get this campsite set up before the kids revolt."

Taryn turns back to the camp and is shocked when she sees Marcus has two of the three tents already set up. She looks at Liz who just shrugs and goes back to throwing grapes in the kids' mouths.

"Must be his photographic memory. Apparently, he read up on how to erect tents and other such wilderness nonsense before we left. I guess the train encyclopedia bribe was worth it huh?" Liz asks.

"Hands down, best $30 ever spent. Should we tell him they are all facing the wrong way?" They all share a smile as they realize they are all facing out and not in.

"Oh, but he worked so hard. I think it's fine, at least you didn't have to set it up," Mia points out.

"True. Okay, let's get these kids in the tents so I can start dinner."

So today was not easy, but then again no day ever is. But they saw more genuine smiles, and fewer meltdowns, at least from the kids than they have in a long time.

They also learned that Liz hates anything creepy or crawly... which is kind of hilarious since she has two boys.

The women were able to get the kids fed, somewhat washed, and in bed all without too many problems. Since Taryn's kids were dubbed the hardest, the girls decided to take the extras in their tent. Max went with Mia and Jasper with Liz.

Taryn had a hard enough time getting her kids to calm down and not hit one another. Finally, she had enough and made a barrier of suitcases between them, pretty much isolating poor Gavin to the back of the tent.

Taryn was so worried one of her kids would try to sneak out while she slept, that she waited until they were sleeping and then tied bells on their wrists. She also tied bells to the zippers of the tent, since you can never be too safe.

It's about three in the morning before both kids are finally asleep and Taryn drifts off. It only feels like minutes before Taryn is awoken by a tiny tinkling sound.

She thinks she's dreaming until she remembers the bells. Just as she shoots to an upright position, Taryn sees Tacoma tear off across the tent to run out the front, ripping the zipper open.

"It's okay Tacoma, it's only a kitty." Jessie's sweet little voice says before Taryn's heart drops to the floor.

Gavin is fast asleep behind his barrier, but Jessie is making her way toward a mother-effing raccoon.

"Sweet kitty. Kitty love Cheetos. You hungry kitty?" Taryn looks down to see a torn open bag of Cheetos on the ground, which must have been what attracted the freaking thing to begin with.

Some protector Tacoma turned out to be. Taryn has to swallow hard and take as deep of a breath as she can, because everything in her just wants to scream bloody murder.

Looking over to make sure Gavin is safely secured behind the barrier, she scoops Jessie up and practically drags her out of the tent before she gets her face ripped off by the, with her luck, rabid raccoon.

"Kitty, I want kitty." Jessie screams as she fights her mom to go back into the tent.

"Dammit Jessie, stop kicking. I'm going to drop you."

When that didn't work, Taryn was ashamed that her only thought was to give good old bribery a go. "Jessie, you want ice cream?"

"Ice cream!"

"Yeah honey, mommy will give you ice cream, but you have to stop fighting me and go to Auntie Liz's tent."

Jessie instantly stills in Taryn's arms, and she thanks the Lord above. The idea of Gavin being trapped in there with that thing is actually giving her hives.

Taryn runs like she's on fire, right into Liz's tent. She tosses Jessica in before her. Unfortunately, it happened to be right on top of a child, who then starts to wail. Liz jumps up, looking around like a madwoman.

"Wha?" Liz mutters, trying to blink the sleep out of her eyes.

"Liz there's a mother-effing raccoon in my tent right now! It's in there with Gav, Liz, how the hell do I get it out?"

"Crap! I have no clue. Food?"

"That's why he's there to begin with."

"I go get kitty." Jessica stands up, ignoring the wailing child she was sitting on and makes her way to the front of the tent.

"Sit!" Both Liz and Taryn demand.

"Marcus, you make sure Jessie stays in here, you understand me. Nobody and I mean nobody leaves for any reason." Liz leaves no room for questioning in her tone.

A sleepy, scared looking Marcus nods once, and holds his arms out for Jessie to come to him. Poor thing is also crying, because they yelled at her, but that's the least of their worries at the moment.

They make their way back to Taryn's tent as fast as possible and see Mia come out of her tent bleary-eyed.

"Raccoon... Gavin... tent..." is about all Taryn can manage through the tears.

"Oh, Jesus! Um... Mia looks around and runs over to the food cabinet, coming back quickly with chocolate.

"Where the hell is your dog?" Liz asks.

"He ran out at the first sign of trouble!" Taryn says, not able to worry about Tacoma right now when that beast is in there with her child.

"If we all make it out alive, I think Mia should sue that therapy dog company for sure, yours is useless," Liz points out.

"Okay, Taryn, you open the tent and I'll throw the chocolate in, then Liz, stand ready with the broom just in case." Mia throws a chunk of chocolate in and starts making kissing sounds.

"What the hell are you doing?" Taryn asks, looking at Mia like she's crazy.

"Well, that's how you call a cat isn't it?"

"My child I understand, but don't tell me you, a grown ass woman, think that's a cat too?"

"Obviously not, but it's in the same family, right? I don't know how to call a freaking raccoon," Mia argues, throwing her hands up in the air.

"Toss another piece of chocolate in, a little farther this time." Liz coaxes.

Mia does as instructed, but the little creature is just taking his time nibbling away.

"Forget this jazz!" Taryn takes the broom and starts hitting the side of the tent with it. That's when all hell breaks loose. The raccoon flies out like its tail is on fire.

Taryn drops the broom and instantly burst into tears. She runs into the tent to hold her son who is now biting and pinching her in between sobs.

105

Taryn can hear the other kids crying in their tents too. There's just enough of a lull in activity to hear Liz say, "camping, what a fabulous idea, Taryn."

Yeah, when Taryn said everyone needs a Liz... she lied.

CHAPTER

The Only Thing Worse
Than Exercise, is Snakes

As hard a time as they give each other, there's nobody Liz respects more than she does Taryn. It doesn't matter if your kids are typically developing or not. Spectrum or not. Motherhood is straight up hard. Sometimes it feels impossible, like you have to do brain surgery with only a plastic knife, kind of impossible.

Even though she can be a hot mess most of the time, Taryn mothers flawlessly. Sure, her kids are out of control, but they are massively loved and cared for. She never lets them hide behind the autism label like Liz tends to.

Liz just wants to shelter her kids, hide them away from the world where they will be safe, and accepted.

Taryn tackles the world like she does life, with gusto. And the best part is, she encourages her kids to do the same.

Liz can only laugh when they are outside some random CVS at seven in the morning eating ice cream out of a gallon container.

"You officially get mother of the year," Liz says, motioning to Taryn with her plastic spoon.

"I can't tell if you are mocking me or not."

"Not." Both Mia and Liz say at once.

"Seriously Taryn, I don't know how you do it. If there was a raccoon in with Ashton, I would have died right there on the spot, not promised ice cream."

Mia takes a big bite of the chocolate and peanut butter ice cream that they are sharing. The kids are sharing their own container because, well, kids are gross.

"Honestly, the ice cream is just as much for me as it is for her, that was freaky."

"Do you regret the trip now?" Liz asks scooping up another bite.

"Do you know what? I don't. Is it hard? Sure. But our daily life is hard. Is Jessie going to get into everything and cause trouble? Sure, she does that everywhere she goes. Will Gavin meltdown nonstop? Again, will happen no matter what." Taryn looks over at her kids, devouring their ice cream and smiles.

"Since those things will happen anyway, at least I can give them some good memories. We will have funny stories of me chasing out raccoons, and amazing memories of eating ice cream out of the tub before eight a.m. At least I can give them that."

Liz looks over at her own boys, devouring their ice cream with huge smiles on their faces. She can't help but be grateful for the crazy woman next to her.

Liz is not an adventurous mom. She is a nervous mom, by nature. The hovering helicopter mom that lives by schedules and routines. Not necessarily by fun and experiences. Everyone needs friends that can widen their views and bring fun into their lives. Liz looks over at Mia who is watching her son with tears in her eyes.

"How are you holding up, Mia?"

"Honestly, I'm good. Better than I should be, probably. You know this is our first time camping."

"Like ever?" Taryn asks surprised.

"Yup. It was one of those things that Tyson and I said we were going to do as soon as we got through law school. And then as soon as we passed the bar. Then once we made partner. Well, you get the drift." Mia puts her spoon down and wipes her hands with some wet wipes.

"After we accomplished all those things, I had Ashton. Ty didn't think it'd be worth it to take a baby and then once he was old enough, he said there's no way would could take him because of the meltdowns and running away."

She gestures to where her son is happily eating, making a huge mess with the ice cream.

"But here we are. I never thought I'd be able to live without Tyson. I never thought I could do it alone."

"Yet here you are, killing it." Taryn bumps her shoulder and smiles.

"Well, I'm doing it anyhow. And thanks to you ladies, I know I can."

109

"Of course you can. Will life be easy? Probably not, but who needs easy? You've got this Mia, and we will be there every step of the way." Liz reminds her with a tight hug. After their embrace, Liz takes a look at all of the messy kids.

"Well, what do you say we get these kids cleaned up? What's on the agenda for today, Taryn?"

"There's a little private watering hole I know of, but it's a small hike away from the camp. Do you think the kids are up for it?"

"The kids, sure... but are we?" Liz asks, eying all the kids.

"I don't see why not. Corina gave me her Moby Wrap so I can wear Jasper on my back. If you and Mia can carry the snacks, we can pair the kids two to each adult. One hand each, would that work?"

Liz laughs, Taryn is so much more adventurous than she is, but that's why they're good for each other. You can see intimidation on Mia's face too, which actually makes Liz feel better, oddly.

"Alright, let's go for a hike."

————————

The only thing worse than exercise, is exercising with children. Marcus took Max, who has actually really taken to him. Taryn got stuck with Jessie, Tacoma and Jasper, leaving Liz with Mason and Gavin. Mia with just her son, but she's been keeping and eye on the other boys as well.

Gavin keeps pinching Liz every time one of the other kids makes a noise... and this bunch is a noisy lot. She looks down at her arm, and groans. Great, she looks like a junky with track marks all over her arm. Taryn sees and gives Liz a sympathetic smile.

"Do you want to trade? You can wear Jasper and I'll take Gav?" Liz looks over at Jasper's sweet, sleeping face and shakes her head no as she pulls down on her sleeve.

They finally make it up to the water hole, not a minute too soon. Liz is dripping in sweat, not to mention blood, by this point. Mason's shoe has come untied and he starts squealing.

"Stay right here Gavin, I'm just going to tie Mason's shoe okay?"

Liz lets go of Gavin's hand for just a minute, ties Mason's shoe as fast as she can and when she looks up, he's gone.

"Taryn!" Liz screams. Taryn looks her way, with eyes wide.

"Did anyone see where Gavin went?"

"He was right there with you."

"Well, he was. I had to tie Mase's shoe and then he was gone."

"Damn! Mia, take Jessie." Taryn runs off and Liz feels horrible.

"I'm so sorry Mia, do you think if Marcus helps, you can watch the others? They will play in the water, I just need to help Taryn."

"Of course, of course. Hurry go."

Liz runs in the opposite direction as Taryn, running as fast as she can.

Hopefully, Taryn finds him, but since they didn't see which way he went, Liz thought it'd be best to go the other way.

Liz is about ten feet away when she finally spots him and sighs in relief... until she sees what he is playing with. *Jesus Christ on a cracker, what the hell is with Taryn's kids and dangerous animals?*

At his feet is a snake, and from this distance, she has no clue what type, but Liz. So. Doesn't. Do. Snakes!

Liz takes out her cell to see there are no bars, she curses and screams for Taryn as loud as she can, hoping she will hear her.

Gavin's head jerks to Liz's direction and she tries to smile, but it's shaky at best.

"Gavin come to Auntie Liz." She motions with her arm, and he gives her a fleeting glance before his eyes go back to the snake. *Damn!* Luckily, he hasn't touched it yet, but that means Liz is going to have to get close to the freaking thing.

She has tears rolling down her face at a rapid pace, because snakes are her second worst fear. Dead children are her first, and Gavin is now eye level to this freaking snake, and if it is poisonous, well she can't even think about that right now.

Liz takes stock of everything she has on her at the moment, which isn't much. She has her cell phone and a tube of travel sunscreen... yup, totally screwed.

She's about a foot away when she holds her hand out to Gavin.

"Come on Gav, let's go swimming."

"Swimming?" He asks, without making a single movement. However, the snake does, he coils and shakes his, Oh God, it's a mother-effing rattler.

Liz runs as fast as she can and takes Gavin down football style. They crash to the ground as Liz protects Gavin's body with her own the best she can, as she rolls them as fast as she can down the side of the hill.

OMG we are going to die, is pretty much the only thought running through her mind at the moment, over and over again. But eventually they stop rolling. Gavin is laughing, the little sadist.

Liz takes a moment to take stock of everything. She is full of cuts and probably bruises. So is Gav, but otherwise they are fine. No broken bones and, thank God, no snake bites.

"Gavin look at me, babe. Snakes give owie okay. Snake bad."

"Snake, owie?"

"Yes, snake owie. No more snakes."

He blinks at Liz like an owl for about a minute, but then gives her a nod. "Okay, it's time to go find mommy now, and then Auntie Liz is going on strike."

"Strike." He mimics.

"Yup, we are getting the hell out of Dodge, buddy."

Nature Hates Me

Taryn doesn't understand how everyone she knows can take a nice little camping trip with no issues, and she can't even make it a day without a life-threatening disaster. She swears, nature hates her.

She's searched the entire side of this mountain and Gavin is nowhere to be found. She's sobbing, running and searching, in that order, when she finally makes it back to the water hole.

"There you are. Liz went that way. I heard her yelling a bit ago, I think she has him, but I didn't dare leave the kids." Mia throws over her shoulder as she sprays Jasper down with sunscreen.

"Oh, thank God! Okay, thank you Mia, I'm going to go check over there."

Taryn runs as fast as she can down the little hill, and her heart finally starts beating again when she sees her little love. Liz has what looks to be a death grip on his hand, sticks in her hair, and blood dripping down her arm and legs. *What the hell?*

Taryn takes off directly for them when Liz puts her hand up to stop her friend. Taryn freezes as Liz points down. Taryn's gaze follows her point to the ground, what the heck? There's nothing there.

Taryn watches Liz as she looks at the ground the whole time she makes her way over.

The closer they get, the more Taryn can see how banged up they both are. She puts her arms out and Gavin runs directly into them.

"Hey baby, are you okay? Let me take a good look at you."

Taryn looks him over, and beside some bumps and scrapes, he doesn't look too bad. Liz however, looks like she's been to a war zone and back.

"You found him! Thank you so much. What happened?"

"I don't do snakes!" She literally screams, even though she's only a foot away from Taryn.

"Um... okay?"

"I don't do mother-effing snakes Taryn. I don't do garden snakes, gopher snakes, or water snakes. You know, the kind that aren't deadly! I don't even do those. So what do you think about rattlesnakes? You know, the kind that can kill you?" She's screaming again, but not at Taryn, more like in just some type of weird panicked mania.

"Did you see a rattler?"

"Sure did. Gavin sat down and invited one to tea."

"Oh, boy!" Taryn frantically starts looking him over again, checking for any sign of bites.

"Oh, no, he's fine, because I risked my damn life for him. We are leaving right now Taryn. I don't do nature and I sure as hell don't do snakes!" Liz yells as she marches back over to the water hole.

Mia looks at us surprised, since the usual mild Liz is having a full-blown freak out. Taryn just shrugs back as Liz grabs her two kids and starts shouting at them to get out of the water and get dressed.

"I'm pretty sure I broke Liz," Taryn whispers to Mia.

"Sure looks that way to me," Mia whispers back.

"Kids doing okay?" Taryn looks over to where all the kids are splashing and playing in the water. Jessie laughs as she splashes Tacoma who is trying to eat the water droplets.

"I hate to make them leave while they are having such a good time," Mia adds.

"Me too, give me a second, let me go talk to her." Taryn finds Liz shoving everything she can get her hands on, blindly into two bags. "Liz honey, come over here for a second and talk to me."

She's shaking so bad, with tears streaming down her face, Taryn's pretty sure she's seconds away from a full-blown nervous breakdown.

"I don't do snakes, Taryn, I don't do snakes. And Gavin, and the rattlesnake, and…"

"I know love, I know." Taryn brings her in and hugs her shaking little body tight. "You did so good though. You found Gav, and you protected him Liz. I'm so very grateful for that. You saved my little boy." Liz bursts out in full-blown tears now. Taryn feels so guilty for bringing her here that she doesn't know what to do but hold her tight.

"Why don't you head back to camp and take a moment? Mia and I will be fine with the kids. Go ahead and take a breath, and then we will decide what to do from there, okay? We will figure something out. You go back to camp, leave the rest to me."

"Okay." Liz takes a deep breath, one last look at her boys and then heads back to camp. Taryn makes her way back over to Mia, who is playing with Jasper happily on the bank. "Everything okay?"

"She's seriously freaking out. She wants to go back home."

"After just a day?"

"I mean, both of my kids could have died already, so yeah... nature just hates me. I don't know if I should push my luck anymore."

"True. I promised Tyson the four days to get his stuff out, so I don't think I can go back yet." Mia bites her bottom lip.

"I know, not to mention Max, we promised Corina the week? I just hate that Kevin was right."

"About what?"

"He said we wouldn't last a day. I hate when he's right!"

"Well, then let's not let him win. We will figure something out."

CHAPTER

That is Not Lemonade

Once Liz finally calmed down and talked to the camp ranger, she learned that the snakes stay in the higher elevation. As long as they stayed near camp, they should be safe.

She will never for the life of her forget the sound of that rattle, or the quick flicks of that snake's tongue. Liz is pretty sure she'll never sleep again.

But after she calmed down and cleared her head, Liz realized that leaving wasn't the answer. At least not in the heat of the moment. So they decided to stay for at least the night. Lasting two nights, feels so much less defeatist than only one.

After what felt like fifteen trips to the bathroom, the ladies finally get all the kids settled in for the night. All the food has been secured in the locked cabinets, and hopefully they won't have another repeat of last night.

Liz is exhausted, today's excitement wore her out, not to mention how sore her poor body is. She's much too old to be rolling down mountain sides, protecting children from venomous snakes.

Everyone finally settles down, and Jasper snuggles in close. She misses baby cuddles. Liz almost forgot how sweet and snuggly the little ones can be.

"Hey mom. *Moooom*." Marcus whispers from the corner.

"What Marcus?"

"I think Mason has to pee."

"We just took everyone to the bathroom."

"But he didn't go then and look at him now."

Liz looks over at Mason who is holding himself and squirming. Then she looks down at Jasper, who finally settled in and just fell asleep on her lap, and her mind is made up.

"Sorry bud, you should have tried, I can't risk waking the baby or we will be up all night. There's an empty water bottle in the corner, have him use that."

"Ew, mom, how is he going to pee in the bottle?"

"That's what train conductors used to do on long trips."

"You are making that up."

"No, I'm not." *Liz totally is.*

"They couldn't walk away from their post, so they would pee in a can. A water bottle is just as good as a can. Go in the back corner and make sure he aims well."

"Well, okay, I guess. Come on Mason, you better not pee on me." Mason giggles and after a few more laughs both boys are back in their sleeping bags.

Liz sighs, and snuggles in for the night. It takes her several hours to get comfortable enough to fall asleep. The sun rises much too early, and she's so not ready to be awake when Jasper starts squeezing her cheeks.

"Ju, ju, wiz."

"Okay baby, once everyone wakes up, we will get you some juice. Go back to sleep now."

He gets up and goes over to the back of the tent where the boys are sleeping. Liz rolls back over and tries to get a few extra precious minutes of sleep. That is until she hears someone make a noise.

"Yummy ju."

Her eyes pop open and she jumps up just in time to see Jasper pick up the bottle of pee. "Oh, sweet Jesus, Jasper no. Don't drink that!" Liz yells as she dives across Mason, just in time to smack the bottle out of Jasper's hands.

Liz gets there just in time, so he didn't drink any, but unfortunately, when she hit it, the bottle cap was already off... meaning the entire tent, and all of their bedding, is drenched in pee. Liz picks up Jasper and runs over to Mia's tent.

"Mia, Mia wake up!" Liz whisper yells.

"Can you watch Jasper for a second, there's pee all over everything in my tent, I need to clean it up."

Liz can hear Mia moving around and then unzips her tent and pokes her head out. She's blurry-eyed with her eye mask hanging around her neck and her hair in a head scarf. She looks much too adorable for camping. But then again Liz is not a great comparison since she's crazy haired and covered in pee.

"Can't you guys just go one morning without some kind of crisis?"

"Apparently not."

Taryn comes out of her tent holding Gavin's hand as she gives me a triumphant, yet, sleepy-eyed look.

"Looks like I'm not the only one who can't control my children."

"Well, technically, this one isn't even mine, so there. Make yourself useful and watch the kids while I figure out this mess will ya?" Liz asks Taryn.

"Yes, ma'am." Taryn fake salutes her, and Liz rolls her eyes as she walks back to her tent.

"Mason, Marcus, go play with Aunt Taryn while I figure out what to do with this mess."

"If you would have just let me take him to the bathroom last night, none of this would have happened, you know," Marcus says, narrowing his eyes at his mother.

"Yes son, I realize that now, but it's too late."

It's her son's turn to roll his eyes at her now, as he exits the tent. Liz looks around at the horrible mess and plugs her nose at the smell. Good Lord, she just might puke. She tosses all the bedding outside just in time to hear Marcus greet Taryn.

"Good morning, Taryn! Did you know that the railroads are responsible for the US standardized time zones?"

"Good morning Marcus, no I didn't. Did you know that mosquitoes have forty-seven teeth?" Taryn asks him back, as she slaps her arm to rid herself of said pest.

"Do they really?"

"They sure do."

"Did you know that a snail's teeth are arranged in rows on its tongue? A garden snail has about 14,000 teeth while other types can have over 20,000," Marcus states proudly.

"No way!" Mia joins into the madness that is Marcus and Taryn's fact hour.

"Yup!" Marcus says as factually as ever.

"Did you read that on a Snapple lid?" Taryn asks, confused that she didn't already know that one.

"A what? My teacher taught us that, in biology."

"Oh, yeah that's where I learned all my facts too, biology." Taryn smiles brightly as she makes the instant coffee.

"You would be a great fact checker, Marcus."

"What's that?" He asks as he pours a bowl of Cheerios.

"A lot of companies use them. Like reporters, lawyers, insurance companies. They are people who are devoted to making sure someone's facts are real."

"And they get paid to do this?"

"They sure do. Maybe we can set something up in the office when you are a little older."

"Really? Man, that'd be great. So you would just pay me money for being smart?"

"Pretty much," Mia giggles.

"Hey, maybe Taryn can fact check for you too, she's pretty smart, and she's already old."

"Hey!" Taryn scowls at Marcus, who is totally oblivious of his rude comment.

"Yeah, maybe if someone sues Snapple, we can do that." Mia laughs, even she has picked up on Taryn's cheating.

Allergic to Life

It turns out that there was nothing to be done with Liz's tent and the bedding. Since they didn't bring any extra, it looks like they were going to have to go with plan B. They are three moms with autistic kids, so there is always a plan B, C and D.

Mia doesn't think anyone is super broken hearted about having to cut the trip two days short. In her eyes, two nights and three days is a huge accomplishment with this many kids.

They have the camp and all seven kids packed up in record time. Since she got the short end of the stick on the way in, they decided to change things up for the trip back.

Mia is driving Taryn's car with Gavin and Ashton, while Taryn has Mia's with Jessie, Jasper and Max.

Mia is pretty sure poor Liz is going to need a break, so the plan is to drive until they find a decent hotel and regroup there. Mia is going to have to call her husband, ex-husband. *Lord, she's not ready for any titles yet.*

She has to figure out what to do next, but for that she's going to need some major privacy. *A little alcohol wouldn't hurt either.*

They find a nice enough hotel about forty minutes past the campground. Taryn pulls in and they all follow her.

"Stay in the car kids, I'm going to talk to Taryn real quick."

Mia hops out and Taryn and Liz do the same. They make sure they can keep an eye on the cars.

"What do you think? Will this work for the night?" Taryn asks.

"We'd have to get three rooms, and that's going to add up pretty quickly." From what Mia can tell, Liz and her husband pretty much live paycheck to paycheck. She knows this is going to break the bank for her, so Mia's about to speak up when Taryn does.

"It's on Kevin for jinxing us."

"I'm the reason we had to go so—"

"Seriously, I've got tonight. Then we can go from there."

"Sounds great to me! I need to find a quiet place to call Tyson, let's get checked in shall we?" Mia cuts in, before they can argue any longer.

"I'll go get the rooms, you guys stay with the kids," Taryn says as she heads inside to check in. As far as hotels go, it's not the nicest she's been to, but it's not horrible either. At least it will have hot water and a mattress.

Mia goes back to the car and takes a few deep breaths. The last thing she wants to do is call Tyson, but it has to be done. She looks in the backseat at Ashton who is fast asleep. He looks so sweet while he sleeps. She wonders how this divorce is going to affect him.

Will he even notice? Mia can't think of the last time all three of them did anything together, let alone ate a meal together. And that alone saddens her deeply. He's missed out on six years with this fantastic kid, even though it was his own choosing, it still makes her hurt for him.

Taryn comes back with keys for all of them, pulling Mia from her sad thoughts.

"Hey, do you mind taking the boys to your room?" Mia asks as Taryn hands over the room key. "I need to make a call."

"Of course. Would you mind calling Michael and updating him?"

"No problem, I'll just be a few minutes." Mia unstraps Ash and carries him into Taryn's room. Once he's out, he is totally dead to the world. He doesn't even budge when she lays him down on the bed.

"He should nap until I'm back, I'll be quick."

"Take your time, we have iPads and television, we are golden."

Mia smiles her thanks and heads directly for her room. She's startled when the door in front of hers pops open, and all she sees is a hand sticking out holding what looks like a sippy cup. Upon closer inspection it's actually a wine shaped glass inside of a sippy cup.

"What the heck?" Mia asks Liz who is the owner of said arm, and on the other side of the door grinning.

"I figured it would help with the phone call. I don't think I'd want to call my cheating ex without a little liquid courage."

Mia takes the sippy cup and smiles. "You are my new best friend."

"I won't tell Taryn." She winks and shuts her door. Mia takes a healthy sip of the Moscato once she gets inside her room. Sitting on the edge of the bed she takes a deep breath and places the call to Tyson.

"Mia, is everything okay?"

"Yeah, it's fine. I was just checking to see if you got all of your things out yet." He lets out a hard breath.

"You said I had four days, Mia."

"I know, but we had a few issues at the campground."

"Is Ashton okay?" Mia is surprised he sounds worried.

"Ash is fine. We are no match for the wilderness, it seems. We are in a hotel tonight, but we can't afford to keep staying here for another three nights."

"Well, I don't know what to tell you. You said I had four days, and I need them all. It's only been two and I have a lot of stuff to get out. Just stay in the hotel."

"The other ladies can't afford it. You have until tomorrow, that's technically the fourth day and should be plenty of time."

"Dammit Mia, it's bad enough you are kicking me out of my own home, I won't be rushed," he snaps and Mia has to take a deep, steading breath.

"Alright, forget it then, I'll figure something out."

"Do you still have my credit card?"

She doesn't say anything because the last thing she wants is to use his money. He sighs at her silence.

"Just book a cabin on the beach or something and use my card. I'll be out in two days."

"I'm not taking a dime of your money, Tyson."

"You aren't. It's for the kids, Mia. I don't want Ashton staying in some seedy hotel. And like you said, this mess was my doing, so I'll cover the cost."

She doesn't know what to say, but he hangs up before she can come up with a reply anyway.

Well, that went better than expected. She dials Michael's number and waits four rings until he finally picks up.

"Hello?"

"Hey Michael, It's Mia."

"Oh, uh, hi Mia. Are Max and Jasper doing okay?"

"Yeah, they've been great, but we had a change in plan after the first few days at the campground. It looks like we are going to go to a beach house instead. Less wildlife and dangers for the kids to get into. I wanted to check to see if you guys were comfortable with that."

"Oh, um, yeah, whatever you think is best is fine with us, Mia."

It's not like she knows him super well, but he sounds very weird, and she's almost afraid to ask, but needs to know.

"Is everything okay Michael? How is the recovery going?" They only touched base very shortly after her surgery to find out if it went well.

Dead silence.

"You there?"

"Um, sorry... yeah, there were a few complications with the surgery." Mia's heart drops to her throat.

"Is Corina okay?"

127

"Yes, they think they were able to get all the cancer, but they cut through a nerve and she was allergic to the anesthetic they used. She ended up ripping her stitches when she threw up, so they had to go back in. She's in more pain than I've ever seen Mia, it's so bad."

"Oh, Michael, I'm so sorry. Is there anything they can give her?"

"That's the problem, she's allergic to all the pain meds they've tried. Since she is even sensitive to the anesthesia, they can't risk her throwing up again and breaking more stitches... so they said she can't take anything else. I've never seen her like this, she's sobbing non-stop. I don't know what to do." His voice breaks, and it tears Mia up.

"Just hold her. There's nothing you can do, it sounds like. Maybe try ice packs, that might help the swelling at least. The older kids aren't home right?"

"No, they are staying with friends for now. But now the doctor is saying she has to be out of the house for one, possibly two months to heal. It was bad when it was two weeks, but longer has her freaking out."

"Well, you let us know what we can do. We will keep the little ones busy, and if you need me to take at least Max for longer, I can. I have to work, otherwise I'd take both boys."

"Oh, no, don't worry about that. I do appreciate it, just this week will be perfect. I'll figure something out after that. I think my mom is going to try and come help out with the kids, but I know Corina would probably appreciate some company. She's going to be hotel hopping for a bit until we can figure something else out."

It occurs to Mia that she might have the perfect solution. She never liked how big her house was. It always seemed ridiculous to have a separate office, but it might just pay off now.

"We have an office that's separate from the house, like a little mother-in-law house. Why doesn't she stay there? It's private, and I can check on her often. That way you won't have to pay for a hotel."

"Really? I'd hate to put you out, I know you have a lot going on right now too."

"Honestly, I've never lived alone, so it'd be nice to have someone there for a while. It'd be a good distraction for us both I think."

"Mia, you are seriously a lifesaver. I had no clue how we were going to swing it. You don't even know how much relief this is to me."

"It is to me too. The idea of going home to an empty house, even though Tyson wasn't there much... well this will be good for everyone."

"I'll let Corina know, I'm sure she'll be thrilled. Or as thrilled as she can be right now. Give the boys hugs from us and tell them we love them please."

"Will do. I should have cell service now, so feel free to call anytime, and I'll send lots of pictures."

"Thanks so much, Mia."

"Bye."

Mia hangs up and washes her face real quick, before she goes and gets the boys. She can't imagine that kind of pain. Two surgeries without any meds, it would be absolute torture.

CHAPTER

They Must Have Dug My Uterus Out With a Rusty Spoon

Corina opens her eyes, after being put under for the second time in three days. All she does is take a breath and moans at the horrible pain that the small movement causes her.

"Hey love, welcome back."

"Babe? Hurts. So bad." She can barely rasp out, as tears flood her face. Did the doctor run out of scalpels for God's sake? They must have dug her uterus out with a rusty spoon.

"I know love, I know. They can't give you anything but Motrin. They were able to go in and do the repair, but we can't risk you throwing up again. They are going to keep you for a few days, so they can keep an eye on you."

"Kids?" Corina rasps in question, and he jumps to give her a small sip of water.

"The kids are fine. The older two are staying with Shantel and Mark for a few days, and the younger two are with the girls. They had a great time camping and are going to spend the rest of the time at the beach."

"Sounds like there's a story in there somewhere, but I hurt too bad to care right now." She tries to move to get more comfortable, but it only makes the pain worse.

"Maybe try to sleep, you'll hurt less that way."

"The cancer?"

"The doc thinks he got it all."

"He said it was nice and contained so he's pretty confident. You're going to be just fine love. We just need to get you better."

"Mmm."

Corina closes her eyes and prays for oblivion. Being a woman seriously sucks. You take away a man's ability to have kids, and all he needs is fifteen minutes and a bag of frozen peas. Corina had to have two surgeries, with a two-month recovery. Yup, women get the shit end of the stick for sure.

It's been four days since Corina's second surgery, and seven days since she's seen her kids. She's one vital organ down and has zero shits left to give.

Bless her poor husband for putting up with her during all this, because Lord knows, nobody else would.

"Good morning Mrs. Sanchez, it looks like you'll be able to go home today."

Michael clears his throat and not so subtly shakes his head at the poor nurse, whose eyes get as big as saucers when Corina bursts into tears.

"Uh..."

"Discharged, she's getting discharged today."

"Oh, uh, I'm sorry..." Her look of confusion would almost be comical if Corina wasn't so upset.

"It's fine, I'm just hormonal and in massive amounts of pain. It's not your fault you didn't know I'm to be sent away like a prisoner."

"Oh, well, we can get you some pain meds before you lea—" Michael's death glare stops her mid-sentence. And Corina can't help but burst into laughter this time.

The frightened nurse runs out of the room and Michael's glare follows her all the way out.

"Jesus, what is this her first day?" Michael asks, his eyes never leaving her retreating form.

"It's fine, they obviously aren't used to having such a freak of nature and it was shift change."

"Yeah, well, you are my freak of nature." He kisses her forehead and then stands as he grabs his phone.

"I'm going to call Ma and make sure the kids are okay and she has your stuff ready for me to pick up. We are going to stay in the car while she brings the kids out to give you a quick kiss before I take you to Mia's place."

The idea of seeing even half of her kids warms her greatly. "I'll be so much better once I can see at least some of my kids."

"They've missed you for sure, but at least the older

ones understand. I will take them to visit you at Mia's when I can. Okay time to make the call. I'll be back, love."

He takes his phone and leaves her room, and Corina takes the moment to sneak her cell phone and call Mia.

"Hi Michael."

"Hey girl, It's Corina."

"Corina, hey! I didn't think you were up to talking just yet."

"Michael doesn't want me to have any undue stress right now, but wondering about all the ways in which disasters are happening is causing just that, so give it to me straight."

"The boys are doing great."

"Okay, now for the truth? It'll be a good distraction from the pain, and I guarantee anything I am imaging is probably worse. So out with it, and quick please, before my warden comes back."

Mia sighs on the other end, and Corina knows she's trying to decide if it's smart to tell her anything or not. Corina also knows Mia's a mom and is putting herself in Corina's shoes right now. Corina wins when Mia sighs deeply.

"Okay, it's been a very colorful trip. But honestly, the boys are doing surprisingly well. There's been a few meltdowns, but for the most part nothing too bad."

"Jasper?"

"Is fine until bedtime. Then he whines for you, but he stays asleep once he goes down. Liz has taken to him and him to her, so she's been a good fill in for the week."

"Okay, I can handle that." Sadly, it actually makes Corina feel good that he misses her.

"Max?"

"As far as our kiddos go, besides Marcus, he's had the least amount of issues actually."

"Meltdowns?"

"He's had mostly insignificant ones. The major one was set off by my son, so I felt pretty bad about that."

Max is super sensory sensitive, so any noise, especially screaming sends him through the roof.

"I assumed that'd be the biggest issue, going with so many kids on the spectrum."

"It's like the worst game of live dominos ever. One gets triggered, and it sets off a horrible motion of meltdowns. But you know what, we've gotten through it. I feel like we are going to come out better, stronger women for it. And the upside is I haven't thought about my sham of a marriage once."

"Well, that's a definite plus."

"Sure is."

"And Ashton?"

"Seems the same as usual, but then again, he has no clue about Tyson moving out. His meltdown was because he wanted waffles and the store didn't have Eggo Blueberry. They had Eggo Chocolate Chip or Buttermilk only. You'd think we were waterboarding him. He got into such a state, that every kid, even Marcus had an epic meltdown."

"What'd you do?"

"Taryn, heaven bless her, took all six screaming kids out back, and laid them each in the sand with noise canceling headphones. She told them to bury their hands and feet into the sand and feel the breeze on their faces. She slowly drizzled sand over their hands and legs until they calmed."

"That worked?"

"Surprisingly, yes. After they all calmed down, she and Liz were able to take them out to the water while I took Ash on a very long drive, until we found a store with Eggo Blueberry Waffles."

"I hope you bought them out." Corina says laughing.

"I sure did. But being here has taught me a huge lesson."

"Oh, yeah? What's that?"

"To stop caring. I'm always so worried when Ashton has a meltdown or to even take him in public. I worry what people think of me, I worry they will judge me, my parenting, my kid. I am so worried that he feels it, and it makes him tense. Liz put it perfectly when she said, *who cares. They are going to judge you no matter what. They don't live your life, so their opinion doesn't matter. We live our life, and we are right there in the trenches with each other.*"

Corina chuckles, because it's a fear she's always had, too. She hates feeling like she's being judged, or worse, that Max is.

"And you know how freeing it is to not care? I don't have to worry if Ash melts down, because Taryn's kids are busy trying to cuddle a raccoon or kiss a rattlesnake."

"Wait, come again?" Corina must have heard her wrong, but Mia just laughs and tells her she will catch her up later.

"My husband is coming back in, and I have to go home but thank you so much for being honest with me. It honestly does make me feel better."

"I'm glad. And Corina?"

"Yeah?"

"I'm sorry they took your baby house." Corina about chokes on a laugh.

"Yeah, bad stuff happens, but life goes on."

"That it does."

"I'm sorry your husband is a cheating scumbag." It's her turn to laugh.

"Yeah, well, bad people happen and life goes on."

"I like this new honesty, not giving a crap feeling."

"Me too! Freeing isn't it? But you might want to keep that within our little group. I wouldn't try it out on your mother-in-law just yet."

Flying by the Seat of my Pants

They are finally home, alive and mostly uninjured. Taryn can't believe they made it. She's laying in bed sharing all the week's mishaps with Kevin, who is laughing so hard, he has tears running down his face.

"I don't know how you ladies did it. Honestly, I'm pretty sure if it were the dad's, we would have tapped out."

"Uh, of course you would have. We did it just like we did childbirth. With the power only a woman can possess." Taryn shoots him a smirk and he leans down and kisses her forehead.

"You are goddesses, I've never questioned that."

"It was actually a very good learning experience for me."

"How so?"

"Watching how all the other moms do it. It's funny because we all have our own way of dealing with everything. The meltdowns, behaviors, crisis. Just like any other mom I guess. I've never had the opportunity to compare the way I parent to how someone else does, none of my other mom friends have kids on the spectrum."

"I mean it makes sense. So many moms have play groups, and friend groups where they can watch how other moms do it and learn. I'm really glad you finally have that now."

"Me too! I mean don't get me wrong, I'm still that crazy mom who is flying by the seat of her pants... even in our group. But at least I know they get how hard my life is, so they don't judge me for it. You know they even admired me a bit this week."

"That's not a shock at all, I admire you every day."

"Okay, cheesy much?" Taryn snuggles in close as Kevin laughs. She's missed this big ball of cheddar.

"We all have our own way of dealing with each situation, and our own strengths. It took a few days, but once we realized who is strong in what area, we became a well-oiled machine. Almost like a marriage in a way."

"I mean it makes sense. This isn't your way of telling me you are leaving me to live on some all women commune is it?"

Taryn jabs him in the rib with her elbow.

"I'm serious, Kev. Liz is the super nurturing, compassionate one. Not just to her kids either, but all kids. She honestly treated each and every one of those kids, like they were hers at all times. I'm not gonna lie, I felt a little guilty because I'd look over and see Ashton or Mason having a meltdown, and I'd instantly feel relief that it wasn't Jessie or Gavin. Where Liz would see a child meltdown and jump right in like they were her own."

"That is a special quality for sure."

"It is, and one I'm trying to develop, although it sure doesn't come natural to me." She thinks back to the start of the trip and chuckles.

"Mia is just a cool cucumber. She had a mini meltdown when we first got there, but I'm pretty sure that was all about her ex and not the kids. Once we were there, she was always calm no matter the situation. And she always came up with a logical solution. I blame that on her lawyering skills."

Kev laughs. "I don't know babe, I don't think you give yourself enough credit. You manage to come up with a solution for things, too. I've never seen you stumped."

"Solution, sure. But not logical."

He laughs, much harder than I'd like at that. "True. I love you for your creative and insane ways... but logic usually isn't high on your list."

Taryn doesn't get mad, because he's not wrong. Her ways have always worked well for them, but they are a bit crazy. Then again, so is she. She's learned to embrace her weird from a very early age. She doesn't think there is a single weird bone in any of the other ladies' bodies.

"So you've talked about their strengths, how about yours?"

"To be honest, I never saw it as a strength until Liz and Mia pointed it out. I still think they might have just said it so I felt better and wasn't the slacker in the group."

"I'll be the judge of that, go on," Kevin prods.

"It's just that I've never seen autism as a bad thing. Does it have its challenges? sure. Is it the reason why I'm exhausted 99.9 percent of the time? Probably. But I've also been able to see the beauty in it."

Kevin snuggles her closer and Taryn can feel his smile against her head.

"The ladies and I were talking one night after the kids went down, about our reactions to our kids getting diagnosed. I was surprised that I was the only one that didn't cry or grieve."

"Everyone reacts differently, and none of it is wrong or bad. But I've always loved that you never saw it as a big deal. If it wasn't for that, I probably would have had a much harder time dealing with it myself," Kevin admits.

"Really? You never mentioned being upset by it." Taryn is shocked this is the first time they've had this discussion.

"Because you weren't. Remember, I never had nieces or nephews, I was an only child. I never grew up around kids. Our kids are the only ones I've ever known, so I've deferred a lot to you. You didn't seem upset or shaken by the fact, therefore, either was I. I just thought, well okay, this is them, this is who they are and who they were meant to be. So, I didn't feel like I could be upset by it. To me it was as if they were born with blonde hair and blue eyes. Just another part of them."

"Which is what we love about you." Taryn smiles over at him and talks about one of her favorite moments of the week.

"One of the hardest days was when Ashton flipped out over the wrong waffles. He went into orbit, of course, sending all seven kids into orbit as well."

"Lord, I can only imagine. I know how hard it is with just our two, I can't imagine five more."

"Yeah, safe to say, the moms were about seconds away from our own meltdowns. Suddenly, it hit me that we have a beach in our backyard. So many different sensory tools right at our fingertips. So I led the crying, biting, stimming kids out the back door and plucked them in the sand."

"I bet the neighbors loved that," Kev chuckles.

"At least it wasn't nighttime. We were far enough away from the beach that it wasn't a horrible spectacle. Anyway, so I have them each dig their hands and feet into the sand, and then I pick up handfuls of sand and I slowly dribble it over each kid. It was crazy how fast the crying stopped," Taryn chuckles, remembering the trickle of screams until it was dead silent.

"I'm pretty sure Liz and Mia thought I murdered them all, with as quiet as it instantly got."

"You joke, but I'm sure they were alarmed."

She laughs and shakes her head. "They looked at me like I was their hero."

"In that moment I'm sure you were."

"Anyway, after all the kids were down for the night, I led the ladies out to the back and made them lay in the sand. I slowly dribbled sand over them, and had them sink hands and feet into it, and asked how it felt." Taryn smiles, remembering the weird looks they both gave her.

"Then we looked up into the sky, closed our eyes and took in the sound of the waves, and the smell of the saltwater, and I've honestly never felt so relaxed and I don't know... grounded maybe."

"How about them?"

"They loved it. I think it was our favorite night of the whole trip. I told them this is how I get through the hard times. I see the world from my kids' eyes. I take little moments to experience life like they do."

"And that's what you bring, your perspective. You gave them a gift, babe. You taught them how to see the world through their kids' eyes."

"Can autism be challenging? Of course it can. But it can also be extremely beautiful. In a world of cell phones, and video games and instant gratification, it's amazing how our kids can find beauty and pleasure in the smallest of ways."

"You are such a good mom, babe. The kids and I are so lucky to have you."

"I'm a weird, crazy mom who is flying by the seat of her pants."

"You are that." Kevin chuckles and hugs Taryn tight. "And I wouldn't have you any other way."

Taryn smiles and snuggles into him, getting settled for the night. This is why they work. She's the wave, crashing through life, taking out those who stand in her path. And Kev, well, Kev is the sand. Warm, comforting and always there for her to crash into.

CHAPTER

It's Always the Quiet Ones

It's the first time in three weeks that they've had group. First, Corina had surgery, then they had the camping trip, then they needed a week just to recover from their camping trip.

They are finally getting together tonight, and it's much needed. Everyone dropped the kids off at Taryn's, where Emily is watching them all, along with Kevin's help, of course. And then the ladies went over to Mia's house and are hanging out in her guest house since Corina is still here recovering.

"How are you feeling? Any better?"

"I mean, honestly... not really. This no meds thing sucks so bad."

"There's one silver lining at least," Taryn adds, as she passes out glasses of wine.

"What's that?"

"You can drink!" she cheerfully says, as she hands her a very full glass of wine. Liz eyes Corina's glass and Taryn just shrugs.

"The woman is in pain, let her find a few moments of numbness at least."

"Bless you," Corina says before she takes a large sip of the wine, and leans back in bed.

"Maybe you guys should have had group at Taryn's, I'm afraid I'm not good company lately. All I want to do is complain," Corina states through tears. Poor thing, Liz can't imagine being away from her kids for almost a month and being utterly alone and in pain.

"That's perfect if you ask me. We all need a good complaining session, so that's what tonight will be. We each get a turn at bitching." Liz announces.

"Here, here." Taryn says, as she raises her glass. "You start Liz."

"Okay, my grievance is with math."

"Math, like all of math, or any number in particular?" Taryn asks.

"I am fine with old math, but new math sucks! It doesn't even make sense; I mean who decided to take a good thing and change it up?"

"Common core?" Mia asks, nodding in understanding.

"Yup, that's crap. I was great in math, too. I was always in advanced classes, because it made sense. This stuff does not even make sense."

"You are homeschooling though. Do you have to use common core?" Mia asks me.

"Technically no, but I am homeschooling through a charter school, so I'm following their curriculum. Plus, I don't want Marcus to suffer because his mom is too old to teach him new math."

"Raise your glasses ladies, to old math. May you rest in peace, you are greatly missed." Taryn toasts, and we all raise our glasses.

"To old math."

"Oh, this is so much fun, okay, my turn." Taryn jumps in.

"My annoyance lately is having to stop and think about what I refer to Emily as."

"What do you mean?" Liz asks.

"The way people look at you when you say nanny. The looks and comments we get, like we are rich people who don't love our kids. As soon as you say *nanny*, all we get is judgement. Yet if I replace the word with *sitter*, we get none of that. Same person, same job... but sitter is totally fine!"

"That's actually so true. We've always used a sitter, but since Tyson left I've been looking for a special needs nanny and the looks people give me as soon as I say nanny are night and day." Taryn throws up her hands like Mia just proved her point.

"Think about it.'Sitter?' You're fine if I pay for someone to sit on my child? That's acceptable, because everyone uses a babysitter now and then. But nanny, a name which some people call their grandmothers, and is used as a loving term, well those are looked down on. WTF people! WTF!"

"You make a valid point, but I just don't see that changing anytime soon. People are judgmental, that's just a part of life," Liz reminds her.

"Well, after those wine, I mean water, cups that I made for you, I'm also going to make a shirt that says, *yes, I have a nanny, go ahead and judge me!*"

"Oh, sign me up for one of those!" Mia says, taking another sip of her wine.

"I might have a nanny, but I also get all of my clothes at thrift stores, and my purses at Walmart! The last lady to openly judge me for having a nanny said, *I wish I could afford a nanny, that must be nice,* while rolling her eyes. She had a freaking Louis Vuitton bag, from this season, not off the rack. But nobody judged her!" Taryn just keeps on ranting.

"She could stick her kid in front of a tv with an iPad, while she's off buying her $700 purse, and that's acceptable, but heaven forbid if I spend my money on someone trained in ABA, who will help me take my kids to the park, and go on walking trails."

"Preach it, girl." Mia cheers Taryn on, and Liz is starting to think switching to water right about now might be a good idea.

"Lord this is liberating! Who's next?!"

"I guess it's my turn. Well, unfortunately I don't have a nanny, but I totally understand what you are saying about judgment and offering unwanted opinions," Corina states.

"I'm always getting judged along with horrible comments made about having four kids."

"What? Seriously?" Mia asks surprised. "But you only have four, it's not like you are the Duggars or anything."

"Right? And it's always the same damn comments every time! *Oh, you have your hands full. And bless your heart, that's a lot! And you know what prevents that, right?* Like, seriously? You don't know my life story lady! You don't know my kids' story, and yet if I were to lay it all down and say that their mom died of an overdose and their dad is in prison and I stepped up so they wouldn't go into the system... well, then I'm a hero and not just some horny old lady. But screw that! I love those kids, I want them, they are all mine."

Liz isn't sure if it's the pain talking at this point, or the Moscato, but based on the looks around the room, nobody has ever seen sweet, mild mannered Corina this fired up.

"And yes, four is a lot, and yes I know what prevents having more kids... prison... as in you keep these rude-ass comments up, and I'm gonna cut you, and end up there myself!"

It's dead silent in the room, and after about a minute, everyone bursts out laughing. Liz has tears running down her face as Taryn passes the unopened bottle of wine to Corina as her prize. Which Corina happily accepts.

"Who would have thought she had it in her," Liz whispers to Mia.

"It's always the sweet, quiet ones," Mia says, throwing Corina a wink.

147

It's All Fun and Games Until Someone Gets Poisoned

It's Taryn's favorite time of day, ten o'clock. That means her kids are at school, she's already done the dishes, the laundry and is finishing up her second cup of coffee. This is the cup she gets to savor and enjoy. Not the one she pours down her throat in order to get her eyes to open.

She feeds Tacoma his special dog food, then makes her way to the bathroom. One hot, uninterrupted shower? *Yes, please.*

Taryn sets the water to the perfect temperature, steps in, and is just starting to lather the soap in her hair when the phone rings. She sighs and tries to ignore it when the number on the phone catches her eye.

"Oh, crap!" Jumping out of the shower soaking wet, she grabs her cell.

"Hello?"

"Hi Mrs. Leighton, this is Jessie's teacher."

"Hi Cheryl, what happened? Is she okay?" This is obviously not her first rodeo. With a kid like Jessie, there's been many calls home.

"Well, she seems okay... That isn't ominous or anything.

"Seems okay?"

"I just got back from my break, and the aids told me that Jessie was at recess and they noticed she was picking berries off the ground."

"Berries?"

"There's a tree that hangs over the fence, and they have these small little purple berries. Jessie was picking them up, and then one of the aids noticed she put it in her mouth. She went over and when she asked her to spit it out, Jessie chewed it."

Taryn takes a deep breath and tries to calm her nerves. Obviously if they are calling her, Jessie must be fine, otherwise poison control would have told them to call an ambulance. But it doesn't hurt to check.

"Okay, what did poison control say?"

"Uh... poison control?"

"Yes, you did call poison control right?"

"Well, no. I was on break, and the aids told me when I got back, so I instantly called you."

Jesus Christ!

"So you don't know if the berries are poisonous or not? Okay, I'm on my way. Please get a clipping of both

149

the tree and berry if you can and meet me out front with Jessie."

"Oh, um... okay. I didn't think it was that big of a deal..."

"She ate a berry that you aren't sure what it is. That's always a big deal, Cheryl."

"Right yes, um, I'll bring her right out and get that sample."

Taryn hangs up and puts her phone on speaker as she tells Siri to call Kevin. She throws on the quickest thing to wear, that she blindly grabs, which just so happens to be a cocktail dress.

"Hey, babe."

"Kev, code red!"

"I'm on my way."

"Meet me at Jessie's school ASAP, we will need two cars."

Taryn hangs up and runs for the shelf with her keys and purse. Once she has those, she puts her feet in the first shoes she finds, running shoes, as she yells for the dog.

"Come on Tacoma, we might need you." Not even caring that she still has a massive amount of soap in her hair, which is currently running down her back, she jumps into her car and heads toward Jessie's school.

Luckily, the school is closer to Kevin and he's already loaded her into his car just as Taryn pulls up.

"Take her to the hospital now, I'm going to go straight to the nursery to identify what she ate, I'll call you as soon as I know." Taryn turns to the very nervous looking teacher standing on the sidewalk wringing her hands.

"Did you check in her mouth?"

"Um, no I didn't. I just called you." Lord help her, that seems to be the only thing this woman is capable of doing.

"Kev." He opens Jessies mouth and swears.

"Sores?" Taryn asks, knowing.

"Yeah, they are large and white." They share a look, and Taryn takes a deep breath and tries not to lose it on this poor teacher. It's her first year, she's still learning.

"Go Kev. I'm right behind you." He jumps in the car and peels out.

"We will talk later Cheryl, but if she already has white sores in her throat, it's poisonous, I just need to find out how much. You have the clipping?"

The teacher now has tears running down her face, and Taryn figures there's nothing else she can say that's going to matter. Cheryl's got the point, it's serious. She nods and hands over the branch that Taryn takes and jumps in her car.

Luckily, the nursery is on the way to the hospital. Taryn runs every red light, carefully of course, and makes it there in a record two minutes. She doesn't even bother turning off the car as she parks and runs right into the nursery.

The lady at the front jumps when Taryn comes crashing in with crazy eyes, and sudsy hair, caring less.

"My daughter ate this berry and I need to know what it is. Can you identify it?" The woman's startled look turns to worry as she picks up the intercom.

"Todd to the front, Todd please come to the front, we have an emergency."

She looks back Taryn with caring eyes. "He is the best we have, he should be able to identify it for you in a heartbeat."

"Oh, thank God! Thank you so much, I'm sorry I'm a mess, it's just my daughter ate it at school, and they didn't call poison control, and it doesn't matter anyway because we don't know what it is and—"

"It's totally fine, love, I understand. We will get you sorted."

Just then Todd comes running out from the back with purpose, making Taryn want to practically kiss him. "Potential poisoning?"

"Happens a lot, huh?"

"More than you'd know."

She hands over the berry and leaf and within seconds he says, "pokeweed."

"You are sure?"

"Positive. They look edible, and it won't kill animals, but they are dangerous to humans." Taryn's heart sinks to the floor and she instantly breaks out in a cold sweat.

"How much did she eat?"

"We think just one."

"Okay, if it was just one you should be okay, anything more and it could be deadly."

"She had white sores on her tongue and in her mouth though."

"Any probably down her throat as well. It's not the berry that's poisonous, it's actually the essential oil that's inside. Once it's chewed the poison is released. If she swallows it whole, the sores won't happen."

"My husband is at the ER now. I'm going to call him with the name and head over. Thank you so much."

"Your daughter should be alright, as long as it was just the one. She will have an upset tummy and sores for about a week. You can pass that on, or have the doctor call me." He hands Taryn his card, and she surprises him by hugging him hard and then running back to her car.

Taryn calls Kev and relays the information. They are already back with the doctor who says she will be okay, but they are keeping her overnight for observation.

Taryn totally forgot about Tacoma, and almost went into another panic attack, until Kevin tells her that he grabbed him out of her car before they left. She didn't even notice in her state of panic.

Taryn makes her way toward the Hospital and calls Liz since, luckily, Gavin and Mason go to the same school. She looks at her clock, realizing he's about to get out in twenty minutes.

"Hey Taryn."

"I'm a total basket case, but can you pick up Gavin and take him to your house?"

"Of course I can. You okay?"

"I am, but Jessie ate a poisonous berry at school." That's all it takes for her to burst into tears.

"It's okay hun, are you driving? Should you pull over?"

"I'm okay. Kev is at the hospital with her now, that guy at the nursery thinks she will be okay since she just ate the one... but Liz, she could have died. One tiny little berry more, and she could have died."

"But she didn't Taryn. She didn't. She only had one, and she will be okay. Don't go there, not now. She will be okay, say it."

"She will be okay."

"She will. It's okay to freak out, but not now. You need to make it to the hospital safe, and in order to do that you need to calm down, okay?"

Taryn takes a deep shuttering breath. She's sure Liz can hear her because she tells Taryn to take another one. She does and starts to feel herself calming. *Jessie's okay. She's okay.*

"I'm going to go now so I can get Gavin before Mason. I'll stop and get the boys a treat on the way home, so he doesn't freak out too much about the change in routine."

"You are a lifesaver, Liz, thank you. They are keeping her overnight, so I'll have Kev come get Gavin as soon as I get there and get filled in."

"Take your time. I made a lasagna so I'll just feed him here before they go home."

"You are the best, I love you so much, you know that right?"

"Of course I do, I love you, too. Now take another breath and text me with an update when you can."

"Will do, thanks Liz."

Every Moment is a Teaching Moment

Liz takes a moment to say a little prayer for Jessie, and then a quick one for herself, too, because Gavin is going to flip out when it's her picking him up and not his mom.

"Marcus, we need to leave to go get Mason."

"It's too early, mom."

"I have to make a stop first and then pick up Gavin, too. Come on, we gotta go."

"We leave at 2:17, we get to the school at 2:28, and then the bell rings at 2:30. It's only 1:45 mom."

Liz does not have it in her to deal with this today. She takes her own advice and takes a deep breath. Every moment is a teaching moment, she reminds herself.

"You're right Marcus, on a regular day we leave at 2:17. But sometimes things happen that are out of our control, remember us talking about that? About when things happen and sometimes we have to leave early or late, and the schedule has to change a little, and that's okay."

"We leave at 2:17," he states, staring right back, almost daring her to correct him.

"That's if we aren't getting ice cream. Wouldn't you like an ice cream?"

"Yes, I would love an ice cream, we can get one at 2:17."

Sweet Jesus, help me out here.

"We leave at 2:17 to pick up Mason. We leave at 2:10 to get the mail and then pick up Mason, and we leave at," Liz looks down at her watch, "1:47 to get an ice cream, and then pick up Gavin and Mason." She holds her breath waiting to see what he will say to that. He looks over at the clock that says 1:47 p.m. and he stands.

"Okay, it's 1:47 time to go." *Oh, thank you Lord!*

"Perfect, let's go."

Liz drives through and buys soft serve ice cream for the three boys. She decides the best way to do this is to have Marcus go in and get Mason, and for her to have an aid bring Gavin to her in the office.

They get to the school at 2:20 p.m. Seeing Marcus open his mouth, Liz hurries and beats him to it.

"On special days we get to school at 2:20, and you go pick up Mason early, while I get Gavin and then we eat ice cream in the car."

"Is today a special day?"

"It is. Can you be a good big brother and get Mase, then walk him directly back here to the car?"

"Of course I can, I'm not a baby."

"Thank you, that's very helpful."

"Well, just so you know we are late." Her son points out.

"What?"

"On special days we get to school at 2:20, and I go pick up Mason early, while you get Gavin and then we eat ice cream in the car. But it is now 2:22 and we are late."

"Then we better hurry." Liz says, trying her best not to roll her eyes. Like always, he takes her literally and takes off fast for Mason's class.

Liz walks into the office and explains the unique situation and that she's going to need a little help. She hoped by getting here early it wouldn't be as crazy with the other kids, but either way Gavin's gonna flip.

Two minutes later she sees Gavin make his way to the office with an aid. As soon as he sees Liz and not his mother, he flops down on the floor.

Liz walks over and kneels down, staying out of swiping range.

"Hey buddy, Aunt Liz is picking you up today okay? Dad is going to get you from my house."

"Mom, *moooooom, mooooooooooooooom*."

He starts biting his arm, and the aid quickly replaces his arm with a chewy, shooting Liz a sympathetic look.

"Come on Gavin, let's walk to the car. You are going with Liz today, and then you will see mom later." The aid lifts him up and ducks the arm that he swings at her, never losing her smile.

157

"There we go, let's go see the car. What color do you think it is? I think it's red."

"Bue car."

"That's right Gavin, I drive a blue car. Let's go see the blue car and get some ice cream." He doesn't stop his fidgeting and biting of his arm, but his eyes light up.

"Eyeee cweem?"

"Yep. Mason and Marcus are waiting for us in the car with ice cream."

That seems to do the trick, thank the Lord above, and they are able to get him to Liz's car without further incident. He gets in and Marcus hands out the ice cream while Liz gives the aid a very grateful smile.

"You are an angel, thank you for your help."

"Anytime. Give Taryn our love, we hope everything goes okay with Jessie."

"You know Jessie?" I'm surprised since Jessie is in a different grade, but the aid just laughs.

"Everyone knows Jessie." Liz smiles and hurries to get in the car to take these boys home.

Kevin shows up a few hours later. They were the longest hours of her life. As soon as Gavin sees his dad, he starts pointing at the door.

"Go bye-bye, go car."

"Okay buddy. Go get your shoes and go to the bathroom while I talk to Liz."

Gavin runs off to do as he's told and Liz takes in how exhausted Kevin looks.

"Come on in, I made dinner. I'll make you up a plate since I don't think Gav will last much longer." Kevin chuckles and runs a hand through his hair.

"That's the truth. Thanks again for doing this Liz. Normally we'd call Emily, but she's on vacation visiting family."

"No problem, I'm happy to do it. How is Jessie doing?"

"She's okay, I don't think she's ever been more scared in her life, luckily Tacoma was able to calm her down a bit. They had to restrain her in the ER and it gutted me." His eyes tear up and Liz instantly pulls him in for a hug.

"I know that's the scariest thing ever for our kiddos, but the important thing is she's going to be okay. You are such a good dad Kevin, and you got her there in time." He wipes his eyes and nods.

"The doctor checked her out, he said she has sores all in her mouth and throat, which is why she doesn't want to eat or drink. They put an IV in her arm, and had to strap her to the bed."

"I can't imagine."

"Yeah, Taryn about lost it when she walked in and saw that."

"I bet, poor thing."

"She's all settled in now with her mom, dog and cartoons. She's refusing all foods and drinks, even milkshakes, so they said she won't be able to leave until she will take at least water by mouth. The doctor said once the sores close up a bit, it shouldn't hurt as bad, but that she probably won't eat for a week or two."

"A week or two? Can she go that long?"

"Apparently, as long as she is taking in fluids. He said she might take Jamba Juice in a few days, so that will help."

"I can't believe this, what a mess. Have you talked to anyone from the school?"

"Yeah, the teacher called and talked to Taryn, so did the principal."

"What did they have to say?"

"Basically, they are making excuses that the teacher was on break, and the aids did what they are supposed to do and wait for the teacher for major decisions."

"Even life-threatening ones? That's ridiculous!"

"I know. Taryn said she wants an emergency IEP meeting, so hopefully we can get this worked out soon."

"I hope so, keep me updated, and let me know if there's anything I can do."

"Will do. Thanks so much Liz, we really appreciate it."

"Come on Gav, time to go home. Say thank you to Liz."

"Bye, bye, go car. Fhank you wiz."

Wow, that's the most I've ever heard out of Gavin. "You are welcome. Bye, sweetheart."

CHAPTER

There is Power in Peer Pressure

Mia grabs the chocolate cake she picked up from the bakery earlier in the day and rushes Ashton out the door. She figured chocolate just might be in order tonight.

It's their first night back to Taryn's since Corina is officially allowed to be back around the kids. Apparently, she has another month to go until she's pain free, but luckily she's doing a lot better.

Mia picked Corina and Max up on her way so she didn't have to drive. They pull up to Taryn's, at the same time as Liz.

"Hey, how's it going?"

"We are good." She looks back and the house with a worried expression. "I picked up some reinforcements though. It's been a hard week for Taryn."

She holds up two bottles of wine and Corina and Mia laugh. Mia holds up the chocolate cake, and Corina holds up the candy.

"Great minds think alike."

"There's not much that wine, cake, and chocolate can't solve." Liz says, as she ushers the kids into the backyard.

Once the kids are all settled and playing with Emily, the three of them make their way downstairs. Mia's not surprised to see Jessie, Tacoma and Taryn cuddling on beanbags in the corner, watching *The Wiggles*.

"Hi ladies, sorry, I can't get her to leave my sight right now."

"That's exactly where she needs to be then, we understand." Mia says, walking over to hug her friend and wave to Jessie.

"Hey little love, how are you feeling?"

"Popsicle?"

"How about a smoothie?" Liz asks handing Jessie a Jamba Juice.

"Yummy!" She takes it and Taryn gives her a look.

"Jessie, say thank you to Liz."

"Thank you, Liz."

"You're welcome sweet pea." Taryn gets up and Jessie narrows her eyes.

"Mommy will be right over there, talking to her friends. Drink your smoothie and cuddle Tacoma."

The ladies go over and sit on the couch, where Taryn can still keep an eye on the two troublemakers. Although sadly, they both look like they've lost their spark.

"It's been tough, huh?"

"It almost breaks my heart how docile she's been. I mean, it's been nice not having to wonder what disaster she's gotten into, but she's just not my Jessie. She cries all the time, and I can't get her to eat anything."

"She hasn't gone to school yet?" Liz asks.

"No, it's been nine days now and we refuse to let her go back until we get this mess figured out."

"They still haven't come to their senses?" Mia asks, getting settled on the couch and taking a glass of wine from Liz.

"It's been an absolute nightmare. Because the tree isn't actually on school property, and just hanging over from the other side of the fence, they are saying it isn't their responsibility. They can't remove it because it's not school property."

"But a kid almost died, there's got to be a clause for that," Mia states, already running through every zoning law she can think of.

"Luckily, I have a friend on the school board who is fighting for it. They are calling an emergency meeting this week to discuss it. I told them until that tree is cut down and better safety protocols are in place, Jessie will not be returning to that school."

"Good for you." Corina says, as she tries to make herself comfortable on the couch, and then gives up and stands in the corner.

"The worst part is how patronizing they were in that meeting. *We are sorry this happened to her, but there's nothing that could have been done.*"

"Are you kidding me? They could have called poison control before they waited a half an hour to call you."

163

"Thank you, Liz. I made that very same point. I also asked about safety protocols, get this… they don't have any."

"Come again?" Mia asks totally dumbfounded.

"Yep. I asked why poison control wasn't called, or at least the nurse, and they said that it didn't occur to them. Then I said, It's basic first aid." Taryn takes a large sip of her drink then throws her hands up in the air. "And get this, it is not legally required in California for the aids to go through first aid training."

"Are you freaking kidding me, even fourteen-year-old babysitters need CPR and aid training," Mia says.

"Yup! And get this, for teaching certification, the teachers have to be first aid certified, but it doesn't have to be renewed. And when a teacher is out on break, not a single person in that classroom has any safety certification."

"That's insane."

"FAPE requires them to offer only what is required by law." Everyone turns and looks at Mia, who throws her hands up in the air. "I think that's just as insane as all of you, and since that isn't my specialized field, I'm not sure, but I'll look into it and get back to you, Taryn."

"Thank you, I appreciate that."

"In the meantime, what's your plan moving forward?"

"I'm keeping her home until at least one classroom aide is first aid certified and that tree has been cutdown. Because there's no guarantee she won't do it again, and next time it might be two berries." They all cringe at the thought of that.

"You fight for whatever you need to, Taryn. Let me know when the next meeting is and I'll come with you."

"I hate that I have to lawyer up just to get them to take me seriously."

"Sadly, that's just how it is sometimes."

"We refused to sign the IEP terms, so we are waiting for a supervisor to call us back. In the meantime, I'll be keeping her home and teaching her myself."

"Oh, we can do playdates, and her and Marcus can be home school buddies." Liz perks up.

"Lord knows I'm not as patient as you, so I'm hoping it's not going to be for that long, but that works for me, for now."

"Until I look into the laws, I can't advise you on how to move forward, however... there is always media and other parents. There is real power in peer pressure, even at our age."

"I hate to fight dirty."

"Agreed, but other parents have the right to know that their children may be in danger, and as a mother at that school, I bet nobody is aware of the first aid certification laws. You could have a real fight on your hands."

"I'm going to give them the benefit of the doubt, but if that doesn't work out, I'll let you know."

"Sounds good, I'll look into those laws and get back to you."

Burning From the Inside Out

Holy hellfire batman! Corina shoots out of bed, like her lungs are on fire. She strips down fully naked and runs downstairs to put her head in the freezer, taking a deep breath as the cool air kisses her overheated skin. Heaven, it feels like pure bliss.

"Head in the oven is a 911 call. Head in the freezer... well as long as it's attached to someone breathing, I'm not really sure what to do," Michael says as he smirks at his wife from the doorway.

"Ha, ha! But if you were burning from the inside out, you wouldn't think it's so funny. I swear I can smell my kidney's burning."

"Another hot flash?"

"No, flash sounds like it's quick. This is more of a heat wave. It rolls over you, until you feel like you will burn up, then you are in instant cold sweats."

"That sounds absolutely horrible. I'm so sorry, love."

"I'm not sure what's worse, having my uterus taken out prematurely, having my abdominals ripped to all hell, or having these horrid heat waves." Corina pops an ice cube into her mouth and sucks on it, moaning in pleasure.

"That all sounds like pure torture."

"You're lucky you are a man."

"I thank God every day for that small fact." Corina shoots him a wink, as she turns to start walking back to their room.

"So do I." She heads up the stairs without waiting for him but hears him chuckle from behind her.

"You realize you are stark naked right? What if the house caught on fire?"

"Then it'd pretty much feel like I do now. I don't even want to think about clothes."

"Until you are freezing in about two minutes."

"Yup! Welcome to hell."

"You really have taken this like a champ. It's also given me a whole new appreciation for everything you do daily that I take for granted. Raising kids? Hard."

"Yup." Corina says, climbing back into bed.

"Cooking three different meals every night because they don't eat the same things? Hard."

"Preach."

"Grocery shopping with four kids? Impossible."

"I'm sorry honey, I know it's been a hard few months for you."

"That's not what I'm getting at. I had to do it for two months, you do this stuff daily, and you never complain."

"Because I love it. I honestly love my life, and you help me. You were all on your own and you rocked it."

"Yeah, not so much. Poor Carissa came home crying every day because she said the kids teased her about her hair. Do you know how many hours of hair tutorials I watched? Just for her to get laughed at?" Corina can't help but chuckle.

"You are a good man."

"I'm just glad you are back now. So are the kids."

"Well, most of the kids." She can't stop the melancholy that comes over her when she thinks about Max.

"He'll come around, babe."

"I've been home for two weeks now, and he still won't even look at me. It absolutely kills me."

"He's just trying to punish you. The other kids understood when I said you were sick and getting better. To Max, you were just gone one day. He doesn't process why, and all of a sudden you're back and he wants you to pay. He will get over it, I promise."

"I know he will, but it hurts so bad to know I put him through pain without him knowing what was going on."

"He'll come around."

"I hope so. One thing I am glad about is that I can cook again! I love your mother, but that woman can't cook to save her life."

"She's not that bad." He couldn't even say it with a straight face.

"I honestly don't know how you survived growing up on that food."

"A lot of cafeteria lunches and eating over at friends' houses."

"When she made *spaghetti*, I legit almost gagged."

"Why do you think it took me seven years to try yours? I just thought spaghetti sauce consisted of tomato paste on noodles." He cringes just thinking about it.

"And that's not even the worse thing she makes."

"I'm pretty sure it is."

"That's because she didn't make you *soup* to feel better." Michael starts cracking up laughing because he watched her make it. "I still can't believe you let her make that and didn't say anything at all."

"What am I gonna say? *Uh Ma, I'd appreciate it if you gave Corina store bought soup, I like her and don't want her to die?*"

"Yeah, that would have been a great place to start."

"I don't care if I'm thirty-five or not, my ma would have whooped my butt."

"Michael, she put potatoes in water, and boiled it. That was her soup. No cream, no chicken stock, not even salt for goodness sakes. It was like the mashed potatoes before you drain it. That was my soup."

"And you ate every drop, because you are a good person."

"Because if I hadn't *my* ma would have whooped *me*." Corina smiles closing her eyes, now that her body no longer feels like it's on fire. There's nothing like drifting off to bed knowing you are home.

Sometimes Being the Smaller Person Just Feels Good

Three months, in the grand scheme of things, is a drop in the bucket. When Mia thinks about it, she'd been questioning her marriage for much longer than that but it seems like that was a lifetime ago. In a way, she guesses it was.

Ashton sees his dad on Saturday mornings, which was pretty much the only time Tyson really spent with Ash before. That was always their family time.

They'd have breakfast, sometimes go to the park or beach, or just cuddle up on cold days and watch movies together.

Saturdays were what used to get Mia through the week. Now, they are the day she dreads. They decided it wasn't best to put Ash through joint custody and, to be honest, Mia doesn't think Tyson would have a clue what to do with Ashton alone anyway.

So they keep up with their Saturday tradition, and of course Tyson is welcome and encouraged to come to anything that has to do with Ashton: award ceremonies, doctor appointments, IEPs, birthdays, holidays, etc.

He hardly came to any of those while they were married, so she doubts he will start now, but if he does, Mia will be the first one cheering him on.

She keeps telling herself that she refuses to be the bitter, jilted ex. Is she hurt? Of course. But she won't let her son suffer for her pain.

Which is what she chants over and over in her head as she sits across from Tyson at the breakfast table.

She looks down at her untouched pancakes and all she can think about is picking up her pancake and slapping him across the face with it. She doubts anyone as serious and refined as Tyson Mathews has ever been pancake slapped.

And just like that, Mia is able to smile. She takes a slow, satisfying bite as she keeps the image of a shocked Tyson in her head. She has to swallow down the giggle along with the pancake at the vision of syrup slowly oozing down his face.

"It's nice to see you smile again." Well, he had to go and kill that nice image. She doesn't bother giving him a response, but turns to Ashton to wipe his face with his napkin.

"So how was camping buddy?"

"Ash had a great time, didn't you little love?"

"Oh, yeah, what'd you do?"

"He discovered he is a frog whisperer, aren't you?"

Ashton smiles wide at that, and repeats, "fog," the best he can.

"Why don't you go grab your pictures and you can show your dad. Run along and go get them. Frog pictures, on your desk."

He runs off and Mia is now wishing she would have rethought that and grabbed them herself.

"Frogs? I hope you didn't let him touch those dirty things." His handsome face is twisted with a judgmental scowl, and for the first time ever, she realized how often he makes that particular face. And just how unappealing it actually is.

"Of course, I let him touch them, he's a little boy, it's important to let him discover things."

"Mia, do you know how many diseases those things carry?" *Let it go Mia, don't go there. Be the bigger person.*

"Probably half the amount as women who are fine sleeping with married men." Yeah, she totally went there, and it felt great. Tyson visibly swallows and then glares down at her. Not allowing him to intimidate her, she goes on.

"At least Ashton can just wash his hands, without needing a shot of antibiotics after." His mouth drops open and she takes that as her cue.

"I'm going to go switch the laundry over. Please try not to kill your child's joy when he shows you his pictures."

Mia walks out of the room with the biggest smile on her face. Sometime being the smaller person feels good.

Mia relays the situation to the girls later that week and can't help the sick satisfaction she feels at their cackles and high fives.

"Oh, I would have loved to see his face once you dropped that bomb," Taryn says, giving Mia a high five.

"I've always prided myself on not stooping to others' levels. I never want to be that petty woman." Mia shakes her head, trying not to be disappointed in herself.

"Oh, please, sometimes petty is just what you need," Taryn defends.

"I tend to never agree with Taryn, just for principles sake, but she has a point here," Liz adds, tossing a wink at her best friend, despite Taryn's cold stare.

"I think everything has its time and place. You were being the bigger person by letting him back into your home, and into your sacred Saturday morning routine. He needs to know how his life choices have affected you and Ashton," Corina adds.

"If you think that comment shocked him, I can't wait to see the look on his face when you start dating again," Taryn adds, as she pops a chocolate into her mouth.

Dread instantly fills Mia. She's sure the panic is all over her face, for her friends to see.

"Whoa, are you okay?" Liz asks, putting her drink down and turning Mia to face her.

"Dating?" Mia manages to barely squeak out.

"I don't mean now necessarily, but eventually," Taryn adds, looking rather sheepish.

"I am not ever going to date again. I mean, forget that I'm damaged goods, I have Ashton."

"Okay, I'm going to stop you right there." Corina speaks up. "You better never refer to yourself as damaged ever again. You are seasoned, wise, but never damaged you hear me? And you have Ash, big deal. Lots of single moms date."

Mia turns surprised to hear her best friend supportive of this idea. "Even you think I should date? Corina, it's hardly been three months!"

"Yeah, but he moved on, while you were still married. Don't you think that gives you a pass?" Taryn bluntly adds.

"Taryn!" The other two yell.

"What? It's the truth."

"It is, but it's also tacky to point it out," Liz admonishes, and Taryn shrugs.

"She isn't wrong, Mia." Corina moves over and puts and arm around Mia. "There's no right or wrong amount of time to move on. Just know if and when you ever decide you are ready, it's okay. It's good for you and even Ashton to move forward."

"I'm so not ready. Even if I were, being a single mom is like the kiss of death in the dating world, nobody would give me a second glance."

"That's a bunch of bull," Taryn says.

"Not even close," Liz pipes up.

"Um, not exactly. I know someone interested now," Corina mutters more to herself than the girls, but it was enough to shock everyone.

Too Much of a Good Thing is Wonderful

Taryn's never been known for her tact, it's true. But she also has never seen the point in it. People are always spouting off about being truthful, upfront and honest… but they never mean it. What they mean is be nice. Don't lie, but be nice while you sugar coat everything.

Well, which one is it? Do you want the truth, or want nice? Because usually those things don't go hand in hand. There's also a small chance she's also on the spectrum, but that can be looked at another time.

Currently, they are all gaping at Corina like they are a bunch of fish.

"What do you mean you know someone interested? I've been divorced for all of five minutes," Mia squeaks out.

"I can't believe you've been holding out. Share the juicy gos." Even Liz doesn't admonish Taryn for being nosy, because she's just as curious as Taryn is. Corina turns a bit pink but takes a sip of her wine and squares her shoulders.

"You know the behavior therapist at Max's school, Hudson? Well, I'm pretty sure he'd be interested, that's all."

"Hold up, you are skipping way too many important details here. Like how old is he? Is he single? Is he hot? Does he have any creepy, serial killer type personality traits?" Liz nods along with my questions, while Mia looks like she wants to sink into the floor.

"I'm sure you've mistaken, Corina."

"No, I haven't Mia, he is totally interested."

"How would you even know that?"

"Based on something he said."

"Hold up!" Taryn places her hand out in front of her stopping whatever weird interaction these two are having.

"You need to back up. How does Mia even know Max's therapist? And how do you know he's interested? And for God's sake is the man good looking? I need details here, woman." Liz pushes Taryn's wine glass away from her, but doesn't ignore the fact that she wants the answers to every question Taryn just asked.

"Well, as you know Mia dropped Max off and picked him up from ABA for me for the last two months. When I started taking him again, Hudson mentioned how nice it was to see me, but that he would miss seeing the beautiful woman with the sad eyes."

Everyone but Mia turned into a puddle of goo at that

comment. Taryn opens her mouth to speak, but Corina cuts her off before she can ask the same question for the third time.

"And yes, he is gorgeous!"

"Oh, picture, picture!" Taryn demands as Corina goes looking through her phone frantically.

"I have no clue who you are even talking about. I'm sure you are embellishing a bit."

"Not at all."

"Wait on the gorgeous part? Or the being interested part?" Taryn asks, because well, that's important.

"Both," Mia says.

"Neither," Corina glares. "Look." She shoves her phone at us and Liz and I both gasp as Mia sits there looking totally unaffected.

"That man is pure eye candy." Taryn says, taking a second and third look.

"Uh, yeah." Liz looks just as affected based on the fact that she hasn't blinked once.

"Oh, please. He's a hippie and a child," Mia says, taking a quick glance at the phone.

"He's neither and you know it."

Taryn looks back at the photo of the man caught in mid-laughter and thinks he might be the most beautiful sight she's ever seen. Although she's smart enough not to voice that out loud, since she does love her husband... but she can also appreciate God's creation. And this man was created well.

He has dark skin, which cause his light hazel eyes, that are alight in laughter, to pop. He has long dreads that are pulled back, and a well-kept goatee.

"Mia, this man called you beautiful? You seriously need to get on that," Liz says as she takes a long drink from Taryn's wine glass and then fans herself.

"He also called me sad."

"But you have been sad, babe," Corina gently points out.

"And most men aren't observant or care enough to notice," Liz points out. Taryn winces when she sees how the words take a direct hit right to Mia's heart. Taryn takes her wine glass back and it's her turn to give Liz a pointed look.

"Oh, no, I didn't mean…"

"It's okay. It's true, Tyson still has no clue how he has hurt me, or that I was ever sad. I just don't think I'm ready to date."

"And that's totally fine. As long as you know you can, if you want," Corina says.

"And when you are, you should totally start with him. Or you can steal Kev from me and this beautiful man can console me and my sad eyes," Taryn says, pouting her lips and fluttering her eyes. It did as hoped and Mia starts to laugh.

"You are too much."

"Yes, but too much of a good thing is wonderful," Taryn replies, passing Mia the wine bottle of the meeting.

"For your sad eyes and a gentleman caller." Mia rolls her eyes but snatches up her prize and sticks it in her purse.

I'm a Woman...
And Have a Pulse

Mia looks at the clock on the dash and groans. She was stuck doing depositions all afternoon and is verging on late to pick up Ashton from therapy.

He takes a bus from school every day straight to therapy now, so Mia doesn't have to leave work midday to take him. It's weird working for a new firm. She didn't just lose her husband; it feels like she also lost herself.

Mia is no longer with the firm she worked hard to become partner, she's no longer a wife, or partner... motherhood is all she has now, and she'll be damned if she fails at that too.

She pulls up with three minutes to spare and signs Ashton out. As she waits for them to bring him out, her phone rings. Mia quickly answers without looking at the ID.

"Hello?"

"Hey Mia, I'm so sorry to bother you, but there's been an emergency."

"Hey Corina, no bother at all, what's up?"

"Mateo was climbing trees in the back and fell. I'm pretty sure he broke his arm. I'm taking him to the ER now, but I should be picking Max up from therapy right now. Do you think you can get him?"

"Sure thing, I'm grabbing Ash as we speak." Mia nods to the therapist who brings Ashton out and rushes him to the car to strap him in.

"We are getting in the car now, I'm across town from Max's center, so it might be a bit."

"That's okay, I called the center and they said they will keep him until you can get there. Go around back, I think they are going to let him play outside to keep him busy. I'm so sorry."

"Don't be sorry, just get that sweet boy of yours taken care of. Did you want me to take him home with me or to your house?"

"My place, if you don't mind. Taryn is there now with the other two, and Michael is heading straight from work to the ER."

"It's the perfect impromptu playdate. I'll pick up a pizza after I grab Max."

"You are such a lifesaver. Thank you so much my friend."

"Anytime. Keep me updated."

"Will do."

"Come on Ashton, we are going to go get Max."

"Max." Mia smiles at her sweet boy and off they go.

Pulling up to Max's center fifteen minutes later, there's only a single other car in the lot. Mia grabs Ashton and they take off toward the back of the building.

Of course, her horrible luck holds strong when it is none other than Hudson out there with Max. Mia takes a deep breath and prepares herself for the awkward situation that is surely about to take place, as they make their way over.

Max starts happy shrieking when he sees Ash, and that's all the invitation her little man needs to run over to the play structure with his buddy. Hudson whips around on guard, instantly relaxing when he sees it's only them.

"Hey there, the cavalry has arrived."

"Sorry it took me so long, Ashton was across town at the other center, so it took us a bit. Come on boys, time to go home."

"Oh, that's okay, let them play for a bit, they are having a good time." Mia looks over at the two boys swinging side by side and can't help but smile. They both have come such a long way in just a few months.

"That looks good on you."

"Excuse me?"

Hudson laughs and her reaction and shakes his head. "The smile, it suits you."

"Ah, yes, me and my sad eyes." Mia gives him a pointed look, he doesn't even have the shame to look embarrassed.

"I had a feeling that was going to come back to get me, although, to my credit I didn't think I'd see you again."

She laughs at his honesty and takes a moment to take him in. He really is a beautiful man, there's no denying that. But they are worlds apart.

181

His posture screams relaxed, even if it didn't, his whole laid-back look would. He sports long black dread locks, hanging free down past his shoulders. He is wearing skinny jeans with a fitted black t-shirt. The white frames of his glasses really pop against the dark color of his skin.

Mia glances down at her fitted pencil skirt, silk blouse and blazer and has to stifle a laugh at how different they are from each other. Where he is laid back in his style, she is about as uptight and professional as you can get.

"Thank you for staying late, I appreciate it, but I gotta get this little guy home and everyone fed." Mia watches as his eyes move to her left hand, and the lack of ring there. He doesn't say anything, but she can tell he's noticed the tan line from where her ring used to be.

She looks him straight in the eyes, almost as a challenge. *Yes, I'm newly divorced and vulnerable. Do you really want this baggage? Nope, keep dreaming surfer boy.*

"It was very nice to see you again Mia. I'm Hudson, by the way. Maybe we will meet again." She picks up on the question in the inflection of his statement, but just smiles.

"Have a great night Hudson. Come on boys, time to go." She gets the boys in the car, but something has drawn her attention. She turns to see Hudson putting a box in his truck, leaning over to push items out of the way. Because she is a woman and has a pulse... she might have let her gaze linger, but she'll never admit it.

Fear and Respect go Hand and Hand

Taryn is on her seventeenth round of hide and seek. Of course, she's the seeker this time, so she's relaxing on the couch looking through a magazine, yelling every so often.

"Nope not there, hmmm, where are you. Man, you are good hiders." She hears a few giggles, so she knows they are still in the house. Man, typically developing kids are fun.

The doorbell rings and Taryn jumps up to answer it. "What is this motley crew? No thanks."

She pretends to shut the door and Mia yells, "We've got pizza."

"Oh, why didn't you say so? Come on in then." Max, Ashton and Mia come into the kitchen as Taryn yells out.

"Carissa, time for dinner. Mia brought pizza."

That's all it takes for her little partners in crime to come running down the hall and into the kitchen. Mia made a waffle for Ashton, thank the Lord above they happened to have Eggo Blueberry here. The ladies send the kids outside to play, while they take their food to the couch where they can sit and still see the yard where the kids are eating outside.

"Any word from Corina?" Mia asks before taking a bit of pizza.

"She texted earlier, it was a clean break. They are waiting to get the cast on now."

"Thank God it was only his arm, and not his neck," Mia adds.

"Seriously. That poor family has had their fair share of trauma lately, that's for sure," Taryn agrees.

"At least they will hit their deductible this year," Mia jokes.

"Hey, with a family of six, that's probably a pretty big deal. I'm sure it'll come in handy."

"So come sit down, I am glad you are here. I actually wanted to talk to you." Taryn brings her in the living room with their plates and takes a seat on the couch.

"What's up? Everything okay?"

"Um, not really. I haven't even had a chance to talk to Kev yet. I got the letter right before Corina's phone call." Taryn pulls the letter from the school out of her purse and hands it over to Mia. Taryn watches her read it, as Mia's eyes grow wider by the minute.

"They can't get away with this can they?" Taryn asks while worrying her bottom lip between her teeth.

"They most certainly cannot," Mia answers with passion.

"Even though they said we refused services?"

"But you didn't, Taryn. All you said was that you didn't agree with the IEP and were waiting for the supervisor to contact you. Did she ever get in touch with you?"

"No, I've called the program specialist, the one who told me she was waiting on her supervisor, but so far nothing. I've left about five messages and hadn't heard a single word until we got this letter." No longer having an appetite now, Taryn puts her hardly touched pizza down on her plate.

"I can't believe they are dropping Jessie from the program. What am I going to do? I can't homeschool her full time, Mia. I'm not like Liz."

"You shouldn't have to. Don't worry Taryn, they legally can't drop you because you have a concern for your child's safety. We will sue them so fast, their head will spin."

"So I'd have a case?"

"A very strong one. I did some digging, and what they are doing, dropping Jessie, is very against the law. They are within their right to only have the teacher CPR first aid certified. But if there is a legitimate concern, a parent has a right at any time to bring it to the school's attention, without fear of repercussions."

"So now what do I do? I really don't want to sue the school, they don't have much money as it is. I don't want other kids and teachers to suffer. We don't want money, we just want what's right."

"And I'm going to write that in my letter," Mia assures, rubbing her friends back.

"Your letter?"

"Yup, my letter to the superintendent of special education in Carwin County."

"You'd be willing to do that? When I called, they said it would be months before I could meet with her."

Mia's smile is slow and cunning. It's the first time Taryn's ever seen how fierce she must be in the courtroom.

"I'm going to fax the letter over first thing in the morning. Be ready to have a meeting with her before the day is out."

"You think she will drop everything to fit me in, all on the same day?"

"Oh, I know she will. What they are doing is illegal, you can't just drop a child like that from a special needs program in California. Our laws protect you, and lucky for us, I know all of them now."

Taryn hugs her tight, feeling the tears of relief spring to her eyes. "Thank you so much Mia, I was terrified."

"I know hon, but it will all be fine. I'll get everything ready tonight and send the letter first thing tomorrow."

"Do you think you can send me all of your information that you've collected? I want to be informed on all the laws and rights we have."

"Of course I can, but I'm willing to go with you tomorrow too." Taryn grabs Mia's hand in hers, pulling her into a tight, grateful hug.

"I love you for that, but this is my fight. As long as I am armed with the facts and the laws, I'll be fine. I need them to know that I can fight my own battles for my kids. I am Jessies greatest advocate, I want them to fear and respect me... not you."

"Fair enough. You will have it all in your inbox as soon as I get home."

"Thank you so much."

Kids Don't Come With Instruction Manuals

"I wonder if we can get frequent flier cards at the hospital. You know, give us a discount on pain meds, or buy one, get one free coupon at the cafeteria, something." Corina asks her husband. Michael just laughs and kisses her hand.

"At least we've hit our deductible now."

"Oh good, so we can break all the bones!" Corina mocks.

"Shush woman! My heart can't take anymore disasters."

"Sorry babe, you've been a champ the last few months, that's for sure. Let's get this kid home to bed, and release my poor friends from duty, what do you say?"

"Sounds good to me. Although you never told me about your follow up appointment this morning. It got lost amongst all the craziness."

"Oh, that's right. It went really well. The doctor said I'm pretty much fully healed now, and the labs came back clean, they got it all." Michael reaches over and squeezes his wife's hand.

"That's fantastic babe, I'm so happy to hear it. So you are totally out of the woods now?"

"Until my next test in a year to make sure I stay that way."

They both take a full breath and let it out in relief. It's been such a hard journey, but they are finally seeing the other side of the mountain.

They finally arrive home, and after the pain meds he received, Mateo is about ready to fall asleep standing up. Michael takes him to bed, and luckily her friends already have the others down.

"Oh, my God, you guys are lifesavers! I'm sorry it's so late. Thank you again for all your help."

"No worries, but I need to get back home to help Kevin put mine down. You good?"

"Oh, yes, of course, get home. I'm so sorry for keeping you." Taryn waves it off and smiles as she runs out the door.

"Sorry to keep you Mia, did Max do okay with you picking him up?"

"There weren't any problems at all. I think it helps that Ash was there, those two are kindred spirits."

"Nobody would have a single clue, but they do love each other. It's funny how two people can be so close, yet never really interact or engage with each other."

"But you can see the comfort they bring each other by just being near. Kindred spirits. I love that they have that."

"Me too! Everyone needs one. I've found that in Michael, and in you girls."

"Same. I don't think I'd have gotten through these last few months without you girls."

"Before you leave, do you think I can pick your brain on something?" Corina asks sheepishly.

"Of course, legal?" Mia asks, concern taking over her smiling face.

"Unfortunately, yes."

"Well, good thing I've already got my lawyer hat on tonight. What's up?"

"Carissa has been asking more questions about her birth parents lately, I think she's just at that age where she is curious and wants to know where she comes from."

"That's very natural for someone her age. She's what, sixth grade?"

"Yeah, we've known it was coming, but we've had them since Jasper was only a month old, so they are our kids, ya know? It's a blessing and a curse to talk about her parents. Her mom was one of my favorite people of all times, but she had her fair share of demons. We've always just shared the good stories and traits with the kids and left out the bad ones."

"That's smart. Bringing up the bad won't help her at this point."

"She's old enough to remember the drugs, and she knows why her mom died, but we don't focus on that when we talk about her."

"And her father?" Mia asks, almost afraid to hear the answer.

"It's much more complicated. Danica died of an overdose, and Joaquin was her dealer. They wanted us to testify against him, pinning Dani's death on him as well as the drug charges."

"And you didn't?" Corina looks down at her lap. She's not ashamed of what she did, but she's also not proud of it either.

"I didn't feel comfortable saying that he sold her the drugs, because I wasn't there. Had he given them to her in the past? Yes, he had. Did others overdose from the same batch that he did sell? Yes. But I did not know for a fact that he sold those particular drugs to her, so I would not say that he did in a court of law."

"That seems very fair Corina, and you have nothing to be ashamed of."

"My parents didn't see it that way, it's why they disowned me."

"Because you wouldn't lie on the stand?"

"They think I refused because of the kids. And honestly, maybe that was part of it. But I also refuse to condemn someone that I didn't see with my own eyes commit the crime."

"What did the kids have to do with it?"

"After the trial, Joaquin signed over all parental rights to Michael and I, and we officially adopted the kids."

"So your parents think he bribed you with that in order to keep you from testifying?" Corina can't bring herself to look up at Mia, so she inhales a breath.

"Did he use them, to keep you from testifying?" Mia whispers out.

"Not in so many words. He's too smart for that, but it might have been implied."

"That's okay Corina, I'm not going to judge you. That's an impossible situation to be put in, legally you did nothing wrong."

"I know, but I will always feel a sense of… guilt isn't right… but just a dirtiness that goes along with the whole situation."

"That's understandable. You lost your sister, and your family in one swoop."

"He had said if I testified and he got life, his mother would fight hard for the kids and keep us tied up in court and he'd never allow the kids to settle." Corina takes another steadying breath.

"He'd do it, too. Honestly, the man terrifies me, but it came down to I just didn't know for sure, and my sister made her own decisions that night she chose to leave her kids alone. Jasper was just a brand new baby, and she left him, to go get high. That was her horrible decision and she paid the final price."

Mia brings her sweet friend in for a hug. "That's got to be so hard, but you and Michael have done such a great job with them, they are fantastic kids."

"They really are, which is why I'm so terrified to let them know anything about their dad. Carissa has been hinting about wanting to visit him. I can't let her do that, can I? But if I don't, I'm the evil one who kept her from him, and when she's of age, she'll just do it anyway."

"There is that possibility. But you can control the situation, at least now and on your terms. If you keep her from him, there's a good chance you are right, that she will rebel," Mia offers.

"I know you're right."

"Why not talk to her about it, maybe set an age for when she's a little older? You can make sure she can decide when she's old enough to know all the facts."

"I actually really like that idea. But legally, he can't get them back can he? He can't take them from us for any reason?"

"He signed over all rights and they are officially adopted?"

"Yes."

"Then you are safe there. They are legally your children, and he has zero right to them in the eyes of the law. Now in his own eyes, that might be different, but legally he has zero rights forever."

"Thank God."

"Just be honest with the kids and let them make their own decisions and assumptions of him. They are smart. Deep down the kids know who loves them and have their best interest at heart. I'd just tell Carissa that you will answer whatever questions she has and if she asks about visiting him, give her an age in which you are willing to take her."

"That's actually a really good idea and will give me time to prepare myself and her. Thank you so much. It's just been eating away at me. This mother gig is hard, special needs or not, these dang kids don't come with instruction manuals."

"Oh, how I wish they did. Honestly though, Corina, you are doing fantastic and you have it so much harder than the rest of us I think."

"Because of the amount of kids or because of the adoption?"

"Neither actually. For me it's just Ashton, so the spectrum is all I know. Same for Taryn since both of hers are spectrum. Even though Liz has the higher end of the spectrum with Marcus, all our kids are still spectrum. But you have both, so you have to navigate through two worlds."

"I've never actually thought of that before. It really is like two completely different worlds," Corina replies, thankful for her friend's insight.

"So, give yourself some grace, because you are doing a fantastic job. Those kids know you love them and would do anything for them. Even laid up and sick, you've always put them and their needs first. And they have such opposite needs, yet you always manage."

Corina wipes away tears that are flowing freely down her face.

"Sometimes it just feels like I'm almost drowning, you know? Like I have one of those tiny water rings just around my neck, keeping me from going all the way under. But I'm bobbing up and down enough to choke on water."

"I think that's a pretty accurate description on motherhood." Mia gives her another squeeze.

"I know you feel that way from the inside looking out Cor, but from the outside looking in? You are a beast riding those rapids from a lifeboat. Looking straight into the current and taking it on," Mia says. Corina gives a small chuckle and dismisses Mia's comment with her hand.

"Really Corina, you overcame your sister's death, you took on three kids, and the system, you are rocking the autism mom life, and you beat cancer. I honestly think there's nothing you can't do."

33

It's All Fun and Games Until Someone Rolls an Ankle

It's 10:30 a.m., and Taryn finally just got Jessie down. It's been a freaking long night. Jessie has been having night terrors more frequently lately.

The logical part of Taryn's brain knows that she had them before the incident, but the momma bear part thinks the increase is due to all the stress and change that happened.

It's just another reason to hate the school district, and right now Taryn doesn't need another reason. She tries to scoot herself out from underneath Jessie without waking her up. It's close to impossible. Every time Taryn gets more than a few inches away, Jessie reels her back in.

"Tacoma, Tacoma come," Taryn half whispers, half shouts into the living room. The dog finally comes in at a nice lazy pace.

"Make yourself useful will ya? Get up here." Tacoma jumps on the bed and Taryn slowly rolls out, as she pushes him closer to Jessie.

Jessie rolls over and wraps her arms around him, and Taryn holds her breath. Her body is half on, half off the bed but she doesn't dare move another muscle. She waits a few minutes and once she knows Jessie is firmly asleep, Taryn slips out of the room, closing the door behind her.

Taryn does a little victory dance all the way to her bed. She turns off all the lights in her room and draws the blackout curtains.

She can't help but moan at how good the bed feels as she snuggles in good. Taryn's eyes just start to close, when her freaking phone rings.

"Nooooo."

She ignores it, but it keeps ringing and she's afraid it's going to wake Jessie, so she reluctantly answers it with a bit too much heat.

"Yeah."

"Um, may I speak to Taryn Leighton please?"

"This is her."

"Hello Mrs. Leighton, I'm Alesha Caster from the superintendent's office. Superintendent Sandoval would like to meet with you and your husband, can you come in this afternoon?" Holy crap, Mia totally called that.

"Um, yeah, probably, I just have to have someone come watch my daughter. What time are you thinking?"

"Would two hours work?" Like I can say no.

"Yes, that should be fine, we will see you then. Thank you."

Holy crap, Taryn's so not ready for this. She was supposed to be rested, and knowledgeable, yet she can barely tell you her name, let alone Californian laws right now.

Resigned to never knowing the blissful feeling of sleep for yet another day, Taryn hops out of bed and instantly steps on those stupid tiny little princess dolls that Jessie leaves all over the floor. It's like she places them right by Taryn's bed on purpose.

Cursing, Taryn hops her way into the kitchen where she puts on a large pot of coffee, then calls Kev.

"Hello."

"Hey love, how much work have you gotten done today?"

"Uh, oh. Is Jess being hard, do I need to come home?"

"No and yes. No, she's actually sleeping, but if you could take a long lunch? We just got a meeting with the Superintendent, but it's in an hour and a half. It's fine if you can't make it, but I wanted to let you know."

"Taryn, when have I ever missed any meeting at all? Let alone one this important?"

"Well, never, but it's short notice and you are working."

"I'll be there. I can take whatever I don't finish home with me tonight."

"Really? I always do all the talking anyway."

"Yes, and I keep you calm so you don't kill anyone. It's a team effort. I'd much rather take an early lunch, then have to take a leave of absence to raise the kids while their mother rots in jail." Kevin teases.

"Ha-ha. Okay, I'll meet you there, I need to see if Liz can watch Jessie."

"Maybe you should take her along so they see what you have to deal with." He's joking, but that's actually a brilliant idea, too bad she's sleeping.

"I'll see you soon, love ya."

"Love ya too, honey."

Taryn hangs up, then dials Liz, as she adds a good splash of coffee creamer to her coffee. She poured it in the largest cup, *okay, it's technically a bowl,* that she could find.

Taryn drinks down half of the cup in one go, burning her throat all the way down.

"Hey Lady," Liz answers, while Taryn's throat is on fire.

"Hey, you'll never believe it, I got a call saying the superintendent of the special needs department wants to meet with us, this afternoon."

"Seriously? That's amazing."

"Well, except for the fact I've yet to sleep and Jessie just went down. I hate to ask, but would you and Marcus mind coming here for an hour or so?"

"Sure, no problem at all, Marcus can do his school-work anywhere."

"You again, are saving my bacon. Thank you so much."

"No problem, see you soon."

Taryn downs the rest of her coffee and pours another cup. She takes it with her back into her bedroom, but instead of climbing back int her comfy bed, she heads straight for her closet.

After standing there blinking, and getting absolutely nowhere, she calls Mia.

"Hello?"

"You will never believe it."

"You got a meeting with the superintendent?"

"Okay, so maybe you will believe it." Mia chuckles, while Taryn looks down at her watch. Jumping to the point of why she called so she will have time to shower.

"I have no clue what to wear. What do you wear when you take on a school system?"

"A power suit."

"Yeah, I'm a stay at home mom, Mia."

"Right, okay, do you have any nice blouses?"

"Yes, a few."

"How about something in red?" Mia asks, while Taryn fingers through all of her clothes until she comes across a bright red blouse that buttons all the way to the collarbone. She hardly ever wears it because it's so nice.

"Yes, I have the perfect thing."

"Good, red shows confidence, now how about a pair of black slacks?"

"Yep, I have those."

"And it's important to wear heels. It gives you height, but also will give you confidence."

"Yeah, unless I roll an ankle… which, with my track record, is very possible."

"No negative vibes. You get that all out of your system now. You go in there with confidence, and tell them exactly what your daughter needs, and what her rights are as a student in that district. You have the facts, and you have the details down. Go in and rock it."

"Yes ma'am, okay thank you so much."

"No worries, you've totally got it. Also, wear nice panties, lace if you have them."

"I'm not going to stoop so low as to sleep with the superintendent, Mia. I don't even think she swings that way."

"It's for you, not for her you weirdo. It's proven that nice underwear makes you feel better, and therefore you are more confident. Same with makeup and do something with your crazy hair."

"It's not that crazy," Taryn says, while she eyes her out of control curly red hair in the mirror.

"It's almost as curly as mine, and at least I do mine," Mia comes back. And, well, she has Taryn there.

"Okay, it will be done."

"Good luck, call as soon as it's over."

"Will do, bye."

CHAPTER

I've Never Been More Terrified, Or Turned On

Taryn probably should have eaten something along with those three cups of coffee, but it's too late for that now. She pulls in just as Kevin gets out of his car.

"You ready for this?"

"Of course I'm not ready, this is insane, I haven't slept since last Tuesday!"

"You've got this babe." He gives Taryn a quick kiss and they walk into the Carwin County Office of Education and approach the first desk they see.

"Hello, we are the Leighton's, here to see the superintendent of special education."

"Please take a seat, and I'll let Melissa know you are here."

"Thank you."

They sit down, and Taryn's hands instantly start to shake. Kevin holds them in his and smiles over at his wife. It's really not fair that this man can always stay so calm. Seriously, nothing shakes him. He missed his calling as a 911 operator. Although, Taryn would much prefer the money he makes as an architect, but still.

"She's ready for you, if you'd both follow me this way, please."

They follow the secretary down a long hallway, when Taryn stops dead in her tracks seeing the large glass conference room, packed full of people.

"I thought it was going to be just us and the superintendent," Taryn whispers to Kevin. He also looks surprised at the full room, but still doesn't lose his cool.

"I mean, you did send her a letter from your lawyer babe, they messed up once, so they are covering all their basis." *Note to self, do not send letter from lawyer unless you mean business.* Thank God for the power outfit, Taryn will have to kiss Mia for that idea later.

"Hello Mr. and Mrs. Leighton, thank you for coming in on such short notice. I'm Melissa Sandoval, it's nice to meet you."

"Nice to meet you too, thank you so very much for fitting us in. We really do appreciate it," Taryn says with a smile.

"Of course, we are looking forward to sitting down and getting everything ironed out. Let's go around and make introductions, since we have a full house, shall we?"

"That would be very helpful, thank you."

"I'll start, as I mentioned I'm Melissa Sandoval, superintendent." She turns to the woman on her right.

"I'm Naomi Lampton, behavior specialist." The woman on her right speaks up next.

"I'm Annise Karns, school nurse."

By this point, Taryn completely glazes over and misses everyone else's names. But there's an autism program specialist, operations specialist for ASD and a SELPA rep.

"And, of course you know me, Cheryl Trenton, classroom teacher."

"I'm Taryn, the mom," Taryn says turning to her husband. "And this is my husband, Kevin."

"Now that you know who we all are, why don't we hear your concerns. We have an idea, but I'd like to hear everything from you if you wouldn't mind."

"Basically, we got a call around 10:20 a.m. from Cheryl saying that Jessie had eaten an unknown berry from a neighbor's tree that was hanging over the fence, while she was on break. She was calling to let me know." The teachers face is bright red and Taryn knows this has to be embarrassing for her, but she has to give the facts.

"I asked if she had called poison control and she had not. I asked if they had called the nurse, and they had not. I asked how long it had been and she said it was roughly forty minutes from the time Jessica had eaten it until she called me."

Taryn takes a deep breath, because as much as she really does love Cheryl, the entire matter had been handled wrong. Taryn smiles an apology to Cheryl, then turns her attention back to Melissa.

"I feel this was handled very wrong. Things happen all the time. Jessie is a very spirited girl and is always getting into trouble. I want to express that I'm not mad that she ate the berry. I've had to call poison control myself several times, so I wasn't mad that it needed to happen. I was upset that it didn't occur to anyone to call the nurse or poison control.." Taryn takes a breath and pauses, to make sure everyone is following.

"Anytime anything unknown goes into a child's mouth, poison control and then the school nurse should instantly be contacted."

"The staff is trained to wait for the teacher before making any decisions. They did as protocol requires, which was bringing it to the teacher's attention the moment she was off break." The program director pipes in. Taryn internally fist pumps, *glad you brought that up.* Instead she turns toward her, with her most professional smile.

"I'm glad you brought that up. That is in fact why we are here, and why we wouldn't sign the IEP originally, because we don't agree with that protocol. If a child does something dangerous or has a health condition, every single staff member in that room should know what to do in order to save that child's life. Without CPR and basic first aid training, how are they supposed to take the necessary measures to save a child's life?" Taryn asks, and the woman looks speechless so Taryn turns to the rest of the table.

"What if it was a seizure? Or God forbid an allergic reaction from what she ate? If you wait thirty minutes for the teacher, the child would die. It makes no sense to me that they don't require basic first aid training, and I refuse to send my daughter to a place where her life is in danger daily."

Kevin's input is nodding his head once in agreement with his wife.

The room is dead quiet, you could hear a pin drop. After a moment the superintendent once again takes control.

"The students' safety is obviously our number one concern. I wish we could train all of our staff members, but to be honest, it's just not in the budget to do so. It is our hope, to eventually be able to have at least one member of each class trained, which unfortunately at this time is only the teacher."

"So when the teacher is unavailable?"

"The school nurse should be called."

"Yet she wasn't."

"Yes, that was unfortunate in this situation, but we will make sure that never happens again."

"This is why we are here. I want to know how you can make sure it doesn't happen, if you aren't having these aides trained. I don't blame the aid, that isn't their job, and the teacher can't be in the room at all times. I understand that she needs breaks for lunch and bathroom, that's her legal right. But it's my legal right to have someone who knows how to call a single number, if my child eats something that puts her life at risk."

Yes, Taryn took it there. She's getting heated and is trying to keep her cool, but they are acting like she's the one to blame here. It's not her fault they put a value on the safety of the kids they are supposed to protect.

"With all due respect Mrs. Leighton, Jessie is fine. She never stopped breathing, and she remained conscious. So, I think we should maybe take a moment to put everything into perspective here."

And. Taryn. Snaps.

It takes everything in her not to reach across the table and smack that director right in the nose. Instead she takes a very slow breath and smiles her *I'm about to lose my shit* smile. Kevin swears under his breath, because he knows the crazy is about to be unleashed.

Taryn goes into her purse and takes out the pictures she had taken of Jessie's mouth. The pictures that show all the huge white sores inside her mouth and throat. Then she takes out the pictures of Jessie strapped to the hospital bed, and the hospital bill for the overnight stay.

Taryn lays them all on the table in front of this so-called director, and then lastly, she pulls out a single berry from a baggie in her purse.

"You're right, she didn't lose consciences, or stop breathing. Instead, she was strapped down and hospitalized for two days. She had sores all throughout her mouth and throat and couldn't eat a single thing for almost three weeks. But since you won't lose consciousness or you know… stop breathing, why don't you go ahead and have a little snack, so we can see how *your* perspective changes afterwards."

Taryn places the berry down right in front of her and then gives her a cold hard stare.

"Jesus," Kevin hisses and everyone else in the room goes dead quiet for a moment.

"Okay, I see that emotions are running high. Mrs. Leighton, you make a very valid point. We aren't saying that Jessies situation wasn't dire. On the contrary, we know how horrible it was, and we know that other steps should have been taken. You have every right to be upset, this is your child, and you love her." The superintendent is good. She almost makes up for the other one… almost.

"We are here to decide how to move forward in the future. And to find out what it would take for you to be comfortable putting your daughter back into school."

"Well, for starters I'm not even sure I'm allowed to. I got a letter stating they were removing Jessie from the program." Taryn takes the letter out and hands it over. The superintendent shoots a look to the director, who speaks up again.

"You declined services at the IEP."

"I'm sorry that's not true. We refused to sign what was offered and requested to meet with you, as is our legal right," Taryn shoots back.

"No such request was made," she fires back.

"Excuse me?" Taryn looks at Kevin and sees the anger she feels reflected in his eyes.

"We most certainly did, and three of the people in that meeting are sitting right here." Taryn makes eye contact with each person that was there, yet they don't make a single move to back her up. *Cowards*.

"We were told that you would get back to us in a week. When that week was up, I called back and was told you were on vacation. It wasn't until we got this letter that I realized something was up," Taryn replies as politely as she can to this horrid woman.

"I'm sorry, but the program specialist says otherwise."

"It's convenient that the program specialist isn't here, because she is lying." The maddening woman just shrugs.

"I guess it's your word against hers."

"Good thing I came prepared then, isn't it."

Taryn pulls her phone out of her purse and brings up her recorded files. She knew this was going to be an important meeting, so she recorded the whole thing.

She skips forward to the very end and pushes play. Her voice instantly comes through the speaker.

"I'm sorry, we just can't sign this until there are better safety procedures in place."

"I'm sorry you feel that way, but there's nothing I can do," replies the program specialist, not sounding a single bit sorry.

"Then who can?"

"That would be my boss, I can talk to her and have her get in touch with you, but it is officially out of my hands."

"That's fine, if you could please have her call me, we just don't feel comfortable signing anything until we talk to her."

"I understand, she will call you next week. If that is all, the meeting is adjourned." Taryn pushes stop and stares directly into the woman's eyes, then makes contact with the teacher and behavior specialist, both of whom were sitting in that very meeting and didn't speak up.

Nobody meets her eyes, and everyone looks pretty uncomfortable right about now, all but Taryn anyway. She loves being right.

"Well, then, it looks like there was a miscommunication." The director finally speaks up, and Taryn scoffs, but otherwise remains silent.

"This is the first I was told about that, and you wouldn't have been sent that letter otherwise," the director speaks up.

"That is beside the point now. We want at least one aid to be first aid certified, as well as that tree cut down. Also, that woman is to be taken off my children's cases, both children. I will never be able to trust her again. When all of those things happen, we will send her back."

"Consider it done. Mallory will now be in charge of both of their cases." The superintendent states, nodding to the other director in the room.

"I'm so sorry you had such a horrible experience, and I'm doubly sorry you were lied to and treated so badly. Our number one goal is safety, and that's what I can promise will be our focus going forward."

"Thank you very much."

"I will have two aids certified by next Monday. Cheryl, please call for subs that day."

"Of course."

"We will also add an addendum to Jessie's health plan, that the nurse is to be called directly after poison control if anything at all is ingested."

"We would greatly appreciate that."

"Again, please accept my apologies, and I'm glad we could work this out."

"So are we, thank you so much for your time and for making this happen."

Taryn stands and turns without acknowledging anyone else. They leave the instant they get the desired results, no sense tempting fate.

They remain quiet until they are out of earshot and then Kevin leans down and whispers directly into his wife's ear, "my God Taryn, you were so badass! You were also totally scary!" He stops dead in his tracks when something occurs to him. "You don't have anymore of those extra berries lying around do you? Jesus, Taryn, *you want a snack?*" He starts laughing. "I honestly have never been more afraid of you, or turned on, in my life."

Nothing Says Closure Like Another Woman's Underwear

Mia is in the middle of tossing her entire house! It looks like SWAT had a field day in here, but she can't for the life of her find Ashton's stuffed frog.

He has been screaming and biting himself non-stop and slamming his head into the door. It's absolutely killing her. Mia's looked everywhere, and texted all her friends, but still keeps turning up empty-handed.

Her bed is one of those old-fashioned heavy oak ones, so she can't move it alone. Ashton slept with her last night, so it might have fallen behind the bed, since it's the only place she hasn't looked.

Mia calls Corina in tears asking if her husband can come help her move the bed. Within twenty minutes the doorbell rings and Mia answers it, a frantic mess.

"Oh, Michael, you are my hero, thank you so much for coming by."

"No worries, my buddy Mark is in the truck. I thought it might help having another set of hands. I wasn't sure if a stranger would set off Ashton though."

It's out of his mouth and mere seconds later Aston is slamming the walls and stomping around screaming upstairs.

"I'm guessing we are past that point now, I'll go grab him."

"Thanks so much," Mia shouts after him.

The guys go running up the stairs and follow her lead to the bedroom.

"It's got to be there, I've literally checked every-where else."

"Let's find out."

The guys move the bed, and instantly the bright green frog stands out.

"Here we go." Michael scoops it up, but to Mia's mortification a hot pink thong is stuck to it, and now sitting in the hands of her best friend's husband. They both turn bright red and he quickly hands it over to her.

"Sorry, this must be yours." Michael quickly drops the offensive scrap of lace into Mia's hands.

Mia's embracement quickly turns to rage. "Nope, not my size," she says, glaring at the tiny little piece of scrap of material. If it's even possible, Michael turns a brighter shade of red and his friend makes up an excuse to head to the car.

"Oh, God, Mia, I'm so sorry."

"It's fine." Mia walks over to the trash and throws it away as she happily takes the frog from him.

"Thank you so much, you saved my life tonight!"

"You better hurry and give it to your little guy. Do you need me to stay for a bit?" Michael winces at the sound of something crashing down the hall.

"Nah, he will settle down as soon as he sees this. Thanks again, and sorry about the panties thing...

They both look away and he mumbles something and practically runs out the front door.

Mia is finally able to calm Ashton down with Mr. Ribbit, and some popcorn. Within minutes she gets a text from Corina.

CORINA: OMG, call me if you need to talk.

CORINA: Scratch that, call me when you need to rant! That asshole!

MIA: It's fine, really.

CORINA: Call me!

MIA: I'm fine.

Mia doesn't get another text, so she assumes Corina finally gave up. Just as she's getting Ash down for bed, her phone chimes again.

CORINA: Answer your door.

MIA: You did not come to my house!

CORINA: Don't make me use the spare key.

213

Mia sighs and hurries down the stairs to open the door. She finds three beautiful ladies, a bottle of wine, and a gallon of ice cream. So naturally, Mia bursts into tears.

"You stubborn heifer, I told you to call me." Corina scolds.

"I'm fine, really."

"Yeah, you really look it, come on let's go sit down." Corina leads Mia to the couch while Taryn goes into the kitchen and opens every cupboard in sight.

"Wine glasses are above the microwave, spoons in the drawer next to dishwasher."

"Score!"

Taryn comes back with four glasses of wine and four spoons. They all eat directly out of the carton, while drinking their wine, and just that act alone somehow brings Mia unmeasurable amounts of comfort.

"So are we just going to pretend like you didn't find some other woman's panties under your bed?"

"Taryn!"

"Don't Taryn me, Liz, that's shitty and I'm just pointing out how shitty it is."

"You're right, it's shitty. I didn't even think I had any emotions left to spend on that man. He had her here in my house, in my freaking bed. I just feel so violated!" Mia declares before attacking the ice cream with gusto.

"As you should, I can't believe the nerve of that man," Liz agrees, patting Mia's leg.

"Honestly, I'm done. I have nothing left to give to him, he's rung me dry." Mia sadly admits to the women, exactly what she's been feeling all night.

"As horrible as this was, maybe it was good, too. Hear me out," Liz defends when the women all glare at her.

"It's now done. You are done, this might have been what it took to get you to that point."

"You are right about that. Nothing says closure like another woman's underwear," Mia says, gulping down the rest of her wine.

Taryn tops off Mia's drink and then reaches for her phone.

"Hey, what are you doing?"

"Starting your new chapter," Taryn announces proudly.

"What?"

"I'm signing you up for a dating app."

"Oh, God no, nope, no way can I do that."

"Sure you can. Plus, you don't have to actually date any of them, it's just the first step of putting yourself out there, claiming your singleness," Taryn declares.

Mia looks at Corina for backup, but she only shrugs.

"I kinda agree with her," Corina says, not at all sorry.

"What? Liz, tell me you're on my side with this, it's crazy right?" Mia pleads.

"I mean it's Taryn, so it's probably crazy, but I actually think she might have a point. Let's at least just take a look. I've been with Tom so long that this wasn't even around when we started dating, it always sounds like fun."

Mia rolls her eyes. "By all means, knock yourself out then," she says sarcastically as she waves her hand toward her phone.

"Yay! Okay, so this picture is fab, I'm picking that one," Taryn says, scrolling through her friend's phone.

"Awesome," Mia says, heavy with sarcasm, taking the ice cream container and ignoring everything else.

"Bio, Corina you do that. You are better than I am at that stuff."

Liz passes the phone to Corina, where she taps on it for a few minutes then hands it to Taryn.

"It's asking for intro questions."

"Why are you giving it to her then?" Both Liz and Mia ask.

"Hey! I'm super clever." Taryn defends.

"That's why I gave it to you, that and you are funny. Guys like funny," Corina states like it's a known fact.

"But I'm not funny," Mia reminds Corina.

"Yeah, but we aren't actually trying to get you a date remember. You don't think I'd trust some random guy to take you out do you?"

"Then what was the whole point of this again?" Mia asks, refilling her wine.

"To claim your singledom back," Taryn says with a fist pump, while she frantically types on Mia's phone.

"Wait, why is she doing the typing? She makes up fake words," Mia says, pointing the wine bottle in Taryn's direction.

Taryn just shoos Mia away. After a few more glasses, Mia doesn't have a care in the world. The girls start teaching her the difference between swiping left and swiping right, although it makes zero sense to her.

"Gah, stop, you are going the wrong way again!" Taryn points out.

"What, I'm just going back and forth."

"Exactly, it's one way, Mia. Give me that." Taryn starts looking through the phone and instantly starts to squeal.

"What, what?" Liz looks over her shoulder and screams next.

"Dude, that's horrible, I can't believe some people," Liz says in disgust.

"What? What happened?" Mia asks, leaning over to look.

"Some guy sent a picture of his, you know what, after he talked about it a bit." Liz says turning bright red.

"Yeah, seriously I can't believe this. Give me that phone back."

Taryn takes the phone and starts texting frantically and then smiles in satisfaction. Liz looks over and groans.

"Seriously Taryn, you didn't tell him off for the offensive picture?"

"I told him off for his offensive spelling. If you are going to talk about your member to a lawyer, at least spell penis correctly. She's smart! You can use a dictionary if you are going to be crass."

"So it was the spelling that offended you, not the picture?" Corina asks on a laugh.

"My eyes were so accosted by the horrible spelling, I couldn't see anything else."

They all start laughing, and maybe this horrible day isn't so bad after all. Mia makes a mental note to change her phone password before drifting to sleep on the couch.

Match Maker, Match Maker, Make Me a Match

"Ice?"

"Check," Corina's husband says smirking at her checklist.

"Cake?"

"I'm picking it up at ten." Corina writes that on the side while she checks off the other boxes on her sheet.

"Meat?"

"Check. The girls are each bringing a side dish, and the guys are all bringing beer."

"Soda." Corina corrects her husband.

"Excuse me?" Michael asks with raised brows.

"Tell them soda, no beer."

"Rina."

"Don't give me that look. It's a child's birthday party, if they can't go without alcohol for one evening maybe they aren't the right kind of friends for you."

He throws his head back and laughs hard, until he sees her look.

"Oh, come on babe, that was funny. You legit sound like my mother. They are grown men having a beer with dinner, not a bunch of kids out drinking all night at the lake."

"I understand that, but I refuse to be one of those parents that use their kid's party as an excuse to make it about them and their friends."

"Okay, can we compromise?"

"You may keep some beer in the garage, and drink it in there, but I swear if anyone gets drunk, I'm kicking them out."

"That sounds fair enough."

"And if I see it, I'm kicking them out."

"Got it."

"And if it turns into a party for anyone other than Max—"

"You are kicking them out. I got it. You need to relax babe, you've got this. I know it's the first party since your surgery, and you couldn't go all crazy planner mode like usual, but it's Max. He hates that kind of stuff anyway. You got an amazing water slide rental which he's going to be over the moon for, so don't worry. It'll be perfect."

"Sorry I'm going crazy, I swear it's the hormones."

"It's fine, you aren't crazy."

My phone rings and Michael picks it up off the counter and hands it over.

"I'm going to get the cake, tell Mia hi." He kisses her cheek and takes off.

"Hey girly, what's up."

"Hey, so there's a small problem," Mia whispers.

"Why are you whispering?"

"I'm hiding in my closet. Tyson is here."

"Oh, say no more. Is that the problem? I can have Michael go over there and kick his ass." Corina heads for the garage to see if she can catch her husband. Mia laughs and then remembers she's trying to hide.

"No, it's not that, as fantastic as that sounds. It's Saturday."

"Yeah..."

"I promised that Saturdays would be Tyson's day with Ashton. Not that he's ever cared about missing one before, but it's the only day a week he sees him so..."

"You won't be coming." Corina tries to keep the disappointment out of her tone, but Ash is Max's best friend, so she's afraid he will be crushed.

"No, no, of course we will be there. But Tyson wants to come too."

"To the party? That's fine."

"You don't think that's weird? Him hanging out with all my friends like nothing happened?"

"I mean, he didn't exactly hang out with us a ton before, and Kevin likes everyone, so I'm sure it'll be fine. I rather that, then you not come at all."

"Alright, we will be there then."

"See you in a few hours."

Corina hangs up, then gets a delicious idea. She tries to talk herself out of it, because Mia might kill her, but it's too good to pass up. She blames her out of wack hormones when she picks her phone back up and places the call.

Three hours later the party is in full swing. She knew having a party with a bunch of kids on the spectrum means there's for sure going to be a meltdown or fifty, so they kept the guest list narrowed down to just very close friends or people who work with kids, well one person that works with kids, a specific one.

"Hudson, I'm so glad you could make it on such short notice." Corina gives him her most innocent smile and he matches hers with a brilliant one of his own.

"Of course, I'd come. Max asking for me specifically by name, to come to his party? I'd never miss it. Especially since he's never been able to say my name before." He winks and Corina knows she's been caught. As he looks around, she decides to give up all pretense.

"She's not here yet, and this better stay between us, because she will kill me if she thinks it's a setup."

"My lips are sealed. So it is a setup? I wasn't really sure... not that I mind, of course."

"I need to warn you though, her ex-husband is going to be coming with her." His eyebrows shoot up and Corina makes sure to add, "against her will. It's his only day with Ashton, and he's not comfortable with him alone, so she let Tyson come."

Now his eyes narrow in anger. "He's not comfortable with his own kid?"

"He's complicated."

"Yeah, and a total idiot apparently."

"We aren't going to have a problem, are we?" Corina is suddenly second guessing this whole stupid plan.

"Not at all, I'm just here for the birthday boy." He gives her another dazzling smile and saunters off toward Max and the waterslide.

37

Every Woman's Ovaries Have Exploded

The Leightons get to Max's party and it's in full swing. Adding their lot to the mix is sure to be nothing but chaos.

"I call dibs on Gav," Taryn says tossing a smirk Kevin's way. He turns and looks at their little angelic looking troublemaker.

"Are you and Tacoma going to behave yourself?"

"Yes, Daddy." Jessie bats those adorable little lashes at him and he frowns.

"I mean it, Jessica. You are on my watch today, if you act up you don't get cake."

"Cake!" Her eyes light up, but then she quickly frowns realizing she has to be good.

"I be good," she says so downtrodden. "Be good boy Tacoma, or no cake," she says to her dog.

"Bribing the children, that's low Leighton."

"You called Gavin before we made it inside, that was low. I didn't even get a fair chance."

Anytime they go anywhere, they each watch one child. Taryn's learned the hard way to call dibs early on. Once they both thought the other was watching Gavin, and he ended up having to be brought back by the Fed Ex guy... not their most shining moment.

"Okay, we each got a kid, and some of us have a canine." He smirks over at me. "You grab the gift and let's do this thing."

The kids make a beeline for the water slide bounce house they have up. Luckily it's two-sided, and there's another large blow up pool next to it, giving the kids a lot of room to play.

Taryn notices everyone standing over by the grill where they are all keeping an eye on the kids, so she and Kev head over. Everyone but Mia and Tyson anyway, who are standing awkwardly off to the side.

"What is he doing here?" Taryn asks Corina angrily. Corina only shrugs.

"Mia asked to bring him. Something about him not wanting to give up his family day."

"Maybe he should have given up his side piece instead then."

"Taryn." Kevin squeezes my side in warning.

"Yeah, yeah. But did anyone think about the fact that he's going to recognize Liz and I as the ones who gave him up?"

"Too late," Liz says as she frantically sips from her *water cup.* Taryn narrows her eyes at it and Liz just shrugs.

"I needed some liquid courage. You missed the awkward moment when they got here."

"He recognized you?"

"I don't think he could figure out how he knew me, until Marcus came over and loudly yelled, *hey Mom, it's that guy who was with the pretty lady at the golf course. You know, the one you were taking pictures of? He's here.*"

Taryn can't help but burst out laughing. "God, I love that kid."

"Yeah, well it's been like Antarctica over there ever since. We are all too afraid to move now.

Taryn turns to look at Mia, but her eyes are completely captured by the eighth wonder of the world currently playing with the kids about five feet behind Mia.

Taryn shamelessly brings her sunglasses down as she takes in the beauty of a shirtless Hudson. He is splashing and playing with the kids in the pool, somehow miraculously getting them to join in and play with each other.

"Heeeeeellooo, Hudson," Taryn says under her breath, but loud enough for those nearby to hear. All the guys around her groan, while the girls giggle.

"They've had the same reaction each time a new woman has come to the party," Corina says with a smile.

"Mia is an idiot, how is she not all over that?" Taryn asks, as Kevin literally brings his hand up to her chin to pop his wife's mouth back into place.

"I don't know, I mean look at him with the kids, he's magic." All the men groan again, while Taryn takes the opportunity to scream Mia's name from across the yard.

She waves manically until Mia gives Tyson one last awkward look, and then comes over to join her friends. "This was the worst idea ever."

"Yeah, sorry about Marcus, earlier," Liz says, looking down at her feet.

"Oh no, don't apologize Liz. Marcus did nothing wrong. Tyson started to yell at me, and I put him in his place in a heartbeat."

"Ooh, what'd you say?" Taryn asks, loving a good drama.

"I said, before opening your mouth, if you bring up the golf course, I will certainly bring up the panties I found under *my bed.* He shut his trap and has been quietly seething ever sense."

They all chuckle, even the guys this time.

"Good for you. He was a fool, and I'm sure he realizes that now. That's the best revenge you can get Mia," Michael says as he flips a burger.

"Actually, the best revenge you can get is *that,*" Taryn says motioning to Hudson, shirtless in the pool with the kids.

Mia, looking totally unaffected just shrugs. "He's not my type."

She's met with a ton of scoffs, even from the men.

"That's bull Mia, he's my type and I don't even swing that way," says Tom of all people, causing Liz to choke on her *water.*

We all laugh and stare at the poor man in question when Gavin slips on the tarp, taking out three kids in the process. All of a sudden it's defcon five with the kids crying and screaming.

The parents take off in a run, when Hudson yells, "yeah Gavin, slip and slide," and goes running and purposely slips like Gavin did.

The kids all blink for a moment and stop crying as they each try this cool new slip and slide. All the parents are frozen on the spot, mouths are agape until Kevin speaks, "Mia, if you don't marry him, I will."

"Not my type," she says glaring up at Kevin, who surprisingly doesn't shrink back in fear.

"He is so your type. Think about it, Tyson, Ashton, Hudson," he adds with a smirk, "that man is built like a God and is a child whisperer. Two-seconds here, and every woman in a five-mile radius' ovaries have exploded. My wife's have twice." He winks at her and then strolls off to the garage.

Corina tries to hold back a giggle, but one escapes anyway.

"I mean he's not wrong, I don't even have ovaries and I felt a twinge," she says to Mia.

"I hate you people, I have no clue why we are even friends." Mia walks off, but everyone noticed the smirk she was trying to hide, as well as the extra long gaze spent on a certain someone.

CHAPTER

Been There, Done That. And Got Left With Someone Else's Panties

Today has been the longest day of Mia's freaking life, but it was also somewhat cathartic. She thought it would be extremely painful to be there with Tyson, thinking about what they could have been. What they were, just mere months ago. But it wasn't painful, in fact it was rather eye opening.

She watched all the other dads play with their kids, calm them down, know exactly what they needed, half of the time before they did. Hell, Hudson, who didn't even have kids, was incredible with them. Yet Tyson was a nervous wreck, not with just the other kids, but with Ashton.

She watched as he went into panic mode when Ashton started asking him for cake. He was looking around like crazy, trying to guess what Ash wanted.

Mia was just about to walk over to tell Tyson what he wanted, when Hudson handed Ashton a piece of cake, she was pretty sure was meant for himself. He just fist bumped Ash and then walked off with Tyson starring daggers at him the whole time.

It was enough to show Mia that not only did she deserve better, but so does Ashton. And that realization was a salve to her pain like nothing else has been. Even if Tyson is no longer in the picture, Ashton will have amazing men in his life like Kevin, Michael, and Tom.

Luckily, the sun wore Ashton out and he went to bed without a fight tonight. Mia looks down at the clock and sees it's still relatively early. She never has a single moment to herself it seems, so she refuses to waste it. She makes sure all the doors are locked, then checks on Ashton, and smiles when she hears his sweet little snores. Closing the door softly behind her, she decides a little indulgence is just what she needs tonight.

Mia makes her way to her bathroom and starts a hot bubble bath. Grabbing a paperback on her way, she sinks into the warm tub and sighs.

After about five minutes of soaking her phone dings. Mia dries her hand and picks it up and groans. She completely forgot that Taryn downloaded that stupid dating app, that's really more like a game than dating. Swipe this way, swipe that way. All she can think about is *Dora the Explorer*. Swipe or no swiping, swipe or no swiping... awe man. She laughs to herself. That's how you know you are too old for this stuff.

She clicks the little icon and groans out loud when she sees who the message is from. These girls are going to be the death of her. She quickly calls Taryn.

"Hey Mia."

"Don't hey Mia me, what the heck did you say to Hudson?"

"Today? Nothing more than hi, can you pass the dip."

"No Taryn, not today. On that stupid dating app."

"I didn't say anything to him, what are you talking about?"

"I just got a very cryptic message from him that says, the *Princess Bride, Harry Potter* and "The Luckiest" by Ben Folds. What the hell does that even mean?"

Taryn starts shrieking and giggling and *OMGing* like a schoolgirl. "Seriously Mia, you've got to marry this man, he is perfect."

"I'm not marrying anyone, been there, done that, and got left with someone else's panties."

"Yeah, but not all guys are douche bags. That's why you need to find someone Tyson's opposite, enter Hudson. Well, the names are a bit close, but other than that, total night and day situation."

"Are you going to stop rambling and tell me what the weird message was about?"

"Oh, right. So, I used three of my favorite quotes. One from *The Princess Bride*, one from *Harry Potter*, and one from my favorite song. Mia, he knew them all! No man has ever gotten that right, not even Kev."

"Why those three quotes though?"

"Because *The Princess Bride* is not only a classic, it's hilarious. It proves they have a good sense of humor if they can recognize it. *Harry Potter* shows they read, always a plus, but that they have imagination, which is key for our kids. And Ben Folds, because he is the man and that song is poetry."

"This was just supposed to be a way of claiming my life back Taryn, now we are officially cat fishing Max's therapist?" Mia drops her head to her hand.

"We aren't technically cat fishing. It is still your picture, and a current non-filtered one, so technically we are more above board than most. Think of it as just group collaborating."

"That doesn't even make sense. So what am I supposed to do on my dates, text you in the bathroom so you can tell me what to say?"

"I thought you weren't going on dates," Taryn points out.

"Hypothetically."

"So, what are you going to say?"

"To who?"

"To Hudson, he got the answers right, so now it's your turn to talk."

"First off, they weren't my questions, they were yours, so why can't you talk?"

"Come on Mia, look at that face."

Mia brings up his picture, and she can't deny the fact that the man is a work of art. "He is probably a player, I'm done with that type."

"Because all the players I know hang out with special needs kids on their day off," she says dryly.

"Hey, who's side are you on?"

"Team Hud all the way! Think of the babies."

"Oh, heaven help me, fine. You want a question, I'll give you a question."

MIA: You find someone else's underwear under your bed, what do you do?

Mia reads her text out loud after she pushes send, and Taryn groans. "Geez Mia, don't be such a downer."

Within seconds another chime tells her Hudson has written back. "Dang, that was fast, what did he say?" Mia can't help but laugh at his response.

HUDSON: Check to make sure they are a breathable cotton blend, then wash and wear. Hey, free underwear is free underwear.

Mia relays the message to Taryn and she sighs heavily. "He's clever, and beautiful."

"And not right for me at all."

"I don't know, I think he might just be perfect for you, really Mia."

She sends off a quick message.

MIA: I'm not funny.

HUDSON: It wouldn't be fair to be smart, beautiful and funny. You gotta leave something for the other girls.

232

"God Taryn, he's clever, too." Mia hates to admit it.

"You sure you don't want Kev? He did the dishes the other day. I mean he loaded the washer all wrong, but you could train him on that."

They both start laughing and instantly the horrible night with the missing frog, another woman's panties, and having to spend all day with her ex is all just a faint memory.

Mia decides to stop trying to handle everything alone. She finally admits to Taryn what she's been scared to say out loud. "Nothing can happen with him Taryn, because I just don't think I can take it if it did. With Tyson, he wasn't perfect, and he still crushed me. But you know what? I can hold on to those imperfections, and I can remind myself that life with him wasn't great. But if I were to try with Hudson and then something happened…"

"It would obliterate you."

"Exactly," she whispers.

"Well, for the record, anything worth having has a little bit of risk involved, but I also see where you are coming from. Try not to put so much pressure on it. Just let things go where they may."

"Should I keep writing him?"

"If you want, but no need to. Eventually you will pick up Max again for Corina, or he will be at a party or whatnot. Just let it flow. If you think about him, reach out. If you don't, no worries."

"Wow, you sound like an actual grown up."

"Shh, don't tell anyone, I'd hate to ruin my rep."

Mia hangs up with Taryn, eyeing the last message.

She's horrible at taking compliments, but also won't admit that because it's a sign of insecurity. So she changes the subject.

> MIA: You were amazing with the kids today.
>
> HUDSON: They make it easy, it's adults that are hard.
>
> MIA: You'll have to tell me one of these days why you chose your profession.
>
> HUDSON: I didn't, it chose me. However, that's a story for another night. Sleep well Mia.

39

Be the Father Your Sons Deserve

Today was so much fun, but it was also horribly exhausting. Both Marcus and Mason fell asleep in the car, so Tom and Liz have the night to themselves for once.

"What would you like to do? We could watch a movie or something."

"How about we talk for a bit?" *Well, that sounds ominous.*

"Of course, love, anything in particular you want to talk about?"

"Today's party really opened my eyes."

"Oh? How so?"

"We've done get togethers with my friends a few times, but don't do them with yours very often, well nobody besides Taryn and Kevin. Being around so many fathers of autistic kids really opened my eyes today. To be honest, Liz, I felt a bit ashamed of how I measured up against them."

"What? Tom, you are an amazing father. Please don't compare yourself to others, you are just what our boys need."

"I appreciate you saying that, but hear me out a bit." Liz nods sitting quietly, waiting for him to finish. Tom isn't a big talker, especially when it comes to feelings, so she knows this must be tough for him.

"I watched Kevin and Michael today, and they knew their kids inside out. They knew how to help the meltdowns, how to prevent them, what they liked to eat…"

Liz scoots closer and rubs his back, she hates to see him so down on himself.

"I also watched Tyson and saw just how out of touch with his kid he is. He couldn't understand him, he didn't know how to help him, it was like he was meeting this kid for the first time."

"I know, it was so sad. I feel horrible for Mia."

"But the thing is Liz, I felt like I could relate to him more than I could the other guys, and that scared the crap outta me."

"Tom, you are nowhere near as bad as that."

"Maybe not yet, but the hard facts are I don't relate to the boys because I don't try. I want to know what they are passionate about, and what sets them off. I've always used work as an excuse for not knowing them like you, but those other men are hard workers and work just as much as I do. I don't want to keep making excuses and become a stranger to my own kids."

Liz pulls him toward her hugging him tight. "You will never become that man, because of this. Because you care enough to notice and make changes. That is why I married you, why I love you."

"I don't want to be the kind of father I have been, I want to be the kind my sons deserve. Will you help me?"

"Of course, I'll help you."

"I was thinking of a family vacation."

"Really?"

"It's been forever since we've taken one, and we always end up doing something that sends the boys into meltdown mode."

"Just comes with the territory."

"But what if it doesn't have to?"

"What do you mean?"

"I was looking up some things. What to do you think?" Tom turns his computer around and shows her cross-country train tickets, and cities highlighted with train museums and tours. Liz's eyes flood with tears at the thoughtfulness of it all.

"I figured we would get a sleeper car, and take two days getting there, two back home. That would leave three days to explore all the different stops along the way. And I thought, maybe we could take them to a baseball game, you know, introduce them to one of my passions while I learn theirs. What do you think?"

"I think that you'd make your son's life."

"Son? You don't think Mason could handle it?"

"Honestly, it's a lot, but I don't see why we can't try. We can ask him about it, and if he doesn't want to, I can see if Taryn will take him for a week. It'd make sense anyway since we can work this into Marcus's curriculum, and Mason can still go to school if he's with her."

"That's a lot to ask of her though."

"It is, but knowing her, I won't even have to ask. That's the hard thing, if one kid loves something, it usually sets the other off. Taryn totally understands that."

"You've got some really good friends, I'm so glad."

"Honestly, me too. Motherhood is hard."

"I can't even imagine."

"Tom, make sure you are a thousand percent sure that this is what you want to do, that you can take the time off work, and that we can afford it, because once you tell Marcus, there's no going back. I can't stand to disappoint him, and this would be a crushing blow."

"I know, babe. I'm going to talk to Steven tomorrow about taking some vacation. I haven't taken vacation or any sick days in years, so I have every right to take some now. We don't have a huge savings, but it's enough to do the trip and my parents give us a sizable check at Christmas for the boys that we never know what to do with, so that money has been sitting in a special account for all these years."

"Oh, my God, I totally forgot about that money."

No matter how many times they've told his parents not to give them money, that we rather them pick out a small gift, they never listen. When the kids were younger, Liz would just go out and buy them a bunch of stuff they'd never play with. As they got older, Liz and Tom decided to sock it away and use it for something they'd want to do eventually.

"I think this would be a great use of that money. And we can come up with an idea of somewhere to take Mason to make up for missing this trip."

"He's been talking about Legoland, maybe we can do a short trip there one of these weekends?"

"That sounds good to me."

"You are a good man, Thomas Rayne."

40

Bested by my Own Rule

"So I have an idea," Kevin says while Taryn packs lunches and he makes the coffee.

"You are brilliant, I imagine you have lots of ideas, it's why you make the big bucks." His wife replies while wiggling her eyebrows at him, as she zips up the lunch boxes. He hands her a cup of coffee, which she sips, then narrows her eyes at him.

"I'm not going to like this idea am I?"

"Why would you say that? It might be the best idea I ever had."

"One, because the best idea you ever had was marrying me. And two, because you put hazelnut creamer in my coffee, so I know you are trying to talk me into something." He laughs, but then grabs her hands and turns her so she's fully facing him.

"Just hear me out before you say no."

Great I'm really going to hate this, Taryn thinks. "Okay..."

"I think we need to getaway for a weekend."

"After the camping trip from hell, I'm pretty sure I need an entire year to recover before we take the kids anywhere."

"Exactly."

"Huh?"

"I don't want to take the kids. I want to get away, just the two of us." Taryn narrows her eyes, then pulls her hands back like he burned her.

"Kevin, you know my answer is no. I won't leave the kids. Hell, they won't be here when we get back. One will run away, and there's a good chance Jessie will kill everyone by lighting the house on fire or blowing it up using nothing but bleach and pop rocks. I love you, but no."

Taryn knows she shouldn't be so angry, he's trying to do a nice thing, but it feels like he's making her the bad guy. She doesn't want to have to say no to her husband.

She hates disappointing him, but she can't leave her kids. She walks to the sink and pours out her coffee.

"What are you doing?" Kevin asks as she takes her empty cup and refills it, using regular creamer this time.

"You've officially ruined hazelnut for me now. I hope you're happy." She starts to walk away, but he pulls her hand back.

"Rule number four." *Damn hm, using her own rules against her.* She gives him a dirty look but doesn't turn away.

When they were first married and not tainted by life, family, or failed therapy dogs, they came up with ten rules that were important to them. Number four is you aren't allowed to storm off angry. Instead, you have to fully hear the person out, then give a time in which you are willing to discuss it later. Number four was Taryn's… obviously she's not the brains of this household.

"I'm listening."

"Okay, so we will go somewhere no further than an hour away, with our cells on at all time. It will be two days tops, and Emily has already agreed. She's going back to school to get her masters next month, so this is the perfect time to do it. And she could use the extra money."

Kevin brushes Taryn's unruly hair behind her ear and looks deep into her eyes, his eyes pleading. "We need this Taryn, I need this." She doesn't say a word, but he knows the pleading goes straight to her heart.

"We are doing great Kev, we don't fight or have problems like other couples do."

"Okay, let's have a conversation then. Right now, talk for five minutes about something that doesn't include kids, dog, school, autism or household issues."

Taryn opens her mouth, then narrows her eyes at him. He gives her his superior "I told you so" look as she crosses her arms.

"I don't want to lose us to our life Tar. I love our crazy life, but I miss us. I want to make memories with you, I want to have experiences with you. After the hard month we've had with Jessie, it just shows me that we need to be strong as a couple before we can be strong parents."

Taryn sighs, feeling absolutely defeated. Now she feels like a crappy wife, but if she leaves, she'll feel like a crappy mom. However, she made the rule, so she'll follow it. "I need time to think, we can pick the conversation back up tonight, after the kids go down."

"After dinner, while they play outside. You know I'll fall asleep before you get both of the kids down." He's figured her out, the infuriating man.

"Okay, fine. Have a good day." Taryn gives him a kiss, put the kids' lunches in their bags and watch as he heads to work.

"Let me get this straight. Your husband wants to plan a weekend getaway, handle all the details, he's already booked the sitter and you are mad?"

"Obviously, Liz."

"I mean, the mad part is obvious, it's just the why that is baffling. If Tom plans what we are having for dinner that night I feel like I won the lottery."

"I'm not mad that he made plans, I'm mad that he expects me to leave the kids and put me in this horrible position of choosing him over them. If I say yes, then I'm a bad mom. If I say no, I'm a bad wife." Taryn takes a deep breath, then takes a huge bite out of her cheeseburger. Carbs and grease always make everything better.

"Marcus, eat some of those veggies first please," Liz tells Marcus as he pushes them to the side of his plate.

"But Aunt Taryn is eating her fries," Marcus points out as Taryn shoves about six fries into her mouth at once.

"Yes, but Aunt Taryn is having a bad day, and has already reached her full growth potential. You have not, so eat the veggies."

"When I have a bad day, I don't get French fries."

"Next time you have a bad day, I'll take you to get French fries Marcus," Taryn mumbles through a full mouth.

Liz glares at her, Taryn glares right back as she takes another large bite of her burger.

"You side with Kevin, I side with your kid."

"How very mature of you. And yes, I do agree with Kevin. It's important to put your marriage first. I'm going to say something that you aren't going to like, but you need to hear me out before getting defensive okay?"

Taryn narrows her eyes, not liking where this is going. She likes it even less when Liz gives Marcus money to go play on the arcade games to give them privacy.

"Not all men tell their wives what they need or what is missing. Some men just go and fulfill that need some-where else. If Tyson had talked to Mia and asked for some one-on-one time before turning to someone else, their story might have ended very differently."

Wow, those words hurt so bad, even if they might be true.

"I'm only saying this because I love you. And Kevin loves you. He might need this time with you, more than you know. He's made the plans and booked the sitter. Don't make him feel like those needs aren't valid Taryn, because next time he might not come to you for those needs…" Liz leaves the rest to Taryn's overactive imagination.

"So you're saying if I refuse, my husband is going to cheat on me?"

"That is absolutely not at all what I'm saying. What I am saying is listen to his needs. Fulfill his needs so that it's not a temptation, in case someone else will."

"I know you are right. I hate it, and I'm mad about it… but you are right. I'm just terrified of something happening to my kids."

"So compromise."

"How?"

"It might seem kinda silly, but maybe stay in town. Do stuff around here, even if it's just a block away. Then each time you do something else, the more comfortable you get, you can go a little further. Who knows, by the time they are adults, maybe you'll actually get out of town!" She mocks.

"Ha ha, very funny. You have a point though, I'll think about it and discuss it with him tonight."

"You don't have to always give in, but at least make him feel heard, and understood. Marriage is a constant compromise, it's when one person is constantly doing whatever they want that it becomes an issue."

"Alright, I hear you. And next time Marcus has a bad day, I'll make him eat a salad before the fries." Taryn gives Liz a big toothy grin, while Liz throws one of her fries at Taryn.

CHAPTER

Pinterest Moms 1, Corina 0

CORINA: I'm not coming tonight, sorry. Give the ladies my love.

TARYN: Are you sick?

CORINA: No, everyone's healthy, it's just been a really bad day. Sorry.

TARYN: Don't be sorry, just be here. That's why we do this. Don't be alone with your problems. Come and drink them away with us.

CORINA: I can drink alone.

TARYN: Only alcoholics drink alone. If you don't come we will come to you. Is your house messy? Cuz I'm going to comment on it if it is.

CORINA: I hate you.

TARYN: As long as you do it in person, that's fine.

CORINA: See you soon.

TARYN: :)

"That woman just doesn't know the word no. I bet she was spoiled as a child."

"And what woman is this?" Michael asks as he comes into the kitchen and kisses Corina's cheek.

"Taryn. I tried getting out of tonight, and she wouldn't let me."

"That makes her a good friend love, not spoiled."

"Whatever. I'm just in a bad mood, have had a hard day and don't want to be around people."

"Isn't that what friends are for? Have they ever told you not to be in a bad mood?"

"Well, no."

"From what you've always told me, even at your lowest, they joined in and made you feel better. So you felt not as alone. Maybe that's exactly what you need tonight."

"Gah! You're just as bad as she is."

"That's why you love us both."

"I guess. Well, I better get a move on if I'm going to make it. There are enchiladas in the oven, we will be back later."

"Love you."

"Love you, too."

Corina pulls up to Taryn's, seeing she's the last to arrive. She sighs before getting out of the car and grabbing Max from the back seat. He starts arm flapping and babbling, so she knows he's excited. Instantly, she feels guilty for trying to back out of tonight. Just because she's having a bad day doesn't mean this group hasn't been equally, if not more, beneficial for Max.

The kids are all out back, making slime with Emily. Max instantly runs over and dunks his hands into the big bin with the oozing green goo.

"You always come up with the best activities." She just smiles and shrugs.

"It's my day job. I really have the best life, I get to play all day at work, and then come here and play... and get paid for both. Shh." She giggles, like it's a secret. Sometimes Corina daydreams about what it would be like to have a nanny. She knows Taryn's kids are so much harder than hers, so Emily's for sure needed, but man, that'd be nice.

Corina makes her way down to the girls who are already around the circle and drinking wine.

"You're here!" Mia says throwing her arms around Corina's neck.

"Sorry, I'm late."

"Better late than never," Taryn says with a wink.

"So what type of group is it going to be tonight? Ranting, crying, secrets? I'm ready," Liz says, cracking her knuckles. Corina can't help but laugh. She's been here two minutes and already feels lighter. Taryn was right, she would have just wallowed at home.

"Up to you," Corina says with a shrug.

"I'm always down for whatever, but you are clearly burdened tonight, unburden yourself my friend."

The other two nod.

"I just feel like I'm failing, and I know it's stupid and that I have a lot on my plate, and I'm doing my very best, yet I still feel like a subpar mom. Not all days, but this month for sure."

"Why are you feeling this way? Anything in particular? Because from where I sit, you are rocking the mom thing," Liz says, giving Corina a bright smile.

"That's the thing, the autism mom thing I've got down. It's funny, because having a kid on the spectrum you get used to looks and comments, and you become almost immune to them. And since being friends with you guys, I can pretty much ignore everything and feel accepted and like I'm doing well."

"Cuz you are," Taryn adds.

"Well, thank you. But ever since I've been home, I'm not sure if I'm having a hard time getting back into the swing of things, if it's my hormones or what, but I just feel like I'm failing the mom thing. I can't help but compare myself to others." Corina replies, dabbing at her eyes.

"It could very well be a mixture of a lot of those things, but you for sure aren't failing," Mia says as she bumps her friend's shoulder.

"Mateo had a class party today, which I totally forgot about until he reminded me this morning. So, I didn't have time to make anything, or get a sitter for Jasper. I didn't want to just not come, because I've been so absent lately. I just picked up some store-bought cookies and took the baby with me."

"Nothing wrong with that."

"You'd think. Except Jasper is cutting his molars, and has been super fussy, so I had to bribe him with a juice bar just to get him in the car. I picked him up out of the car seat and realized only after I got into Mateo's classroom, that his shirt was covered in juice bar, as was my white t-shirt. I had three moms ask if my child was bleeding, one asked me if it was laundry day, and another tried to rub my breasts with a shout wipe."

Taryn bursts out laughing, while the other two have the decency to stifle their giggles at least.

"Then I put the store-bought cookies down on the table and I legit had everyone side-eye me."

"Why?"

"Because there was a clear theme that I didn't stick with."

"Which was?" Mia asks.

"Pinterest."

"Huh?"

"Like everything was themed and cute and picture worthy, homemade masterpieces. Like one of the moms made a zoo out of fruit!"

"What? That's not a thing."

"Apparently it is. She had little animals cut out of fruit, and dolphin bananas, and an ocean made out of Jello. Who has the time to carve fruit? I don't even have time to buy fruit."

"Just because they are overachievers doesn't make you a bad mom."

"I know that, deep down I do. But it's just that feeling of being judged, and then you start to look at yourself through their eyes you know. Here's this hot mess mom with a screaming baby, in a dirty shirt, with store bought cookies."

"I can totally see how upsetting that could be," Liz says, and hands her a tissue, "but you can't judge your parenting because you didn't spend five hours making a fruit zoo."

"Word!" Taryn says, raising her wineglass.

"To flip it around a bit, just think. You were spending quality time making breakfast for your family, while they ignored their kids for five hours to carve out fruit. You know it was just to impress other parents."

"Taryn you don't know that," Liz says, "maybe their kids helped."

"Doubtful."

"Oh, I didn't even tell you the worst part."

"Oh, yay, there's more." Taryn doesn't even try to hide her excitement.

"Jasper only had on one shoe. So I go to put him down and one of the moms comments, *oh, you only put on one shoe? That's a new fashion statement.*"

"Wow, rude much?" Liz points out.

"Right? I was like, no, of course I put on two shoes, obviously, it must have fallen off in the parking lot. So Pinterest mom goes, *okay, I'll hold your baby while you go and get it.* Like it was a challenge right? So I said fine, I hand Jasper over and march out to the parking lot ready to shove that shoe in her face."

"But...?" Mia already sees where this is going.

"But it wasn't there. And then I search the car, and it's nowhere. I'm starting to panic now thinking, there's no way I just put one shoe on my kid. It's here, it's got to be here. So I'm looking under seats, and I get down and look under the car."

"Uh, oh."

"Yeah, so I have to come back now covered in dirt, and juice bar, with no shoe. It was so humiliating. So I said, maybe someone picked it up." They all look at Corina with sympathy now, while Mia fills her glass up.

"So the mom says, _yeah maybe,_ but then I hear her turn to the mom next to her and say, _if I ever take my kid out without a shoe and covered in filth, just put me out of my misery._"

"Oh, honey!"

"She said what?"

"That bitch!"

Liz, Mia and Taryn all yell at once. And as crappy as it feels having to relive that moment, their reactions do make her feel a little better. Yes, especially Taryn's, because that's exactly what Corina thought at the time too.

"What did you do?" Mia asks as she passes Corina another tissue.

"I held my head high, I made it through the party, kissed Mateo and walked out to the van with Jasper in his one shoe, strapped him in, drove down the street, pulled over and burst into tears."

"No, you don't let them make you feel small. I want to punch them all in the nose. This, this whole Pinterest era makes moms feel less than and that's not right," Taryn states with passion.

"It's like a site dedicated to other moms not being able to live up. And it's not just you, there's an entire google page dedicated to Pinterest fails, because that's not real life."

"She has a point," Mia says.

"Damn right I do. Moms are supposed to lift each other up. We live in the trenches. We all have hard, crappy days. They should have been creating matching stains in solidarity."

"Here, here, sister!" Mia pumps her fist in the air. Liz and Corina just roll their eyes, but the others are too entertaining not to smile at them.

"It's so true. We get broken down daily. By our bosses, kids, men... we should be standing up for one another. Building each other up, not adding to the breakdown."

"You three can validate a woman like none other. Thank you for that! And thank you for hating them for me. It helps."

"You just tell us next time your kid has another party. We will all show up with stains wearing one shoe and a *come at me* scowl."

"By we all, Taryn means she will, and we will be on standby with bail money," Liz says.

"Whatever works."

Taryn raises her glass. "To the moms who buy store-bought cookies and spend time with their kids. May I never make a single animal out of fruit!"

"Here, here." *Man, I love these crazy women. Only they could make me feel normal after a day like today.*

"But I've got to know," Taryn asks leaning forward like it's a secret, "did you ever find out what happened to his other shoe?"

Corina buries her face in her hands and groans. "I found it all right. That was the worst part, she was right."

"Where was it? Mia asks.

Corina looks out from between her fingers and sighs. "It was right on the shoe bench, I legit only put one shoe on my kid and then left the house."

They all burst out laughing. *So much for solidarity.*

Has Telling a Woman to Calm Down, Ever Made One Calm?

Mia flips the last pancake and tries to calm the nerves in her stomach. She replays every second of the two-minute phone conversation with Tyson over and over again in her head.

His parents are in town, they want to spend time with Ashton, can they take him out, without her? She goes over it again and again, yet somehow she still can't figure out what their angle is.

He asked if they could all come to breakfast today to discuss things. What things are there to discuss? Her child? Her divorce? Her cheating ex who they raised?

Personally, Mia doesn't want to discuss anything with those people, she didn't even like them while they were married. Now, she's no longer contractually bound to pretend.

Mia takes the stack of pancakes to the table and places the best smile she can manage on her face. Based on Tyson's smirk, she failed at making it look genuine, but whatever.

"Everyone dig in," Mia announces as she walks back into the kitchen to make Ashton his waffles.

"What are you doing dear?" His mother knows exactly what Mia is doing. The same thing she's done every time they've come over for the last six years.

"Getting Ash his breakfast. Don't wait on me."

Mia takes the waffle from the toaster and walks back into the dining room, where she is met with two matching scowls. Tyson is staring down at his plate, like the pancakes hold the answer to the universe, as Ashton happily bangs his hands on the table.

"Ashton, stop that," Jack admonishes and Mia swallows back the anger that rises in her.

"Here baby, eat your food."

"He really should use a fork and knife. He's much too old to be using his hands."

Mia sighs and says the same thing she has for the last six years. "He doesn't have the motor skills for that yet. We are working on it, but it's frustrating for him, and since he doesn't use syrup or anything on it, he eats it like you would a piece of toast. You don't cut toast."

"Well, you could," his mom says.

"It just doesn't look polite is all, using your hands and having to have special meals," his dad adds.

Mia takes a deep breath and looks to Tyson, who as usual stays quiet.

"He's never going to be normal until you make him act normal." *Yeah, not putting up with this.*

"Ashton, go eat your breakfast in the living room. You can watch a movie, okay?"

"Movie!" Ashton chants, taking his waffles and running to the other room.

"You really should keep food at the table you know," Laura admonishes.

"No Laura, I don't know. Since this is my house, I will run it as I see fit."

"Mia."

"No Tyson, you don't get to scold me."

"Technically, it's Tyson's house, he's just letting you live in it," Jack mumbles. And Mia snaps.

"Actually Jack, it isn't. We shared a banking account and mortgage. I paid just as much as he did for this house, and the minute I found out he was sleeping with someone else and he left, I took over the full payment. So it's my house, and I refuse to be disrespected in it."

Mia stands, walking right out of the toxicity. Tyson follows her to her bedroom and tries to defuse the situation. "You seriously need to calm down. I don't know why you always let them rile you up so much."

"Maybe because they act like my son is defective? Or like everything he does is wrong. Out of respect for your relationship with your son I allowed this, but I'm done, Tyson. You can come anytime you want to see him, but I want them out of my house."

257

He runs a hand through his hair and starts to nervously pace. "They are my parents Mia, and like it or not, they are going to be in Ashton's life. They think me only seeing him once a week is unfair, that we should have joint custody."

"I could care less what *they* think Tyson Mathews, what do *you* think?"

He just keeps pacing and when he doesn't answer right away Mia keeps going.

"To them you may have checked out months ago, and I'm fine with letting them think that, but we both know that you checked out the day Ashton was diagnosed. I've never said a word about it to you, because I didn't want to make you feel bad, but I'm done walking on eggshells, Tyson." She walks right up and puts her hands on his shoulders to make him face her. She softens her voice, but the words are strong.

"You don't know him. You know nothing about what makes him tick, or what sets him off, or calms him down. You know nothing about what fabrics hurt his skin, or what noises hurt his ears. I don't hold any of this against you, and anytime you want to learn these things, I'll be right here to help."

Mia lowers her voice, making full eye contact so he can see how serious she is. "But what I refuse to do, is allow you to use my son as some pawn to show your parents what a good father you are. You can have as much involvement as you want, and I'll even let them be in his life, but the moment you try to use him to win their approval again is the moment I will drag your ass to court so fast, your head will spin."

"I don't want this to turn ugly Mia. I haven't fought you because I know you are what's best for him. And I haven't fought for you, because I know I'm not what's best for you guys. I hate it, and it guts me... but I'm not."

That one admission, and maybe the tears streaming down his face, is the one thing that finally sets Mia free. And because he gave her that, she gives him this. "The difference between a meltdown and a tantrum is a meltdown isn't caused by not getting his way. It's caused by not understanding or not able to communicate or get across how he feels. It's because he can't process the way others do and it can be extremely painful."

"I didn't realize that."

"I know." Mia nods and keeps going with truths about his son. "Ashton only eats neutral color foods. I think it's because life is too colorful sometimes. It's too much to process, too many sounds, too many flavors, too many choices. Vanilla, plain, these things aren't too harsh for him."

"I can understand that."

"He doesn't like to be hugged, but he will sniff you. It's his way of showing affection, it's basically his version of hugging. And if you are sad, he will touch your face."

"How did I not know any of this?" Tyson rasps out.

"Because you didn't try, Ty. You were scared and didn't understand and couldn't fix it. Your life has been about knowledge and justice. If you couldn't figure something out, you felt like you failed. But the only way to fail your son is to not show up, to not try."

He doesn't say anything but wipes his eyes and nods once.

"We will continue to do what's best for Ash, and if you ever have any questions, you ask. Don't assume. And never bring those people back here again. If they want to see him it's somewhere public, with no food or talking involved."

He chuckles, but nods again and turns to leave.

"Thank you for being honest with me, Tyson."

"Thank you for being what I can't, for our son."

What you won't, Mia thinks to herself, but doesn't voice. They actually got somewhere today. They talked and listened, and she won't throw that away for the last word. She can finally be free, and move on in the best direction for Ashton.

CHAPTER

Some Have an Emergency Contact, Some Have a Binder

"I've tied bells on the outside of their bedroom doors, so make sure you shut them once they go down. And make sure the alarms are all set to out mode, even though you are home."

"I will," Emily says with a kind smile, even though Taryn's being completely crazy.

"And Gavin likes *Beat Bugs* on the hard nights, but if you give him melatonin he should sleep all the way through. Don't give it to Jessie though or she will have nightmares."

"I understand." Of course she does because Taryn's told her twice, and wrote everything down in the binder. And by everything, she does mean everything.

"I've sent Gavin and Jessie's pictures over to the local police department and let them know we are going out of town, and that they are runners, mostly Gavin, and that he's nonverbal."

"Please tell me you are joking?" Kevin asks as Taryn bursts into tears.

"What if he tries to come looking for us? We've never left him overnight. The last time he got out was when you went away for work, I swear he was trying to find you."

"Shh, honey if you are going to get this upset about leaving, maybe we shouldn't go."

"I have an idea, why don't we take it a few hours at a time okay? You are used to leaving them with me for a few hours at a time, so that's what we will do. I have an activity planned for every block of time, so they will stay busy. I will take lots of pictures and you can call in and see how each block of time is going. If they are doing fine, you go until the next time. How does that sound?" Emily asks.

"Absolutely ridiculous, but I love it. Thank you, Emily. I swear I'll get better at this, I just don't know how to function without them, or being on constant alert. You will stay on alert won't you?"

"Yes, Taryn. Believe it or not, I'm used to more than two at a time."

"Don't forget Tacoma, he's just as much of a handful as my kids."

"Have a wonderful time away, relax, eat food while it's hot, sleep in, take a bath without a child jumping in, the possibilities are endless."

"If we all survive this unscathed, you are getting a raise."

"Okay, it's time to go, babe."

"A really big one," Taryn yells over her shoulder while Emily just laughs at them.

"Call if you need anything at all."

"I will."

Taryn climbs into the car and instantly bursts into tears before they even pull out of the driveway.

"Um, are we doing this? Am I driving around the block a few times first? Help me out here babe."

"I'll be fine, just go, fast before I change my mind."

Kevin puts the car in gear and pulls out. Taryn is still crying when they pull up to the hotel, fifteen minutes later. Her phone vibrates in her hand, she looks down at about ten pictures that Emily sent. The kids are smiling or laughing in almost every single one. The knot in her stomach slowly starts to uncoil and she feels like she can take her first full breath.

"You were right."

"Can you say that again? I swear I must be hearing things."

"I said you were right. If it affects me this much just to leave them across town, we obviously needed a break. I'm sorry that I've made them that much of my world, I probably have given you less time than I should have."

Kevin just sits in the car and stares at Taryn for a few minutes dead silent.

"What? That's the last thing I was prepared for you to say."

"What'd you think I was going to say?"

"Something along the lines of me not loving them as much as you do, or begging me to turn around, or any variation of those two."

Taryn just shrugs her shoulders, because those really are the things she wanted to say but didn't because she knows they aren't true. Instead, she leans over and kisses his cheek as she climbs out of the car.

"Last one to the room has to go get the ice and order room service."

After six thousand pictures, and about eight thousand texts confirming the children are still alive, Taryn finally calms down enough to enjoy the quiet. Funny thing about living on adrenaline, it's almost impossible to check out or calm down when you are always in a state of heightened awareness.

They take a walk after dinner. Taryn eyes a child walking next to their mother, not holding hands with the mom, and maybe two steps behind. Her panic instantly kicks in. How could that mom not hold her daughter's hand? What if she darts into the street? What if she jumps into the water and drowns? All these horrible scenarios were going through her mind, when in reality the little girl was totally fine walking by her mother's side, without incident.

Then fear turned into bitterness. *Must be nice not to be in a constant state of paranoia.*

"This is nice," Kevin says, pulling his wife from her thoughts as they turn the block and head back to their hotel.

"It really is. Thanks babe, there's no one else on earth I rather do nothing with than you." He chuckles, because she's probably the only woman in the word who would turn down a fully planned, action packed weekend, to stay a block away from the house and do nothing. But it feels fabulous.

"Are you going to actually sleep tonight?" He gives me her the side eye and she smiles.

"Of course. I'm going to sleep twelve full hours." He narrows his eyes and she can't help but laugh.

"In Taryn speak, that means you'll toss and turn all night, watching the cameras to make sure the kids don't wake up and sneak out."

"Yes, but just knowing I could sleep is a win for me."

"You would die from boredom if you had any other life."

"Probably."

I Asked Out a Man

It's been such a long day. Mia is on her third cup of coffee that has yet to kick in, when she looks down at her watch and swears. It's taken her twice as long as usual today to get through all these depositions. Ashton was up most of the night last night and she is dragging.

Mia shuts down her laptop, throwing it in her bag before grabbing her coffee and keys as she makes her way to the center to get Ash.

Mia's not paying any attention at all as she hurries into the center, texting something to her paralegal on her phone and walks smack into someone.

"Oh, my God I'm so sorry—Hudson?" He laughs at her frazzled, surprised expression, steadying her by grabbing her shoulders so she doesn't fall down.

"Hey, you alright?"

"Yeah sorry, crazy day... oh no, did I show up at Max's center instead? That's just like me to do something like that today."

Mia hurries back to the parking lot when Hudson breaks out in a full belly laugh.

"Wait, Mia, wait, wait." He grabs her arm, just as she's about to get back into her car.

"You are at the right place, I'm just not." Mia looks back up at the building and joins him in laughter.

"Nothing would surprise me today. I've been walking around like a *mombie* all day." He laughs at her mashup of words and holds the front door open for her to go back in.

"Ashton isn't sleeping?"

"Not last night, and he's been struggling to go down all month. So by the time I get him down, and finish work, I get maybe two hours in."

"Yikes, that's rough. Do you get any nights off, like when he's with his dad or anything?" Mia studies him a moment before she answers to see if he's fishing, but he looks very sincere so she answers truthfully.

"I have full custody of Ash for now. Anytime with his dad is spent supervised by me."

"That makes sense." That wasn't bad, she was expecting some judgment. "That's gotta be rough on you though, not having a break or any help."

"I'm working on getting a special needs nanny, I just haven't had time to do any interviews. And my hope is that eventually Tyson, my ex, will be comfortable with him enough to where I can trust them alone, or that he will even want to take him alone."

"Actually, this is pretty fortuitous timing then. The reason I'm here is because I'm offering a parenting class to all the parents in town. I was just here dropping of fliers."

"A parenting class?"

"It's more of a behavior class for parents. I don't think you'll need it, but it wouldn't be a bad idea for Ashton's dad to attend. It's not uncommon for one parent to attend all the meetings and drop off/pick-ups. So, I'm offering a few classes on Saturdays for the parents who would like a little extra information. We will go into a breakdown of what autism is, what it looks like, the different types of behaviors, and the best way to address them and hopefully replace them."

"Wow, that sounds fantastic. I highly doubt he will go to all of them, but I'd be over the moon if he even made it to one."

"It's only once a month for three months, but it's a six-hour class with an hour lunch break, and we will have several stretch and bathroom breaks. I think it would be fantastic for him to come, and if you and the other ladies would like to come as well, we've love to have you."

"I'll have to check to see if we can all get sitters, but I'm sure we'd love to go."

He smiles wide. "Then I'll see you there, because childcare is provided."

"It is?"

"Yep. A few of the therapists will be working so that both parents can be in attendance if need be. We understand how hard it can be for both parents to attend anything at all together, so we are hoping to lessen that burden."

Mia takes her time sizing him up, trying to figure out if he is too good to be true. At first, she was put off by how truly good looking he is, but now that she's gotten to know him a little bit, his authenticity helps to lessen the intimidation factor. Even so, she shocks herself by inviting him out.

"I have to grab Ash before they kick him out. I'm not sure if you have any more places to hit up tonight, but I was going to take him to McDonald's PlayPlace for dinner tonight, try to wear him out a bit before bed." Mia holds her breath and almost takes the invitation back. Until she sees his face light up at the offer.

"McDonald's sounds fantastic. I have one more center to hit, but it's on the way. Why don't you grab him and I'll meet you there once I drop some of these flyers off?"

"That sounds great."

Mia runs in and grabs Ashton, signing him out. As she buckles him into his car seat, she calls Corina on the car Bluetooth.

"Hey girl, I just got home with Max, what's up?"

"I asked out a man," Mia blurts out. And it's dead silent. "Hello? Corina, are you there?"

"You asked out a man? Like on a date?"

"Yeah, well, I think so."

"What man?"

"You're never going to let me live this down."

"Hold on, this sounds juicy. I'm going to have the girls join in one second." Before Mia can tell her not to do that, the line goes quiet and she realizes that Corina is already doing it.

The more Mia thinks about it, the better more opinions will be. She still has time to call it off. Ashton threw a fit, got a fever, emergency at work. She starts naming off all the excuses she can think of, feeling better having a backup plan.

CHAPTER

Why Must I Always be the Voice of Reason?

"Hello?"

"Oh, good Liz, it's Corina. I'm adding you to the call."

"What? What call?"

"Okay, you guys all there?"

"I'm here."

"Still here, but seriously Corina, this is not needed."

"It is too, you asked out a man for God's sake, Mia."

"Hold up! You what?" That's Taryn's shriek.

"Yes, she did, and that's all I know before I added you two."

Okay, even Liz is super intrigued. This is so out of character for Mia. She groans and Liz can feel everyone's excited energy on the line.

"Who did you ask out?" Taryn asks.

"That's the million-dollar question," Corina chuckles. "Hudson."

"What?" Liz asks.

"Oh, my God, you're lying," Corina flat out says.

"Yummy, yes please," Taryn perks up.

"I ran into him at Ashton's ABA center, and we started talking and it was actually very informative and I'd like to finish the conversation, so I thought why not? So, I invited him to go with Ash and me to McDonald's PlayPlace."

All that can be heard is a loud groan from Taryn and Corina chuckling. This multiple caller thing is difficult to follow, so that could be wrong.

"You did not ask the hottest man alive on a date to McDonald's of all places, with your kid along for your first date. Mia!" Taryn chides her, and Liz can't help but laugh herself.

"What? It's not a date, date."

"Let me pick up Ashton and then you guys can go out," Corina offers.

"No way. No, no, no. I need Ashton there. It's too much pressure otherwise. It's not a real date. Really."

"Okay, which one are you going to? The one on Orange?" Taryn asks. *Oh Lord Mia, don't answer her.* Liz sends her as many silent messages as she can, not to answer that question.

"Yeah..." *Well, now you've done it,* Liz thinks.

"Perfect, Kevin just got home, so I'll be there in five."

"Wait, what? No, you don't need to come."

"I want to."

"Oh, Oh, me too! I forgot to defrost the hamburger anyway, so I'll just take the kids," Corina adds, and Liz can't help but laugh as she shakes her head.

"Why must I always be the voice of reason? You guys are not crashing Mia's date."

"It's not a real date."

"You are not crashing Mia's fake date," Liz rephrases.

"Of course, we aren't. I'm just going for moral support," Taryn replies.

"And I'm going to feed my hungry children," Corina defends.

"And now I'm going to end up being roped into going to keep you guys from doing anything crazy," Liz whines.

Mia groans again, the poor thing. This will teach her to tell them anything ever again.

"You guys, he's going to know I called you and that I'm freaking out."

"Did you tell him that we weren't going to be there?"

"Um no, but I didn't say you were either."

"So we will say it was planned, and that way it doesn't look like you were asking him on a date. Lord help me Mia, but I refuse to let your first date with *that* man to be at a McDonald's. I refuse," Taryn adamantly states.

"You know how much I hate to agree with Taryn, but she's right."

"Okay, so we all have our stories straight, this was a planned play date for the kids, and Mia invited him to come to finish their conversation?" Corina double checks.

"I mean, it works, because we were talking about parenting classes, and you guys right before so…"

273

"Perfect! Okay, see you all there. But don't forget to leave them alone a bit for some one-on-one time," Corina admonishes and poor Mia groans again.

"I'm so not made for this. I can't even ask a man out without backup."

They all hang up and Liz texts Tom that she's taking the boys out. The things she lets these girls talk her into!

Normal is Just a Setting on Your Washer

Mia pulls up to the McDonald's and tries to figure out how to not mess this up. Does she tell him this play date was planned? Hijacked? Act like it's not a big deal? Apologize for the ladies?

Mia is fretting so much she doesn't realize that he is standing next to her window until he knocks on it and she screams.

He looks contrite but then she bursts out in laughter and so does he, as she unlocks the door.

"Sorry, I didn't mean to scare you."

"I am such a spaz tonight, it's not your fault. But I've got to warn you, the girls are going to be here with their kids for a play date."

"Had to call in reinforcements, huh?" He doesn't look at all offended, but she can tell he wants to tease her about it. Mia's not the type of girl to be coy or flirt. She's always been direct. In and out of the courtroom, so she doesn't see any reason to change now.

"I don't know what I'm doing, Hudson. I'm a mess most of the time and too old to try to figure out this dating thing."

He leans against her car door, with that adorable grin.

"Who says we have to figure anything out? I'm not one for labels anyway. I say we get to know each other however you are comfortable and go from there. If you want to do it at a six-year-old's birthday party, or a McDonald's playdate, or a parking lot, it's all the same to me."

"Lord, you really are too good to be true."

"Nah, come, let's get Ashton out before he revolts."

Mia looks in the back seat and sees Ashton slapping his thighs over and over. "Sorry buddy, let's go in and play with your friends."

They walk him in and he runs right for the PlayPlace. Max and Mason are already high up in the equipment. Mia and Hudson make their way to where the ladies are sitting, noticing they are two kids short.

"Where's Jessie and Gavin?" Mia asks Taryn, who just laughs like that was a ridiculous question.

"This place is their perfect hell. Gavin would implode at all the sensory overload, and after Jessie got stuck, and then so did I trying to get her out last year, I banned her from all indoor play equipment."

Mia shakes her head and laughs.

"Ladies, can I grab you all something to eat?" Hudson asks, and Mia swears the other three ladies all swoon right there and then.

"That is so sweet of you, Hudson, but I just ordered a ton of stuff for everyone to share. It'll be up shortly, so help yourself," Taryn says while shooting Mia a wink.

After they all eat, and Mia finally gets Ashton to take a few bites of yogurt after she picked out all the fruit, the ladies slowly disperse to *help* the kids, leaving Mia alone with Hudson.

"I've got to say, you probably have the best friends ever. They are hilarious."

"They are something alright. But I honestly don't know how I would have made it through the last few months without them."

"How long has it been since the divorce?"

"Only a month since it was finalized, but Tyson moved out five months ago."

"I'm sorry about that."

"Meh, I was too, but I've realized that it really is what is best for Ashton and me. And possibly Tyson, too. We were always the same type of person, but when I had Ashton, I changed so much and Tyson didn't. It wasn't anyone's fault, but my son became my world and he wasn't Ty's. I didn't realize how bitter and resentful I became until I was able to look back once I had removed myself from the situation."

"I can't imagine. The idea of marriage has never scared me, but I've never quite been able to picture it either."

"So you've never been married? Have you been close?"

"Honestly, no. I don't know if picky is the right word, but I'm very selective. I'm not the type to just date for fun. If I can't see a future with someone, I don't even bother." Mia's eyebrows go up and he laughs.

"You thought I was a player, huh?"

"Well… yeah, I did, I'm not going to lie."

He laughs and brushes it off. "You aren't the only one. Everyone assumes that. But I need someone who is compassionate. She doesn't have to have my job, but I need someone who can understand it, and that's hard to find. And because I'm a supervisor, I can't date anyone at work, so that limits things a bit."

"Is that why you are on the dating app?"

"No. I'm a really social person, and I moved here about a year ago, so I got it as a way to meet people. But then, it was just something I did out of boredom. I don't really meet up with anyone anymore. I was shocked as hell to see you on it though."

"You can thank the girls for that. They stole my phone one night after I found another woman's panties in my room." Mia can't believe she just blurted that out and drops her head to her hands in embarrassment.

"I love that you are so honest."

"Blame it on the profession. I don't know how to be any other way."

"So are you going to tell me how you stumbled upon your profession? I've got to say, from what I've seen, you are amazing at it." Mia quickly changes the subject, she can see the pride fill him at her single compliment.

"Thank you, that means so much to me. I didn't really stumble upon it at all. I really feel like I was born to do this."

"Do tell?"

"I wasn't actually born here. I was born in Jamaica."

"Really? So that's where the accent is from, it's so faint I couldn't really tell."

"Yeah, it gets much stronger when I'm around family or I go back home to visit."

"So how did you end up here?"

"Both of my parents are from there, but my uncle came to the states when I was about five and started his own business. My father followed him out two years later and then sent for my mother and I a year after that."

"Oh, wow, that must have been hard to live without him for a year."

"I'm sure it was, but island life is so much different from here. Everyone helps everyone out, looks out for each other, it was all relaxed and he visited when he could." He shrugs, like having your father in a whole other country is no big deal.

"Moving out here was pretty hard on me though. Everything was different, the pace was so fast, and I was pretty behind in school, so I was put in resource classes." She loves that he has no shame with sharing that fact. He hasn't lost his smile or his easygoing disposition.

"I met a friend in resource name Jacob. Jacob was on the spectrum and used to get teased all the time."

Mia's heart squeezes just thinking about how hard it must have been for that poor boy. She puts her son in his place and can't help but feel compassion for this boy she's never even met.

"I actually could relate to Jacob, not because of the spectrum thing, but I was teased something awful too."

"What? I just can't picture that all."

"My father was born and raised in Jamaica, but his great grandfather was one of the German settlers that came over. So my father is blond-haired, blue-eyed with a Jamaican accent." He smiles wide at the thought of his dad.

"It actually trips out a lot of people when they meet him. In Jamaica, nobody batted an eye. But once I got here, I was the weird mixed kid. I have dark skin, light eyes, dreads, and a laid back chill attitude. I was teased as a child and called a stoner when I got older. The only constant I had was Jacob, and I was his. He taught me so much. How to not care about what people think, how to discard certain emotions just to get through the day." He smiles and pulls out his phone to show Mia a picture of his friend.

"He's still my best friend to this day, but he is why I wanted to become a BCBA."

Mia can't help but smile at the picture. A clearly uncomfortable man is practically folding in on himself as Hudson is draped over him with his arms around his shoulders, smiling wide.

"I started using a similar type method to help him get through the day, before ABA was really a thing. Or at least before I knew it was a thing. When I started looking into colleges and programs, I discovered that it was, and it was like my whole life's purpose had been laid out for me."

"You really are something special."

"Nah. We both helped each other. And I probably get more from these kiddos than they ever could from me."

"I can imagine that must be hard to find someone to date who is as accepting of people."

"It's sad, but it really isn't easy. The first girl I ever got serious about told me Jacob made her uncomfortable and I just couldn't fathom how. He kept to himself, he never bothered her. It wasn't until then that I realized that some people just can't see past the norm."

"Lord, isn't that the truth. I'm afraid Tyson is one of those people, too. I used to struggle with that a bit at times. Wanting Ashton to be able to fit in with his peers. But then we met all these guys," Mia points to her amazing friends and their kids, "and we found our new norm."

"My mom used to always say normal is just a setting on your washer."

"I love that! It's so true, too. There's really no such thing. I much rather my kid be himself and happy than normal."

"The first time I ever saw you was when you picked up Max from the center. You had Ashton with you and he was arm flapping pretty hard, from having to go to a new place, I assumed. He was screeching to go home, and Max stopped halfway to the car and started turning his head upside down."

He smiles at the memory and Mia finds herself turning warm from embarrassment. She had no clue he saw her.

"You stopped walking and asked him what he was doing. When you realized he was trying to see the clouds from a different angle, you brought him and Ashton over to a patch of grass off to the side."

Mia lets out a small awkward giggle. She remembers a few weird looks she got from other parents picking up their kids.

"You laid down right on the grass with the two boys. You had on a really fancy white suit," he lets out a small laugh, "and heels that you just kicked off. All three of you laid there looking at the clouds for a while."

He tips her chin up so Mia is no longer looking at the table, but at his smiling face. "You are someone special, Mia. If anything ever comes of this or not, I want you to know that."

And now she's a pile of goo in his hand. But she has to set something right. "Taryn taught me that, how to see the world from the kids' perspectives. How to find joy and blessings in autism. Most people are too busy looking at the negatives, they don't take the time to enjoy the positives. I'm trying to now."

"I love that. You have some very special friends indeed," he says looking over at the group, just as a shriek bursts out from one of the boys.

He looks over at the kids as Mia looks down at her watch.

"It looks like they are ready to meltdown," he points out.

"Yeah, two hours is usually their max, and we are coming up on that time now. But I've really loved getting to know you a bit."

"Same. So am I allowed to have your number now, or do I have to keep stalking you on the dating apps?"

"Oh Lord, I already deleted that thing. Some guy sent me a picture of his… you know…"

Hudson throws his head back and barks out a laugh. "You are certainly refreshing, Mia."

47

You've Got to Fight for Your Rights

"If it wasn't for Wednesday nights ladies, I'm really not sure I'd make it through the week."

"Hear, hear!"

"I know we've talked a bit this week, but it's all been about kids. I say we focus on ourselves tonight. Let's take turns going around and giving an update. Liz, you start."

"You always make me start, but very well. Things are good with me. Great actually. Tom and I have been talking a lot in the last few weeks, and he really wants to make an effort to understand and connect with the boys better."

"Oh Liz, that's amazing!" Taryn's replies, so happy for her friend.

"It really is. He wants to take Marcus on a week-long train trip. I couldn't believe it. He has it all planned out and is so excited."

"Oh my God, Marcus is going to flip, have you told him?" Taryn asks.

"Not yet. I need to make sure we work out all the details first before we tell him."

"Are you taking Mason?"

"I don't know. That was Tom's plan, but I think it would be way too overwhelming for Mason. So we are talking about just the guys going, and me staying with Mase. Or maybe us going half the time, we're not sure yet."

"No way are you missing any part of that trip, Liz. You've got to go. This is once in a lifetime, and as easy as Marcus is, he still has his flip out moments. Will Tom know how to handle those alone?" Corina asks gently.

"Probably not." She looks so sad, that Taryn can't take it. So she nudges Liz's foot with hers.

"Then you go and show him how it's done. I'll take Mase."

"I knew you were going to offer. No Taryn, that's way too much for you."

"It's really not. I already have a house full of craziness, myself included. What's one more?"

"And I can take him when Taryn has hard nights." Mia jumps in with a smile."

"I'm always down for more play dates. You took care of two of my boys while I was dow,n Liz. It's the least I can do. You are going on that trip!"

Liz starts to tear up, so Taryn pulls her in for a tight hug. "Seriously, we are so happy for you."

"Thank you so much, if you guys really mean it, I'll talk to Tom."

"We mean it," they all chant.

"Okay, my turn, my turn," Taryn speaks up. "I know this is an insane idea, and I haven't even run it by Kevin yet, but I want to see what you girls think."

"Do tell," Corina says taking a sip of her wine.

"It actually comes from our conversation on Monday, Corina." Taryn turns to the girls to fill the others in. "Corina was telling me how Max started picking up weird speech phrases and replacing his words with them." She nods.

"Yeah, it was the weirdest thing. He started saying digga, in place of I want. *Digga bathroom, digger outside*, etcetera. So I mentioned it to Taryn."

"Anyway, I told her to bring me her IEP, and I looked over it. It was pretty similar to my kids, so I told her to ask for his speech records."

"I did, and it turns out he hasn't seen the actual speech therapist for three months."

"What? That's insane, why not?" Mia asks surprised.

"Because they just have too many kids on their docket. She was telling me she is the only one in the district at the moment. They are having a huge shortage. So instead they teach the aides, and then they work on the goals."

"Which is illegal," Taryn points out, and Mia nods.

"So I started looking into it, and into my kids IEPs and their speech records. It turns out they are all only getting half of their promised hours."

"Oh Lord, I need to check Ashton's."

"Yeah, you really do. Anyway, this got me thinking about all the parents who don't know any of these rules, or even how to access the things their child needs."

"So, you came up with some type of plan?" Liz guesses.

"Of course, I did. It's insane, but I really think I want to become a parent advocate."

"Oh, my God, you would be amazing at that Taryn." Corina jumps up to give her a hug.

"You really don't think it's crazy?" Taryn pins her look at Liz because she's always the hardest to win over.

"Not at all. I think it's perfect for you. Look at how you took on the school system for Jessie. You would be such a blessing to other parents."

"Okay, I think I'm going to do it. Mia, you're up."

"Not a lot is new with me. I've been talking to Hudson a lot this week."

Taryn fans herself, then mock faints as Mia rolls her eyes and slaps Taryn's shoulder.

"I really like him, you guys. But I'm terrified to get involved with another man. And how can I do that to Ashton? He doesn't understand any type of change, bringing in another man into his life? That might just turn everything upside down."

"It could, but it could also be a good addition for him. Let's be honest, Tyson isn't the best male role model. If you *are* going to have one for him, who better than one who actually understands him, and knows the best way to work with him," Liz points out.

"Yeah, and think of all the free ABA you are going to get," Taryn teases, earning a few laughs and a glare from Liz.

"Well, we are taking it slow and just getting to know each other for now. Corina, I think it's your turn."

"Yeah, way to dodge a bullet. Nothing new for me to report, Taryn pretty much did. We are fighting to get Max his full speech hours. I asked for an IEP meeting and contacted our regional center rep, who is coming to the meeting. She said his hours should be reinstated by the end of the day."

"I just feel bad for all those parents who don't know about it and how to get it back," Taryn says, thinking about the overworked and under-slept parents.

He's Like a Jedi Master

Tyson was a crappy father and proved to be an even worse husband. But when Mia pushes the bitterness aside, and seriously, that's a feat in and of itself. She can see that he is trying to be a better man.

Sometimes it takes losing everything to realize how much you had. As far as Mia knows, he's no longer seeing Tammy and he always looks a little lost when she sees him.

It's been two months since Mia and Hudson started dating and she still hasn't told Tyson. It seems so silly since he was seeing someone while they were married and she's been divorced for almost eight months, but it still feels like she's betraying him.

Mia was going to tell Tyson last week, but then he agreed to attend the behavior classes and she didn't want to risk it. She also threatened bodily harm if any of the girls or their husbands say anything.

Hudson won't say anything because even though they started dating before the class, it would still look weird.

Everyone gets there a little early in order to sign the kids in and get them all settled. They each grab a name tag and Liz saved everyone seats in the front row.

"Awe man, why are we sitting this close?" Michael complains.

"Shh, Liz was nice enough to save these for us," Corina admonishes him.

"Yeah but that means I have to pretend to pay attention."

"Or you could just pay attention," Liz points out.

"What's the fun in that? Why don't the guys sit in the back, and the wives can sit up front?" Tom offers, earning an elbow to the ribs from Taryn.

"How about you stop being sexist for five-seconds, Thomas. I would be in the back with you lot in a second, while Kevin *McNerdy Pants* would be front and center taking notes," Taryn teases.

"Just for that, I won't let you copy them," Kevin jokes back.

Hudson walks up to the front of the room and there is a collective sigh, that is pretty freaking loud coming from the women in the class. Mia can't help but smile and shoot him a smirk.

"Hey wasn't that guy at Max's party?" Tyson whispers.

"Yeah, he is Max's therapist."

"Oh, that's how you heard about this? Makes sense. I thought that was weird since Ash doesn't even go to this center," Tyson remarks, and Mia ignores his comment and listens to the introduction.

"Hello everyone, and thanks so much for taking time out of your schedule to join me. My name is Hudson Allen. I have a masters of science in clinical psychology and applied behavior. Plus, I'm a board certified behavior analyst." The lights all go out, making the room completely black.

"Don't mind the lights. Everyone relax and settle in." His voice drops to almost a seductive tone. Well, Mia thinks so anyway. Most people would just call it a quiet voice.

"For kiddos on the spectrum, it can sometimes be very hard to focus when there is too much going on. There's too many sights and sounds to distract them. We try to minimize as much distraction as we can, to help the learning process. Some ways to do this at home would be to have a designated quiet area, with very little in the space. No toys or bright colors. Maybe have a bean bag, head phones or weight blanket nearby to help calm them in case of sensory overload."

"Uh, are we going to turn the lights on anytime soon?" Michael asks.

"What, you aren't afraid of the dark, are you?" Taryn teases.

"Your wish is my command," Hudson chuckles and all of a sudden the lights flash super bright and lot of white noise is played at much too high a volume.

The lights then start to flicker, and a fan starts to blow loudly. It's instant sensory overload, and everyone is covering their eyes, ears or combination of the two.

"This is what it can feel like for your child when they are overstimulated or tossed into a busy environment, such as a store or school cafeteria."

The fan blows so hard and cold across their skin that it's actually painful, several people start rubbing their arms.

"Do your eyes hurt from the light? How about your ears? Does your skin prickle from the cold?" Everyone nods their head.

"So would you say you are in emotional or physical pain?"

"Physical." Most people yell.

"I don't know, I kinda want to cry," Liz whispers but Hudson hears her and smiles.

"It takes its toll, both mentally and physically and that was only a few minutes."

The lights and sound go back to normal and everyone takes a moment to ground themselves.

"That is just a small view into your child's world. Some of your kiddos are verbal, but can't really express how it feels, so they throw a fit. The nonverbal guys will have meltdowns or engage in self harm, biting, hitting, or maybe hurting others. It's because they don't understand what's happening or why. So why did I just torture you like this?"

"To show us what our kids experience, so we are more aware when they are overstimulated?" One woman speaks up.

291

"Exactly. I want you to remember exactly how you felt, I want you to bring these feelings up every time your child is in an over stimulating area, and I want you to think about what you can do to minimize the horrible sensations."

"Dude, this guy is like a Jedi Master," Kevin whispers to Taryn who giggles.

"Everyone take a five-minute break and catch your breath and we will start our next exercise."

"This guy is insane," Tyson whispers to Mia, whose back snaps to attention while her eyes narrow.

"He's brilliant. There's no way that him describing all of those things would ever have had the same amount of impact."

"Maybe not, but a little heads up would have been nice."

"That's kinda the point though, right?" Kevin points out. It's why we give our kids a five-minute warning for everything. Imagine having that type of reaction every time something changes and having no warning at all. It's jarring to the system."

"You'd think with all those degrees and stuff that he'd take a little more pride in his looks though. He looks like an average bum," Tyson judges.

Corina squeezes Mia's hand, partly in support but mostly a warning to keep her cool.

"If that's what the average bum looks like, I'm going to have to start hanging out under the overpass more often," Taryn pipes up. Kevin rolls his eyes while everyone else laughs.

CHAPTER

Everyone Else Can Suck It

"Come on boys, we are running late, let's go." That's all it takes for Marcus to come flying down the stairs, he hates being late.

"We are actually ten minutes early," Tom whispers with a grin.

"Yes, but by the time I get their butts down here and we find Mason's missing shoe, we will be late," Liz rebuts.

"What missing shoe?"

"There's always a missing shoe." On cue Mase comes walking in holding one shoe. Liz raises an eyebrow and Tom laughs as he goes on the hunt.

Liz isn't as uptight as she used to be. She isn't sure if it's because of the girls, or if it's the parenting classes, but there has been a serious shift in their household. Everyone is much more relaxed and Tom has been trying so hard.

These classes have been a godsend to them. Originally when Mia mentioned them, Liz was quick to dismiss it. But she wanted Tom to go and thought she would go for support, but she's honestly learned just as much as he has.

It helps that Hudson is a fantastic teacher. He teaches through action and not lecture. It helps that he isn't so hard on the eyes either.

They get the boys dropped off and walk into the classroom. Luckily they are the first couple there, because Tom and Liz walk in on Mia getting a little extra credit from the teacher.

Liz clears her throat and they jump apart. Hudson is grinning ear to ear, while Mia is as red as a tomato.

"Teacher's pet," Liz quips as they take their seats. Mia shakes her head in embarrassment as she takes the chair next to Liz.

"That man can talk me into just about anything. I told him no PDA here. What if you had been Tyson?"

"Mia, it's been nine months, he's got to know that you have moved on. You are a catch, there's no way you were going to wait around and pine forever. He made his choices, and now you get to have some guiltless fun. I think it's about time you told Tyson anyway."

She shakes her head and shoots a look over to Hudson. "Hudson asked if I'd be okay if he talked to him first."

"Before you do?"

"He said it's only respectful, and he wants to make his intentions known, not just with me but with Ash."

"Whoa! I didn't realize things have gotten so serious already."

"I mean, they really haven't. I'm crazy about him yeah, but as far as Ashton goes, I won't be introducing any man to him as anything more than a friend until I'm sure it's a lifelong commitment."

"So he hasn't met Ashton as the boyfriend yet?"

"He hasn't officially met Ashton at all and won't until it's forever. I can't do that to Ash, I just can't put him through that again. But I will start having him over for BBQ's, parties, outings and things like that with other people. I want it to be as natural and fluid of a transition as possible."

"And Hudson? How serious do you think he is?" They sneak a glance in his direction and he is fiddling with his computer. It's as if he can feel their eyes on him as he looks up and shoots them a wink.

"I think it's much more than casual for him too, but we've only been dating four months."

"Yeah, but you are both older, so you know what you want. And time doesn't mean much, it's all about connection. Did you know Taryn and Kevin were only dating for three months when they got engaged?"

"No way. Three months?"

"She said they talked about marriage on the second date, she had a ring just shy of three months and they said I do, six months from the day they met."

"I would have never guessed that."

"I'm sure their marriage isn't perfect, none is, but if I had a couple to admire and copy... it's them. So go on your own timeline, what works best for you guys and Ash, and everyone else can suck it."

"Wow Liz, since when did you get so feisty?"

"Since your crazies started wearing off on me."

"Good morning! Oh, secrets? What did I miss?" Taryn asks as she joins them in the front row.

"Liz just said and I quote, *everyone else can suck it,*" Mia says using air quotations. Taryn jumps out of her seat and throws her arms around Liz's shoulders.

"I knew I'd finally wear off on you. And you are so welcome, by the way."

Does That Mean I Get to Bite You?

Taryn is actually really sad that this is going to be the last parent class. The last three months have been so beneficial to her and Kevin. It's helped them to get on the same page as far as parenting goes, so that they can be an even stronger couple.

Taryn looks over at Mia who is blushing, sneaking little glances at Hudson, she wonders if maybe they can work out a deal where he comes and teaches them how to be parents, and they let him continue to date their friend. Taryn thinks that's more than fair.

"Okay guys, since today is the last day, we are going to celebrate with Legos."

"Yes!" Everyone turns to Tom and his very unTom like outburst.

"What? I'm never good at anything in these classes. Legos are so my thing." Liz shakes her head, but she can't hide her smile.

"That's the spirit, Tom!" Hudson walks over and fist bumps him, and no joke, Tom blushes. Dang, even the guys have man crushes on him. Is nobody immune to the man's charms?

"So what we've done is set up eight different tables in the back. Today you are going to be the kids, and the staff and I will be parents."

"Oh yay, does that mean I get to bite you?" Taryn asks before really thinking about how sexual that could sound... especially since she said it to Hudson.

"Taryn." Both her husband and Mia scold her in unison. For once in her life she gets flustered.

"I didn't mean it like that. I meant because some of our kids bite when they are... you know what, forget it." Taryn slumps down and Kevin leans down to whisper.

"I'll let you bite me later if you're good." He nips her earlobe as he says it, and instantly she's feeling better.

"So everyone break up into groups. Spouses at different tables please."

"Does that go for Liz and I, 'cuz she's practically my wife?" Taryn asks as innocently as she can. Liz rolls her eyes massively and Hudson just shakes his head and keeps talking.

"At each spot is a diagram of something you need to build."

"Yes!" Tom whispers and it's Taryn's turn to roll her eyes.

"Everyone has a different thing to build, but you will each only have one color and style of Lego. In order to build your project, you must ask others for colors and shapes."

"That sounds easy enough."

"There's one catch though."

"Of course there is," Michael groans.

"You can't use words. A lot of the kiddos are non-verbal, so I want you to get an idea of how you can politely ask for something, without words. And you can't just take what you want either."

"Can we make sounds?" Taryn asks, thinking of how Gavin communicates. That question earns her a full-blown smile.

"Yes Taryn, you may. And if anyone is feeling particularly dramatic," Taryn swears he focuses on her again, "then you can even have a meltdown if you'd like. The point of this exercise is to teach you how to get your child to interact with others and communicate successfully. As well as show you how they feel when they aren't understood."

"That doesn't even make sense." Of course that comes from Tyson in the back. Mia wonders when he snuck in. "How can someone communicate effectively without using words?"

"Fantastic question, Tyson. That leads me to our tool table. On the table in the corner you will find resources to help you communicate. There are PECS books, in which you cause pictures to communicate your needs. We also have an iPad with speech and picture technology. There are sign language cards, that will teach you how to sign what you want. And, of course, don't forget nonverbal cuesMost of your kids are highly skilled in nonverbal communication, so it might be helpful for you to learn what that looks like if you don't already know."

"This is freaking amazing," Taryn whispers to Kevin who nods back, already looking excited. He's such an overachiever. She can only imagine how hard it might be for Tyson, or maybe even Tom.

"You may begin."

The Key to Understanding is Education

"I was all for this before the non-talking thing. How the hell am I going to be able to do that?" Poor Tom went from elated to terrified.

"Try the sign language cards. Remember we did baby sign with both of the boys? I'm sure it'll come back to you." Liz tries to help. Based on the look he gives her, he doesn't remember the sign.

"Why don't you come to my table Tom. I'm a pro at PECS, I'm sure we can rock this in time," Corina offers, and Liz shoots her a grateful look behind her husband's shoulder.

"I've always been fantastic at nonverbal communication." Corina's husband teases, wagging his eyebrows at her. Corina just laughs and heads for the communication table. When Michael joins her a second later, she looks over her shoulder to make sure she won't be heard.

"Can you sit at Tyson's table? I feel bad for him, most of the guys ignore him."

"Yeah, for a good reason."

"I'm not saying he doesn't deserve it, but he's here isn't he? I'm actually really surprised he's been coming, and I think he could use someone right now."

"You are a saint, my love. Alright babe, I will for you." He kisses her cheek and grabs an iPad on his way to where Tyson is standing.

Corina watches him say something, laugh, and slap Tyson's shoulder as they head to a table in the back.

"Thank you." Mia surprises Corina by coming up behind her.

"Oh, I don't know what you mean," she says with a smile.

"I know it's got to be hard for the guys to include him, but I'm so happy he's been coming here. Any improvement is improvement."

"Have you noticed any improvement between him and Ash?"

"A little, at least he's trying now. He defers to me more times than not, but he's trying."

"That's all you can ask for I guess." Corina looks again to make sure nobody can overhear them.

"Seriously girl, you hit a goldmine with that one." She doesn't dare say his name, but her eyes go straight to Hudson. Mia ducks her head, but Corina doesn't miss her smile.

"I honestly am afraid to get my hopes up. He's got to be too good to be true."

"I honestly don't think so, Mia. Some people are just genuinely good people. He exudes goodness, light and love. Just let yourself be swept away by it."

"I don't think I can help it at this point. Okay, we better get going."

They grab their tools and head to two different tables.

"Okay Tom, let's do this!"

———

It took them about an hour to get through the project, and everyone is absolutely spent by the time Hudson calls a lunch break.

"You guys did fantastic." He's met with a bunch of dirty looks and groans which he just laughs off.

"Hard, isn't it?" Everyone nods in agreement.

"Can you see now why your kids might have meltdowns or throw fits? Isn't it frustrating trying to get across what you want, when people can't understand you after all that hard work?"

They all nod their understanding. The staff purposely didn't understand what they wanted a few times and grown adults with no behavior issues were actually throwing a few fits. Tyson, being one of them.

"So keep this in mind the next time your child is struggling with communication. Make sure you have tools around your house that make communication easily assessable."

"This has been such an amazing past few months and I want to thank each and every one of you for taking the time out of your busy schedules to give up your Saturdays to learn. It is an amazing investment in your child's life that I promise will pay off."

"How about you who gave up your Saturdays and more to teach us when you didn't have to. Thank *you* Hudson," Corina adds and everyone starts to clap and cheer. This is the first time you can actually see a shyness to him.

"Okay, okay, enough of that. It's my pleasure to be here and teach you all. Now, to end the course, I want to bring up a subject that can be sore to some people. Extended family." At that, there are several groans, Corina's included.

"I know, I know. The reason why I wanted to end with this topic is because it tends to be unpopular and one people tend to be very passionate about." Corina scoffs and Michael elbows her softly in the ribs.

"Raise your hand if you have helpful and understanding extended family." Mia looks around and only sees a few hands raised.

"Now raise your hand if your family tries but misses the mark." A few more hands go up, including Michael's.

"How about those family members that just don't get it and tell you instead about everything you are doing wrong." The majority of the people in the room put up their hands. Liz and Michael are the only ones from their group who don't.

"That's what I thought. Now I'm going to be unpopular for a moment, but hear me out."

He hops up on his desk and sits facing them, looking like his usual relaxed self.

"Parents are fixers, as I'm sure you know. And a lot of people in an older generation don't understand anything about autism at all. They see it as a choice to throw fits, not something unavoidable a lot of the time. When people who are used to offering advice don't understand the reasons for these behaviors, the advice doesn't usually work out, does it?" He smiles and they all laugh, thinking about all the unwanted and horrible advice they've gotten over the years.

"Instead of getting mad and shutting those people out for not understanding, the best thing you can do is educate them. It isn't your job to change them, just teach them. Maybe share with them a few of the things you've learned with me."

You can see a lot of skeptical looks, especially from Taryn, who Mia is pretty sure just snorted. Her in-laws are especially harsh. The moment Gavin was diagnosed, they were cut off completely from Kevin's side of the family.

"It might not work, but the key to understanding is education. Having autistic children can be hard and alienating. You need your people around you for support."

"And if your people refuse? If you try and they don't care?" Taryn asks.

Hudson nods and gives her a pointed look, then looks at each of us. "Then you find your people, and surround yourself with the ones who do, and teach them."

She nods back. If anyone from their group was ever on the fence about Hudson, he just passed all of their tests.

I Want You in All My Moments

Mia seriously needs more hours in the day. She finally gets Ashton calmed down enough to do a quick load of laundry and load the dishwasher. She's surprised when there is a knock on the door.

Mia didn't order anything and shouldn't have anyone coming by. That's the main thing living alone has done, it's turned her into a chicken.

There's another knock on the door, and she checks the camera on her phone to see that it's Tyson. *Hmm, that's weird.* She hurries to the door and sure enough, there's her ex husband standing on the stoop looking oddly out of place.

"Sorry to just show up like this, but can I come in?"

"Of course, is everything okay?"

"I just wanted a chat." *A chat? Well, okay then.* Mia opens the door and steps back so he can enter.

"Ashton's in the living room, I just got him calmed down, so maybe we can talk in the kitchen?" she suggests, not wanting to upset Ash again, or throw him off by seeing his dad. Tyson nods and follows her back to the kitchen.

"So, what's up?"

"I just talked to Hudson." *Crap.*

"Oh, um, okay..." *What the heck am I supposed to say to that?*

"I thought we could talk about it? I was pretty surprised when he asked to meet with me. I mean, I'd have to be stupid not to see that he was into you, but it was the fact that apparently the feeling is mutual that shocked me."

Mia can feel the blush creep up her neck. This is so freaking awkward, and the last thing she wants to discuss with her ex.

"My love life is seriously the last thing I feel like discussing with you, but for the sake of Ashton, I will. As long as you can promise to keep things civil."

"Of course I will. I just don't want to be left in the dark, especially if some strange man is going to be spending time with my kids."

Mia narrows her eyes at him. He's already pushing for a fight with just that comment. "First off, he isn't a strange man, and you know that. Second, I have never brought him into this home, or introduced him to Ashton in any way as a part of my life. He knows him as Max's therapist and family friend, that is all."

"He said he wants to be a part of both of your lives."

"Okay."

"Were you even going to tell me?" He's getting more upset and his voice starts to rise, so she shoots him a warning glance as she looks toward the living room.

"Not until there was something to tell. You lost the right to be a part of my personal life, Tyson. I've been as civil as I can for Ashton. You will always be his father, and I'm not trying to replace you in that role," Mia lowers her voice, "but who I choose to fill the other roles in my life is none of your concern." He stares at her a moment, then drops his head.

"I know, I know it's not. I know that I messed up, trust me. It was the biggest mistake of my life, losing you. But I guess a part of me thought you'd… well, I just didn't think you'd move on so fast."

"What, you thought I'd be waiting for you? That I had such little self-esteem that I'd let you screw around, get it out of your system and then take you back whenever you pleased?" It's her voice now that she needs to control.

"I know that sounds selfish but—"

"But nothing. You are selfish Tyson. You've always been a little selfish, and I've always accepted that. But it's time for me to put myself first for once. I'm not trying to hurt you, I'm really not when I say this, but you aren't what's best for me. It took me a while to figure that out."

"And Hudson is?"

"Yes, he is. And more important, he's better for Ashton."

"Better than me?" He glares and Mia holds his stare with her own.

"At the moment... yes, and he isn't even really in his life." Tyson looks totally dumbfounded, as well as offended.

"Do you remember what you were like as a husband? As a father?" When she's only met with silence, she reminds him.

"We saw you when it worked for you, Ty. I did all Ashton's doctor appointments alone. All his IEP and regional center meetings alone. All his back to school nights and parent-teacher conferences. That was all done alone. When I got the news that my mammogram came up abnormal, you weren't there. When I had to go back two times for testing and ultrasound, I went alone."

"You didn't even tell me."

"I tried, but you were never around. How many conversations started with, 'we need to talk'?" He looks ashamed now and won't meet her eyes. "And how many ended with, 'not now Mia, I'm exhausted, we will talk in the morning.'" The look on his face tells her he knows she's right. The shame she sees there means some of those times he was probably with his mistress.

"Morning would come and you'd be out before I got up. So yes, I've placed Hudson in each of those scenarios, and do you know where he'd be? Right next to me. He'd be asking questions at each of those meetings, and calming down Ash at the doctor, and holding my hand when they say I'm cleared of cancer. That's where he'd be."

Mia wipes a lone tear that falls from her eyes and continues on.

"So, is he in my life for good? I don't know. Will he ever be my husband? Maybe. Will he ever be Ashton's father? I guess that's up to *you* and if you decide to step up or not. Because I know for a fact, if you don't, he will. Now I'm tired, and I think it's time for you to go."

Mia walks a blurry-eyed Tyson out, then she put Ashton to bed. She's so physically and mentally drained all she wants to do is cry, or sleep, or both. But she crawls into bed and calls Hudson.

"Hey doll."

"Don't you hey doll, me."

"Uh oh."

"Don't you think a little heads up would have been nice, Hudson?"

"Sorry. I take it you've talked to Tyson and it didn't go over well? He seemed fine when we talked."

"I don't care that you talked to him, I care that you didn't talk to *me* first. Having to deal with Tyson showing up tonight was not my ideal ending to a crazy day."

"He came over there? Did he upset Ashton? You want me to come by?"

"Calm down, we are all fine. I appreciate you caring, but you've got to let me do things in my own time and way."

"I honestly didn't think I'd make things worse. I wanted to come to him man to man, especially since he knows me."

"I'm a grown woman, Hudson, you don't have to ask permission. Especially from my ex."

"Is that what you think I was doing? Asking his permission?"

"Well, wasn't it?"

"Hell no! I asked you for permission to date you, I don't need his. He was the idiot that walked away."

"Then why did you need to talk to him?"

"I wanted him to know that I wasn't a threat, that I want to make this a smooth transition and that I won't try to replace him in Ashton's eyes. But that if *he* chooses not to step up and be there for Ashton, I sure the hell will."

"That's why you met with him?"

"Of course. Mia, as far as I understand, you two are done right?"

"Completely."

"Then the only common denominator left is Ashton. I'm not going to lie, I want to be there for him. Part of me, and this is going to sound bad, but part of me was glad that Tyson was a bad dad. I wanted to step up and be Ashton's hero. I don't want to have to fight for his affection or come in second. Tyson's biggest mistake just so happens to be my greatest blessing."

"Oh, Hudson," Mia sighs, as she melts inside.

"But the other part of me, the son in me, wants his dad to step up for him. I want Ashton to know that he has more than one man who loves and cares for him. I don't want to be his dad, I want to be the man in his life who chooses to love him, who he knows will always be there."

"We've only been dating six months," Mia lamely states.

"And your point?"

"Isn't this moving fast?"

"Is it? I know after six minutes if I want to see someone again. I know after six hours if I could date them or not. I don't need time to know if someone is right for me,

Mia. I understand if you do. And I'm not saying we have to rush anything. But when you know you want someone, you want it to start right now, because you don't know how long forever might be," his voice softens to almost a whisper, "maybe it's fifty years, maybe it's only two. I don't quantify in time. I quantify in moments. And I want you in all of my moments."

And Mia is now a pile of goo on the floor.

I Have a Crazy Idea

It's finally Wednesday, and Taryn's had this crazy idea floating around in her head all week. She's just dying to get it out. The kids are outside with Kev and Emily making s'mores, and she just prays nobody ends up in the burn unit.

Finally, the ladies all show up, and by this time Taryn is a bundle of nerves.

"What's got into you?" Liz questions.

"You are a bit more... well, just more you than usual," Corina adds, causing Liz to laugh.

"Leave her alone."

"Thank you, Mia."

"So, are you going to share what's got you all wound up or what?"

"I have a crazy idea," Taryn announces.

"Oh Lord, help us all! Your ideas are always crazy Taryn. The camping trip was a *stroke of brilliance* according to you. So I'm legit scared. I need some fortification for this, hold on." Liz pours herself a glass of wine and takes a large sip then passes the bottle to the other girls, who are giggling while they follow suit.

"Must you always be such an asshole?" Taryn pointedly asks Liz as Corina chokes on her sip of wine.

"To you? Yes," Liz says as she scratches her nose with her middle finger.

"Are you done?"

"Go on girl, I can't wait to hear this," Mia says.

"It goes hand in hand with my advocacy idea. And after taking those classes with Hudson, it gave me kind of a crazy but amazing idea that I want to run by you all."

"We are all ears," Corina says.

"When I was pregnant with my kids, I had this book called *The Girlfriend's Guide to Pregnancy. The things your doctor won't tell you.* And it was the best pregnancy book I've ever read. And I read a ton of them," Taryn points out.

"But it was all topics that most people don't talk about. Like the embracing things that happen to your body, and emotions nobody wants to admit to having. After our parenting classes, and how much you ladies have helped me by being in this group, I thought," she pauses, nervous about what they will think, "what if we wrote a girlfriend's guide through autism. You know like a self-help book for other parents, written by parents?"

Taryn looks around and the girls are all wide eyed and silent, so she takes advantage and keeps rambling.

"I thought we could all chime in on things that work for us, you know IEPs, doctors visits, alternative medicine, ABA, and tips on how to reach your children where they are at. I also thought Hudson might share a few activities parents can do, like he showed us, that we can add. What do you think?" Again, she gets nothing but crickets. But after a few more moments they all start laughing.

"Oh, no, that bad?" Taryn drops her head in her hands while Liz cackles.

"Oh my God Taryn, only you could actually have a stroke of genius and think it's crazy. I think that's the best idea you ever had!" Liz exclaims.

"Seriously?" Taryn is shocked.

"It's amazing Taryn, and I think we could help a lot of parents. I scoured bookstores and libraries for months after Max was diagnosed, and all the books were so clinical or depressing."

"I'm for sure down to help. I can be the fact checker, and data girl. And I'm sure Hudson will jump at the opportunity to help, too," Mia adds.

"This is so much better of a reaction than I was expecting. And I was thinking, that any money that we make off book sales can go into a getaway fund for us. Like a well deserved mom's vacation. If the book doesn't sell, we go to the beach. If it goes gangbusters, we go to Rome."

"Now you are for sure talking!" Liz holds up her glass of wine and the other follow suit. "To meltdowns and Moscato. We couldn't have one without the other."

"To meltdowns and Moscato," they all echo.

"And to Taryn finally having a good idea." Liz jokingly follows up.

A Bit of Home

"Hello?"

"Hey Liz, it's Mia. What are you guys up to tonight?"

"Not much, just hanging out."

"Would it be alright if Hudson and I came by with Ashton for a bit? We thought we could pick up takeout so you don't have to cook, and there was something we wanted to run by you."

"Uh, sure. You had me at not having to cook. I'll call Tom and make sure he comes straight home."

"Okay, we will see you around six o'clock? I thought I could come straight over from getting Ash."

"Sounds good, I'll see you then."

As soon as Liz gets off the phone with Mia, she calls Tom.

"Hey babe, what's up?"

"Hey, I need you to come straight home today. Can you get off by five-thirty?"

"Uh, yeah, I think so. Why what's going on?"

"The strangest thing just happened. Mia called and asked if she and Hudson could bring dinner over and talk to us."

"Talk to us? You don't think they are getting married, do you?"

"Lord, I don't think so. Plus, wouldn't that be more of a group announcement?"

"How would I know? You don't think we did anything to offend them do you?" Liz thinks about it for a moment, then quickly dismisses it.

"I don't think so. I mean, they are friends with Taryn, so if she hasn't offended them yet, chances are we are good."

"Well, no sense worrying about it now then. I'll be home as soon as I can."

"Okay, see you soon. Love ya."

"Love you, too."

Unsure what they are bringing over, Liz makes spaghetti for the boys, since she knows they'll eat it. She's finishing feeding the boys and doing dishes, right when Tom walks in the door.

"Hey, I'm pretty sure they pulled up right behind me, so I'm gonna grab a quick shower and be right out." He gives her a kiss, then runs off. Sure enough, the doorbell rings just a few seconds later.

"Hi guys, come on in."

Liz gives Mia and Hudson a hug, but Ashton has his headphones on and is screeching, so she just stands back and lets him in.

317

"Hard night?"

"He was fine when I picked him up. I told him we were coming here, but once we pulled up, he started freaking out."

"Gower." He pulls on Mia's dress and says it again. "Gower."

"When we get home Ash."

"I want gower pease."

"That's great using your words to tell us what you want Ashton." Hudson says to him, then he gives Mia a pointed look.

"This is so embarrassing, but do you mind if he takes a shower? Water calms him, and he just asked in a full sentence which we've been working on," Mia says, embarrassed.

"Oh, of course, you don't have to ask. The boys' bathroom is down the hall to the right. He can help himself to any products in there."

"I'm so sorry."

"Do not be sorry, never with us."

"I'm learning." She smiles and runs Ash down the hall.

"Sorry to crash like this," Hudson says.

"No worries at all, it's great to see you guys. How's everything going?"

"It's been great."

"I can see Ashton is already getting used to you, huh?"

"Ash is a great kid. His language has really been coming along too." He beams like a proud papa already. Man, he's so far gone this guy. Liz looks down and sees he's carrying a bunch of food she didn't notice when he came in.

"Let me take those bags for you." She takes the bags and puts them in the kitchen, laughing when she sees the box of blueberry waffles sticking out. Hudson follows her gaze and chuckles.

"It's the darnedest thing. I bought four different brands, all blueberry waffles the other night. Ashton knew exactly which one was the Eggo. Both Mia and I couldn't tell the difference. But he just sniffed them and knew."

Liz can't help but laugh with him. She loves how easy going he is about everything. Nothing seems to bother him. Mia comes back a few minutes later looking a bit flustered.

"Sorry guys, he just needed to calm down a bit," Mia says as she walks into the kitchen. "He's hanging out with Mason."

"They are hanging out?" Liz asks super shocked and Mia laughs.

"Well, Mason is on his iPad while Ashton plays Lego, but they are in the same room."

"Hey, close enough. I'll take it." Tom finally comes out of their room freshly showered and ready for dinner. Liz opens the takeout bag and smiles.

"You got Chinese food?"

"It's your favorite right?" Mia asks, beaming.

"It sure is. Let's go to the dining room and eat."

They all pile their plates high with noodles, rice and veggies, and dig in. Hudson has everyone laughing over stories from work, and his mom's reaction when he told her he has a girlfriend.

"I mean really who says, *a real one* like I have a bunch of fake ones hanging around."

After everyone cleans their plates and Liz stacks up all the dishes taking them to the sink, Mia calls her back over.

"As much as this has been fun, I'm sure you are dying to know why we showed up randomly."

"You guys are welcome over anytime, you know that. Especially if you bring dinner, but yes, we were curious. Is everything alright?"

"Oh, yes, everything is great. Hudson and I were just talking about the trip you were telling the girls about."

"We haven't told Marcus yet," Liz whispers. Mia nods and lowers her voice.

"We had an idea we wanted to run past you."

"Okay."

"I agree with the other girls, I think this would be a great time for some one-on-one time with Marcus, and I honestly don't think Mason will be able to hang."

"I know, it's our worry, too," Liz says, looking over at Tom who nods.

"So I was talking to Hudson about how I would like to take Mason for the week, that way he's not bouncing around from place to place."

"Oh, Mia, I couldn't ask you to do that, you have enough going on."

"You didn't ask, I was going to offer..." She looks over at Hudson.

"But I think I have a better idea," he jumps in, "Mia would have to have Mason stay with her because Ashton would flip staying somewhere else. I'm not sure Mason would do great staying somewhere else either would he?"

Liz looks down at the table, because no, he'd have a meltdown if he was in town and couldn't go home.

"Not at all," Tom speaks up.

"That's what we thought. So I thought, what if I watch him here."

"You?" Both Tom and Liz ask at the same time.

"I know you don't know me that well, but I'm live scanned and cleared. I've worked with kids for ten years, and Mia and Ashton would come over for dinner every night so he has familiar faces."

"Why would you do that?" Liz asks still shocked.

"Honestly, my first reason was to make it easier on Mia. But then the more I started thinking about it, it just made sense. This way Mason doesn't have to leave his home, and it won't disrupt Ashton's life either." He grabs Mia's hand and looks softly at her for a moment before turning back to us.

"It's also a good neutral ground to get to know Ashton a little bit more. I am trying to be respectful of Tyson, and I don't want to confuse Ashton by having a random man at his house all the time."

"Wow, Hudson, that is such a generous offer," Liz says, still shocked he is willing to do this. They've never left their kids with anyone other than family, and even that isn't more than overnight.

"Think about it and discuss it with each other. I don't want you feeling pressured to do anything you aren't comfortable with. My hours are pretty much his school hours. Since I make the schedules, I can make sure I am out by the end of school that week."

"You really wouldn't mind?"

"I really don't. I would prefer to do a few more get togethers before the trip. And maybe have me take Mason to school or pick him up a few times, so we know he is comfortable doing it. But yeah, I'm down."

"We will talk it over, but that would be such a huge help."

"I miss how close my neighbors were when I lived in Jamaica. We were all one big tribe who helped each other out and did everything together. You guys remind me a bit of home."

Tom nudges his wife under the table and nods once when she looks his way, then raises his eyebrows. Liz hates the idea of leaving Mase for that long, but Hudson is like the child whisperer, so it's kind of a no brainer. So she smiles and nods back.

"You are one amazing guy, bro. We would love to take you up on that offer," Tom says as he fist bumps Hudson.

"As long as you promise we can pay you guys back by taking Ashton for a night or two anytime you want a proper date night," Liz follows up.

"Done!" Hudson and Mia are both quick to respond and they all laugh.

My Breakdown Box

Some days are hard, some are horrible, and others are breaking. Today was a breaking kind of day. It started with Gavin waking up in a fit of rage. There's usually a precursor with Gavin's outbursts. Actually, not usually. There is always a precursor, but they don't always know what it is.

Some days, like today, they don't actually know what happened. That's the hardest part for Taryn. Not that he is upset or aggressive, but that for the life of her, she doesn't know why. Did he have a nightmare? Is he in pain? Is he sick? He can't tell her, and she'll never know.

Taryn went to help him get dressed as usual, and he didn't want to. Instead of saying no, he head-butted her and broke her freaking nose.

Taryn is a pretty dramatic person, and maybe this was God's way of teaching her to not be so dramatic. She must have told Kevin at least a thousand times over the years that Gavin had broken her nose.

So when she went running into the bedroom at five o'clock in the morning with blood gushing down her face and two swollen eyes screaming that her nose was broken, her sweet husband turned over and said, "I'm sure you're fine, Taryn."

She calmly walked out of the room, left Gavin in his room to break everything in sight, then went and woke up Jessie. She called an Uber, since she could hardly see, and dropped Jessie off at Liz's house.

After taking one look at her, Liz rushed all the kids to her car and took Taryn straight to the ER.

Kev started blowing up Taryn's phone shortly after, but she ignored it. Liz texted to say she took Jessie to school and that Kevin came by later with Gavin, both of whom were in tears and a total mess.

Six hours later, Taryn was finally discharged from the ER and waiting on another Uber, with a broken nose, which the doctor kindly reset, and a mild concussion.

Kevin is waiting for her at home with the most contrite look she's ever seen on his face. Gavin's passed out on the couch, probably exhausted from all of his exertion.

Kevin goes to open his mouth to speak, but Taryn just raises her hand and walks away. She knows she's being ridiculous. She's a dramatic person, Kev is used to her being overly dramatic, so she shouldn't be mad at him for not believing her. Leaving like she did was extremely childish. She knows all these things, but at the moment, she just really doesn't care.

She walks right into her breakdown box and she lets herself breakdown. She used to hide in the bathroom, the bedroom closet, the laundry room... but the kids always found her.

She had to get creative when she needed five minutes to breakdown. That's all it takes. Just five minutes to shut herself away from the world, have a good cry, then back to business as usual. Kevin knows to give her those five minutes before he comes looking for her.

The breakdown box just so happens to be the tiny little cupboard that stores the ironing board. Since that would require her to iron, or have an ironing board, the cabinet has always remained empty. It's just big enough to hold a few brooms, mop and iron board... or one hysterical mother. Taryn, of course, opted for the latter.

So, this is where she finds herself now. She takes three minutes to sob. She cries for her sweet son, who she knows is trapped beneath all that anger. She sobs for the little boy who must be screaming inside of his head, but can't access the words to explain. And then, because she is feeling selfish, she cries for herself, and for her pain and exhaustion. Lastly, because yes, Taryn is a little vain, she cries for her poor nose that will never look the same again.

Once she gets all the tears out, and is now a snotty mess, she decides to take her phone out and call something who will snap her out of this.

Taryn's go to is Liz, but after showing up like she did this morning, she'd hate to bother her again. Mia is at work, so she dials Corina.

She almost rethinks it and hangs up. Corina has her plate full and then some. But Taryn doesn't really want to be talked out of feeling bad. So maybe that's why she calls her, because if anyone understands just feeling awful sometimes, it's Corina.

"Hey Taryn, what's going on?"

She greets, and Taryn sobs out a quick rendition of this morning's events. "And now I'm in the breakdown box calling you like a hysterical maniac."

"I wish I had a breakdown box, that's so cool. Where is it?" And this is why Taryn called Corina. No judgment, no telling her what she should do next or how her anger is misplaced.

"It's the ironing board cupboard in the laundry room."

"I'm so jealous of you right now. Not of your broken nose or concussion, of course. But I wish I had my own breakdown room. Do you know what I had to do one time?"

Taryn stifles a laugh and realizes that she's not crying anymore. Taryn wipes her nose with the hem of her shirt, *yeah disgusting, but she's crying in a cupboard, she has worse problems.* She listens to Corina tell her about her own breakdown hideaway, making Taryn feel normal for the first time today.

"I live in a crackerjack box of a house, with four kids and a husband, there is zero place to hide. I can't even remember why I was crying now. Could have been a bad day, could have been the day I found out about the cancer. I honestly don't remember the reason. But I'm starting to feel panicked, like the kinda of panic where if you don't get two minutes alone you might stop breathing?"

"Yep, I totally know that kind of panic."

"So, I end up in the garage looking for a place, and I see the car sitting there looking like a safe haven." Taryn laughs, only imagining what she does next. "I think, if I get in the car, the kids can still find me. Then I see the trunk, like a bright beacon, calling out to me."

"You did not get in the trunk," Taryn laughs.

"Not only did I get in the trunk, but I felt so relaxed, that I fell asleep."

"Oh, my! What did the kids do?"

"Freaked out of course. They swore I was abducted by aliens. They called Michael who searched all over the house for me, and was just about to call the cops, when I woke up and called him on my cell from the trunk."

Taryn bursts out laughing, picturing Michael's face when he finds his wife curled up in the trunk.

"Needless to say, I am banned from the trunk now. But between us," she whispers, "that was the best nap I ever had."

"I'm so glad I called you, Corina. Thank you for sharing your story… and my brand of crazy."

"Any time girl. I love you, and I'm here for you anytime."

"Thank you. And if you ever need to borrow my breakdown box, it's all yours."

"I'm so taking you up on that."

Why Couldn't I Just Have a Kid Who Mows Lawns?

Liz feels so bad for Taryn, really she does. Some people just attract problems, kind of like mosquitos. You know how you can have five people go camping, and one person is always covered in a million bites by the end of the night, while the others only have one or two? Well, that's Taryn, but with problems.

Bless her heart, but the poor thing has one catastrophe after the next. Which is why Liz finds Taryn on her doorstep at 9:05 a.m. asking to hire her son.

"Taryn, that's a bit weird don't you think?"

"Why is it weird?"

"Because he's a child."

"Teenage boys mow lawns for money all the time. Why can't I pay him to do some research?"

"Because that's weird, just ask him for help after he's done with his schoolwork and he will help you."

"Nope. He's not helping me Liz, this is a job. A person gets paid for a job, it's only fair."

"Couldn't he just mow your lawn instead?"

"Liz!"

"I have a feeling this one job is going to turn into a months worth of obsession for him. We leave for our train vacation in three months. What if he's spouting off berry facts the entire time?"

"Okay, never mind, I'll do it myself." Taryn hangs her head and turns to leave. Even though Liz knows she's acting, it still makes her feel like crap.

"Fine, you can ask him. But he has to finish his schoolwork first."

"Yes! Thank you, Liz, you are seriously the best. This has got to work, I know it will."

Liz just shakes her head and goes back to her dishes as Taryn talks her child into researching for her. Liz laughs, just thinking of all the crazy things she gets her and now Marcus into.

Apparently last night while they were on a walk, Jessie found a bush with berries on it again. She swiped one and was about it put it in her mouth when Taryn knocked it out of her hand. She had to drag Jessie home kicking and screaming.

This morning, Taryn got the brilliant idea to have Marcus research all the poisonous berries in California so she can teach Jessie what not to eat. Then they are going to take her to the store and show her the berries that are good to eat.

In theory, it's a great idea. Part of Liz loves how hands-on and creative Taryn can be. But the mother of the son who is usually dragged into these creative projects is a bit leery.

Marcus is smart, he actually has a genius IQ level, but it can also be a curse, he can become easily obsessive about things. Like train facts. By giving him this project, Liz knows he's going to obsess on it, and be spouting berry facts for who knows how long after. But it will help Taryn, and it will give Marcus some spending money for their trip, so Liz lets it be.

"Mom, mom! Guess what?" *And it starts.*

"What love?" Liz asks trying to fake some excitement for him.

"Aunt Taryn just hired me."

"She did?"

"Yup! I'm going to be her nature expert."

"Oh, really?"

"Yeah, she's paying me five hundred dollars."

"Taryn!" Liz scolds, while Taryn just shrugs.

"It's going to take weeks to research, and then he's got to go with us all over the city to point out the good and bad bushes and trees." She shrugs again, "that's a lot of work."

"Yup, and being an expert on things means you get paid more than just an average person," Marcus pipes up.

"Schoolwork comes first, son. If I find out that you are looking up anything that isn't on your curriculum before you are done with your work, you won't get paid a single cent." Liz is saying it to him, but her warning is for Taryn.

"Will I have to give back my deposit?" He asks and Liz narrows her eyes at Taryn who laughs.

"Marcus reminded me that professionals always charge a deposit for their services," Taryn smirks, proud to be turning Liz's sweet boy into an evil genius.

"Oh, Lord help me, why couldn't I just have a kid who mows lawns?"

"I much rather not do manual labor. Thank God I'm intelligently superior," Marcus adds as he runs upstairs to finish his work.

"I blame you for part of his social awkwardness you know."

"The kid is fantastic. I will take credit wherever I can for his awesomeness."

"You might think so, but you are weird too. The other kids just tease him Taryn. I want him to try to fit in as much as he can."

"Why fit in when you were born to stand out?"

"You read that on a t-shirt didn't you?"

"It doesn't matter where. The point is, it's true."

Taryn Has Created
a Monster

Corina looks forward to Wednesday every week. It's actually helped her hustle the rest of the week. She sets a goal for herself during her weekend online parties and has Monday and Tuesday to bill and ship out so that she's ready for Wednesday nights.

She's done three Norwex parties this week, and two Pampered Chef parties online. Her goal is to be able to drop one of the jobs so she can help write the book. She's been busting her butt to save up as much as possible. Four kids are expensive.

"Hey Lady, come on in." Taryn greets Corina at the door. Max has already run out back with the rest of the kids, and she joins the ladies at the window as they watch them all play together. Sure, they may not look like typically developing kids when they play, but the joy is still present. They just interact differently.

"I can't believe it's already been a year," Mia states.

"Has it really? That went by so fast," Corina sighs.

"But think of how much has happened, and how much we've accomplished in that short amount of time. This last year has changed my life, ladies," Taryn says as she gets all misty eyed.

"Don't you start turning on the waterworks, or I will too," Liz teases, as she takes tissue from her purse and hands one to Taryn.

"Jessie has come so far. I mean, she still lives for trouble, but I think she's learning to harness her energy a little. And I never thought I'd see the day that Gavin would be around this many kids without totally freaking out."

"It's so true, Max is the same way. And his speech is improving. Every day it seems like he's using more words."

"It's the same for Ashton."

"Is that because of our play group or your new hunky man though?" Corina teases her.

"Stop. Of course, it's the play group... Mia turns red, "and probably has a bit to do with Hudson, too. He's so fantastic with him, it actually makes me feel like the bad parent for once."

"Oh, stop, you are a great parent."

Marcus notices us all standing there watching and comes up with a large grin on his face.

"Ladies, I have a wonderful learning opportunity for your kids." Liz's eyes about bug out of her head, while Taryn grins proudly. "For the low price of one hundred dollars each, I will train your child in the dangers of poisonous berries and other edible harms."

"Marcus Anthony Rayne!" Liz yells, while Taryn bursts into laughter.

"What? This is a very important lesson for kids of all ages, and I'm giving them a huge discount. Aunt Taryn paid me $500, but since I had to do the research for her anyway, I gave them a significant discount."

"Go, right now young man." She points to the yard.

Marcus looks crestfallen and turns to leave, but stops. "How about fifty?"

"Marcus, now!" She then turns her icy glare on Taryn who is bent in half, cackling her head off.

"This is your fault. You are turning my kid into some kind of nature pimp," she accuses. Taryn can hardly catch her breath through the laughter.

"A nature pimp? And people call me dramatic?" Taryn finally gasps out. "He's a young entrepreneur. You won't be mad when he makes his fist million before he's twenty."

"It's not a bad idea Liz. I mean, even fifty is kinda steep, but I wouldn't mind giving him twenty bucks to teach Ashton."

Corina nods, agreeing with Mia.

"It wouldn't be a bad idea for all of my kids to learn. They don't put things in their mouths now, but if we ever go camping or heaven forbid, they get lost in the woods, it'd be a good skill to have."

"See what kind of predicaments you put me in Taryn Leighton?" Liz sighs and rubs the back of her neck.

"He will teach all of the children because it is the right thing to do. You help friends, and part of that is keeping them safe. We are going to have a long discussion on karma tonight."

Liz turns and addresses Taryn, who has finally stopped crying from laughter.

"And no more bribing my kid. I mean it. Not a single dollar or French fry bribe will ever be uttered again, do you hear me?" Taryn starts to open her mouth to defend herself when Liz points her finger right at her best friend.

"If you bribe him one more time, Jessie will get a whole stack of *Denis the Menace* comics. I bet she will get a few nice ideas from those, don't you think?"

"You wouldn't dare." Taryn narrows her eyes.

"Try me."

These two are more entertaining to watch than the kids. Corina nudges Mia, who looks just as amused.

"I'd say it's about time for that wine now, don't you think?" Corina says, ever the peacemaker.

"Awe, man. It was just getting interesting!" Mia protests.

"Exactly. Taryn doesn't need another broken nose. Come on, let's get them downstairs."

Once everyone has had a glass of wine and calmed down, Mia hits her glass with a pen. "I have some news everyone."

They all look over at Mia who is grinning widely.

"You are getting married?"

"You're pregnant?"

"Hudson moved in?" Liz, Taryn and Corina all yell at once. Mia's grin is now replaced with a frown.

"Not even close, but thanks for ruining the mood."

"Then what is it?" Taryn asks.

"I have a client who works for a publishing house."

"Oh, who?"

"You know I can't tell you that Taryn."

"I work on her personal accounts, but I happened to mention Taryn's book idea when I met with her this week. She loved it, and pitched the idea to her boss, who is a big editor."

"Shut up!" Taryn yells.

"Seriously. Anyway, she called me today to say that her boss is willing to have a sit-down meeting with the four of us, to pitch the book idea. That is, if you are serious about writing it."

"Shut up, shut up, shut up!"

Mia looks over at me. "Is that a good shut up or a bad one?"

"Based on her smile, I'd say good. This is amazing, Mia."

"Okay, so wait, are you guys all still on board? I mean I know you thought it was a good idea, but this is actually happening. It is actually happening, right, Mia?"

"If you want it to happen, then yes, it can."

"I mean, of course, I want it to happen," Taryn says looking around, "do you Mia?"

"I mean, I have my hands pretty full, but I'm fine doing the facts and statistics like we discussed. And handling the legal aspect and contracts. Corina?"

"Of course, I'm down. I think this will be amazing. Not to mention, if it allows me to be able to quit one of my jobs, I'm more than down."

As one, they all turn to look at the voice of reason in the group. "Liz?"

She throws her hands up in the air in defeat, and they all shout in triumph.

"Lord knows someone has to reign you all back in. Okay, I'm in. But I have that trip planned in exactly two months. So, we need to have the meeting before then. And I can write now and when I get back, but I need two weeks off for the trip."

"That's totally doable," Taryn says, then looks to Corina.

"It looks like the bulk of the work is going to fall on us, at least for a while. Are you okay with that?"

"Of course, I am. I'm so excited about this guidebook."

They are all practically buzzing. You know that moment of total euphoria, where you can just feel something amazing in the air? Like you are on the cusp of your life changing. That is how all four women feel sitting in the place that started it all.

Girlfriend's Guide through Autism

"Let's shout out what we think it should cover," Taryn says, while Liz grabs a notepad and pen from her purse, thinking to herself, *good thing I'm always prepared.*

"Diagnosis," Corina shouts out.

"Taryn, I think you should write that chapter, since you have such a positive outlook on autism. It doesn't have to be bad news and I think parents would benefit from reading a positive perspective on it," Liz points out.

"Great point," Mia says.

Liz writes it down with Taryn's name next to it. "What else?"

"Early intervention? I can do that one with help from

Hudson. But besides notes here and there, as well as the stats and stuff, I'm probably tapped," Mia says.

"That's totally fine, Mia. That's a ton of work already," Taryn responds.

"After early intervention, I think IEP and navigating the school system would be a good segue," Taryn says, "I'm happy to take those one, too."

Liz writes her name, but then gives her a pointed look. "Don't take on too much now. Make sure you aren't overloading yourself."

"I know, I know. Corina's turn."

"I'm happy to take meds and holistic approaches. I don't know much about medication, but essential oils, chiropractic and diet, have worked great for me," Corina says. Liz writes her name next to the category.

"I can help with the med side of things. We have found a great cocktail that works for Marcus. Mason, we are still trying to perfect."

"Great!" Corina responds as Liz writes her name next to Corina's.

"We have got to have a section on being yourself and not comparing. Like the importance of finding your tribe," Taryn adds. They all look over at Corina who laughs.

"Yeah, I'll take that one, but only if I can use my Pinterest mom story."

"No names mentioned, or school... but yeah, that's fine," Mia adds as their own personal legal counsel.

"I think it'd be a great idea to add our own personal stories and antidotes. We need to keep it light and uplifting. All the self-help books I read when Ash was first diagnosed were so depressing and heavy."

"Agreed. I'd love this to be an encouraging guide-book for parents." Taryn agrees.

"Okay, so we are doing this?" Mia asks, part excited, part skeptical.

"We are doing this," Taryn says with a nod, followed by the rest of them.

"Then, get ready ladies, because we are in for a crazy ride. If this takes off that means book signings, possible television appearances, radio interviews. Are you ready for that?"

"Are we ready for that?" Liz asks the girls. Each of them look a bit worried about those things because they all have hard kids who don't do change.

"Although, it does mean helping other moms and possibly giving them just a small piece of what we have all found this year. That is worth it." Taryn adds.

"That can always be discussed in the meeting, right? They might not even want the book," Liz says, as the voice of reason again.

"Oh, trust me, they are going to want the book. But you are right, everything is negotiable. I say make the meeting Mia," Taryn says. They all nod and smile as they raise their glasses.

"To the *Girlfriend's Guide Through Autism*," Taryn says.

"May it be super successful," adds Corina.

"And help fellow moms everywhere," Liz throws in.

"Dads, too, this is non-gender specific," Mia says with a smirk.

Marcus,
the Drill Sergeant

"Now listen up, because I don't offer a refund for the kids who don't pay attention and end up eating something bad and die. Your parent's paid cold hard cash for you guys to learn this stuff, so make sure you listen." Marcus is walking up and down the line of kids who are all looking elsewhere and fidgeting. But that doesn't deter him one bit.

"I leave on my vacation in two weeks, and I don't have time to reteach you all this stuff, so pay very close attention."

"He might just be the cutest little drill sergeant I've ever seen, Liz," Taryn whispers to her friend who just rolls her eyes at her oldest child.

"The power is obviously going to his head. Cold hard cash? Who talks like that?"

Taryn giggles and grabs Jessie right before she's about to dart into an unknown bush.

"Pay attention, Jessie. You are the reason we are doing this."

They stopped at the store before this, and picked up all the berries, nuts, and beans they needed for the lesson.

Marcus and Liz spent a week, driving all over to find all the poisonous plants. Taryn was afraid if she took her kids, it would be giving Jessie the wrong idea, so Liz offered to do the scouting.

They took the kids to a park, where Marcus has them all lined up on a bench as he begins to demonstrate good verses bad plants and berries.

Max is playing with an ant that is crawling on his hand, and up his arm, as Jessie braids Tacoma's hair. When Gavin runs off to play with a butterfly and Ashton starts to squeal, Marcus throws his hands up in air.

"I did not study and research for weeks just for all of you to ignore me and eat something bad. Do you hear me? I will earn that money for my trip. You. Will. Listen!"

Instantly all the kids' eyes are back on Marcus. Even though three of them are now covering their ears.

"Dang, can he teach us how to do that?" Taryn asks Liz who looks taken back by her own child's authority.

"If you have turned my sweet natured child into a dictator, I will never forgive you, Taryn."

Marcus holds up a clipping of the tree that poisoned Jessie. "Now this is a pokeberry. Jessie, pay attention.

This berry is bad, this berry makes you sick. Say it. This berry bad. Berry makes me sick."

All the kids mimic Marcus like the cutest little parrots.

He opens a container of blueberries that we got earlier and passes one out to each kid. Gavin and Ashton instantly throw theirs, and Max squishes his in his hand. Marcus rolls his eyes and passes out another.

"Now, if you want to eat a berry like this," he holds up the pokeberry, "just eat a blueberry instead."

He pops a blueberry into his mouth and rubs his stomach saying, *"yuuuuuum."* All the moms giggle.

"He's seriously the cutest little drill sergeant I've ever seen," Corina says.

"Again, pokeberry bad, blueberry good." All the kids mimic him again, and Jessie and Mason pop the blueberries into their mouth.

"This one?" Marcus holds up the pokeberry.

"Bad," Jessie screams, "give owie."

"That's right, Jessie. This one is bad, it hurts you."

"This one?" He holds up the blueberry.

"Yum." Jessie says as she grabs a few from his hand, eats them, then gives one to Tacoma.

Taryn notices that Hudson and Kevin must have come at some point and are leaning up against a far tree with Tom. Marcus was so proud of his first paying job, that he made his dad promise to get off work early to watch him work.

Tom has seriously transformed in the last year, probably more than anyone.

Everyone was really hoping that Tyson would. He seemed like he wanted to change, but the closer Hudson and Mia got and the more involved Hudson became with Ashton, the less Tyson did. Now he hardly ever sees Ashton, even their Saturday mornings have fallen to the side.

"Now this one, looks like a green bean, you know what a green bean is?

"Yuck!" Jessie yells.

"Ew." Mason shares her sediment.

"Ugh!" Max makes the noise while scrunching his face.

"Okay, I guess we don't have to go over wisteria then." Marcus moves on.

He grabs another berry off the table and Jessie yells, "cherry! Me, me, me."

"Okay, looks like we need to go over this one. Jessie, this is a bad cherry."

"Cherry, cherry, *cherrrrrrrrrrrrrry.*" She tries to jump and grab at it while he holds it up in the air.

"Jessie, listen. This bad cherry. Say it."

"Bad cherry," she says with a frown.

"See how the colors are a little different. Brighter red, and more yellow?" He picks up a regular cherry to show her the differences.

"This is a good cherry. It's dark red, and all the same size."

You can eat the good cherry, but the wild ones are very, very bad. Say it."

"Very, very bad." All the kids say.

"I might have to hire him as my new assistant," Hudson whispers as he sneaks up behind the ladies.

"Nope, nuh uh. No more *jobs.* Taryn has already made him a greedy little goblin. He can volunteer at the center if you really want," Liz whispers back.

"He is really amazing, Liz," Hudson says again, watching him with awe. Liz stands a little taller, full of pride.

"He is taking this extremely seriously," she replies.

After he taught them all about nightshade, dogwood, and holly, he ends the afternoon with the buckeye nut, which then instigated a walnut war... and Liz called an end to the lesson.

"Okay kids, everyone make sure you thank Marcus for teaching you the good and bad foods," Taryn instructs.

"Thank you, Marcus."

"Fank og Marca."

"Phanx."

"Ank oooo."

All the parents smile proudly at the different thanks, and each grab their child to take back home. Kevin grabs Gavin while Taryn holds her hand out to Jessie.

"So, what did you learn tonight, Jessie?"

"Walnut taste yucky."

"The buckeye is yucky, walnuts are good."

"Walnut taste yucky."

"Well, what about the other things?"

"Cherry squirt." Just as she announces this, she squirts cherry juice directly into her mother's eye, then runs off with her dog to the van.

"That looks like a pretty painful waste of five hundred dollars," Liz quips as she tosses Taryn a wink while she saunters, yes, she actually saunters, all the way back to her car.

Why is Taryn friends with this woman again?

Leaving on a Midnight Train

Liz will never make fun of Taryn again. *Okay, that's so not true.* She'll just never make fun of her overreacting about leaving her kids again.

They just left Mason with Hudson and Mia. Liz's heart feels like they ran it over on their way out.

"He will be fine Liz, take a deep breath," Tom instructs, as she frantically tries to swallow down her tears, reminding herself that this will be worth it.

"You bought him five new sets of Legos and left him with the best behavior director, or whatever the heck he is, in the state." Liz smiles at Tom's attempt to calm her down.

"Just think of all the fun we are gonna have, Mom, all those trains!" She smiles at the excitement that pours off Marcus in the back seat.

346

"I know love, we will. Mom's just sad to have to leave Mason behind," Tom says.

"Why? I'm sure not."

Liz rolls her eyes and looks out the window as they make the late trip to the train station. They hoped by starting this late at night, that Marcus would be exhausted and would sleep right through the first day jitters. Unfortunately, that didn't happen.

"I just hate that I couldn't kiss him goodbye."

"You kissed him goodbye before bed, Liz. We all agreed that it was best to pack and leave once he was asleep."

"I know, I know. It just feels like I'm picking one child over the other," she says, wiping her tears with the back of her hand.

"You are, you are picking me. I love being the favorite." Liz cries even harder and Tom shoots Marcus a look.

"Quiet Marcus. Your mother is upset and you are making it worse. Stay quiet until we get to the train or I will turn back around."

That's all it took for Marcus to zip it. No way would he risk that. Liz takes out her phone and texts Taryn, knowing she never sleeps.

LIZ: Did you regret leaving the kids and going away for the weekend?

TARYN: Yes, it was the worst mistake of my life, one that I'm pretty sure scarred my children forever.

LIZ: WHAT?! Are you serious?

"Tom we might need to go back. I think this is a bad idea."

Tom gives her a *you seriously are not pulling this now are you?* kind of look, while Marcus's eyes are as big as saucers and he's shaking his head back and forth.

TARYN: Gotcha! Just kidding, it was the best thing I could have done, for everyone involved. Go on your vacation, spend quality time with Marcus and Tom. We've got Mason covered.

LIZ: I HATE YOU SO MUCH!!!!!!!!!!!!!!!!!! We almost turned around, you big fat jerk face!

TARYN: I love you too!

"Never mind, I'm fine. Let's just get there already." Tom lets out a breath and gives her a dirty look, while Marcus fist pumps in the back seat.

"Now that everyone is calm, I have a surprise for you. Our trip for the California Zepher doesn't leave until tomorrow night."

"What? Then what are we doing leaving now?"

"I planned a few stops along the way." He looks in the review mirror right at Marcus as he says, "we are going to different historic train museums, and working our way to the train port past LA. That's when we will board."

"Yes! Oh, my God, yes! I can't believe we are going to all of them, I should have done research beforehand. Mom, I need to use your phone."

"No. No phones. I made it a surprise because I don't want you going crazy with memorizing facts, I want you to experience it all new and fresh," Tom tells him, giving Marcus a pointed look.

Liz could tell Marcus wanted to argue, because he doesn't do anything without days of research first, but she shakes her head no and mimed zipping her lips. He wanted to go more than he wanted to press his luck, so he did as she told.

Liz, however, will never forget that moment of Tom making surprise plans for his son. Not only did Tom find something Marcus was interested in, but he did the research himself, something else close to his son's heart.

They may have their issues, and she might have felt alone raising the boys on several occasions, but he's trying now and that's all she could ask for.

They visited the Orange Empire Railway Museum, Barstow Harvey House & Rail Depot, San Bernardino History and Railroad Museum, and Los Angeles Live Steamers Railroad Museum, all in one day.

Liz has never seen Marcus more excited about anything in his life. They could have ended the trip there and it would have been well worth it.

But they don't. They board the train and get ready for their grand adventure on the California Zephyr. They end up in the tiniest room known to man, with bunk beds claustrophobically on top of one another, and a little toilet and shower.

That is where Liz falls in love with her boys all over again.

Look, They're Playing

Taryn called the girls this morning to cancel group since Kevin and Gavin both are at home with the flu. Instead of canceling, Corina offered to have it at her house.

The kids have gotten used to their Wednesday night routines anyway, and so have the moms. Liz is still on vacation, but it's nice to see the other girls.

"Corina, girls are here."

"Be right there."

Corina finishes putting the charcuterie platter together and grabs the stack of mini plates as she heads to the living room. Unlike Taryn, they don't have an extra space to hang out in, so she sent all her kids upstairs to watch movies in her room, while Michael bravely watches the others.

"Hey guys." Corina places the platter on the table and Mia compliments her efforts, while Taryn narrows her eyes at Corina.

"Showing me up already are ya?"

"Never. I feed people, it's what I do."

"True story." Michael comes in rubbing his very flat stomach, and they all roll their eyes at him.

"Keep a close eye on those kids," Corina says with a pointed look.

"Especially Jessie!" Taryn yells as he walks away. He gives a thumbs up over his shoulder as he keeps walking up the stairs.

"Are you sure I shouldn't call Emily to come help? That's a lot of kids," Taryn says, biting her lip.

Corina shrugs and passes out wine glasses to everyone. "He said there was no need, he has Mateo and Carissa to help him."

"The poor naïve man." Taryn takes a sip.

"So how have you ladies been?"

"Busy." They both say at once and then laugh. Taryn puts her hand out for Mia to go first.

"I've had a ton of cases lately, and one is currently in trial, so it's been a madhouse. Plus, I've been trying to help with Mason as much as I can while Liz is gone. Poor Hudson though, he's pretty much been on his own."

"But if anyone had to do it, he's the guy," Corina points out and Mia nods.

"Doesn't it make your ovaries ache? Seeing that beautiful, capable man with a child?" Taryn asks as she fans herself. "Mine ache watching him and I never want to have another child ever again," she adds.

"Not fair! Ooh, wait, you can have one for me," Corina teases.

Both ladies laugh very hard at that idea.

"Do you really want another little Jessie running around? Thank God we had Gavin first, otherwise I'd only have ever had the one."

"You joke, but you love her more than life itself," Corina points out.

"And then some. She's one of my greatest achievements, but like any achievement... it's freaking hard work." They all have a good laugh, and then Mia puts her hand up for quiet.

"Do you hear that? What's that noise? Do you guys have a leaky faucet or something?"

Corina strains to listen, and that's when she hears the drip, drip, drip sound. Sure enough, there's water running from somewhere. They all stand up and walk toward the stairs where the sound is coming from.

"Oh, no!" Taryn points to the water that is now running down the stairs, "I'm so sorry."

"We don't know it's Jessie," Corina says, not at all sounding the least bit convincing. Both ladies look back with raised brows.

"Let's at least go find out before we find her guilty," she adds as the three of them race up the stairs, and Corina gasps when they find themselves ankle deep in water.

"Oh Lord!" Mia looks down at her own feet.

"Michael!" Corina screams out to her husband who comes running out of the kid's rooms.

"What? Oh, my God, what happened?"

"That's what I'd like to know."

They follow the water to her bedroom, where it only gets deeper. Corina gasps when she sees the water level has reached the top of her bed frame.

"Geez, what the heck?"

They wade their way to her bathroom where the water is pouring out of the toilet. Two very naughty kids and a very wet dog are sliding back and forth in the water.

Jessie places her feet against the wall and then pushes off, shooting across the bathroom floor.

"*Wheeeeee.* Your turn Max, try it, try it."

Corina's sweet son follows suit, with the biggest smile she's ever seen on his face.

"Awe, they are playing together," Taryn says.

Michael shoots her the dirtiest, *you've got to be kidding me* look, but his wife can't help but smile at how cute they look playing in filth. *Oh Lord help her, she's gonna have to bath them in bleach.*

If Cancer Can't Take Me Out, Mold Sure Won't

It's honestly one of those situations where you don't know if you should laugh or cry. Taryn went with laugh and Corina looks like she's going to cry. It is her house, after all.

Mia goes into full fix-it mode and straight into action, since the other adults seem too stunned. "Michael, do you have a shop vac?"

"Yeah, in the garage."

"Great, go get it and an extension cord if you have one."

"Taryn, get these kids downstairs and clean them up. You have a downstairs bathtub, right Corina?" She just nods, unable to take her eyes from all the water.

"Corina, why don't you get out of here and go downstairs with Taryn. Call one of those restorative places to see if you can get those big fans out here to dry the floors."

Everyone runs to do Mia's bidding and she reaches behind the toilet to shut off the water valve. When done, she places another quick phone call.

"Hey Mia, group done early?"

"Hudson, there's been a... well, I'm not sure it was an accident, but Corina's house is now flooded. Do you have a shop vac? I know I used to, but I'm not sure if Tyson took it or not."

"Yeah I've got one, I'll bring it right over."

"You are the best, thanks."

She hangs up just as Michael brings up his shop vac and extension cord.

"Thanks. I'll go ahead and do this. Why don't you see if you can find some large towels?"

"Right. Thanks for taking charge Mia, I just can't believe..." He trails off and Mia places a hand on his arm.

"Hey, your house is flooded. You have every right to panic, it's fine. Let's just do what we can before there's damage."

At that thought he jumps and runs to get the towels. Mia starts the shop vac around the most important areas like the floorboards, trying to soak up as much moisture as she can.

Mia has dumped the shop vac twice before Hudson finally arrives with another one.

"Thank God you're here. Can you take the other half of the room? God, I'm so sorry to do this to you after work."

"No problem mon." He says it with a full-blown accent, and she can't help but smile. It's the first time he actually sounds fully Jamaican.

Taryn comes back after they dump several more rounds of water in the tub.

"Kids are all clean. Oh, hi Hudson, thanks for helping. Actually, since it was most likely my kid who did this, why don't we trade spots? I'll help Mia and you can go watch the spirited children."

His mouth turns up at her description.

"I don't want to leave all the heavy lifting for you guys," he says, just as Mia about drops the shop vac she is now lifting.

"Go ahead. I can help now."

Michael comes back in the room, holding something soggy. "Looks like I found the culprit. This is Jasper's little stuffed animal. Looks like he tried to flush it," he says, shaking his head.

"Yes!" Taryn shouts, fist pumping the air like a madwoman. They all look at her like she's crazy, while she just shrugs. "This is the first time in, well ever, that Jessie was not the cause of the craziness."

"Yes, but she was taking advantage of it," Mia points out.

Taryn smiles and shrugs again. "Well, of course she was. That kid is full of mischief. But at least she didn't ruin my friend's house. And just think, it wasn't even one of the kids on the spectrum. It's a good day."

The rest of them groan at that and Hudson puts his hands on her shoulders, walking her out of the room before anything else can come out of her mouth.

Two hours later, Michael and Mia just about get all the water up. Mia's back is screaming, from all the bending over, but she's pleased with the outcome.

"Oh, wow, you guys do fast work." Corina comes back into the room and takes it all in. The pond is now gone.

"We are trying anyway. Any luck on those fans?"

"Actually, yes, but not good luck."

"Uh oh. What happened?"

"Those freaking people want to come and rip up the floors, replace them, and then take out all the drywall in my walls and replace them too. Do you know how much that costs?"

"Isn't that a bit excessive?"

"Yes, it is. And I told them as much. But then they tried scaring me saying that it can cause water damage and start to mold behind the walls."

"Which is true, but we did get to it pretty fast." A thought hits Mia, so she runs over and starts opening all the windows in the room. They are instantly hit with a blast of heat.

"We live close to the desert in California, it's one hundred and nine out there today. Who needs fans?"

"Oh, good point. Dang, it is hot out there." Corina starts fanning herself, and Mia hopes this doesn't send her into another hot flash.

"So, what did you tell them? Are they going to come out?"

"For fifty grand! I told him he was out of his mind. And that if cancer didn't kill me, a little mold sure won't."

357

Mia can't help but laugh. Although she does make a mental note to set up a home inspection visit in a few months to make sure her friend isn't taken out by mold.

What a sad way to go.

What a Difference Three Months Makes

Who would have thought there was a perk to never sleeping. While Taryn's up with her kids at ungodly hours of the night, she writes.

She writes in journals, and notebooks, her laptop. She even takes random notes on her phone. And then when they are in school, Taryn puts all the notes and nonsense together to make a book.

Corina and Taryn have been writing their booties off for the last three months. Liz also has helped out a ton and submitted all of her chapters before she left on her vacation.

Liz's goal was to get a huge chunk of the book done before her trip, so they didn't have to wait on her to finish. She submitted everything as promised.

Corina got the official all clear and is now cancer free. To celebrate the news and to thank her for all her hard work on the book, Taryn bought Corina her very own breakdown box. It's basically just a panic room for a single person that she can put in her garage, but it's better than getting locked in the trunk.

Emily has been a lifesaver the past few months. She has been able to help out more with the kids so Taryn can focus on the book a little more.

The meeting with the publisher was the most nerve-wracking thing she's ever done in her life. Taryn took Mia's advice and bought a power suit, and she was right. Nothing can give you more confidence than a power suit and lacy underwear.

The editor loved their idea, even though the pitch might have been a bit rocky. Taryn's a talker, especially when she's nervous. But they loved the concept, and the finished pages even more.

The first draft is due in three months, and they are right on schedule. The ladies didn't realize how badly they all needed this. Something that was theirs and wasn't all about the kids. The beauty of it is, without their kids, none of this would have been possible. But this is something just for the moms.

Surprisingly, the husbands were all on board with it. Kevin might have had to talk the others into it a bit, once they realized how much more responsibility they'd have to take on. But they started having guys' nights once a week at Kevin and Taryn's place, where Emily watches the kids, so that helps.

The women jokingly refer to it as the *beer and bare it nights.* Really, it's just their way of giving the guys a little of what they have found in each other.

Their kids haven't slowed down at all, which has made things interesting. Jessie's latest obsession has been with cutting her own hair. She finds anything sharp she can get her hands on and has taken small chunks out of her hair. It looks horrible, but she's so proud of her creation that Taryn can't say a thing about it. They've even taken to hiding the knives, afraid she might try to saw it off.

Gavin has made leaps and strides in his speech. He is still hard for most people to understand, but Kevin and Taryn can pretty much understand almost everything he says now. The best part about it is that he's gained a confidence along with his ability to express his wants and needs.

The most surprising news of all is Tacoma. After years of complaining that Jessie ruined their therapy dog, Tacoma finally proved his worth about a week ago.

Jessie was walking with her mom to get the mail when she started chasing a squirrel of all things, right into the street. There was a car that was flying around the corner and would have hit her, if Tacoma hadn't pushed her out of the way and taken the hit himself.

Jessie wailed like she was dying, and in a way, a part of her was, seeing her best friend laying broken in the street. Kevin came out and called Emily to come stay with Gavin while the three of them took Tacoma to the vet.

Jessie never left his side for a minute, and they had to physically restrain her when it was time to take him back to surgery, all three of them with tears running down their faces.

He broke his hip and right back leg. The vet said he will probably always have a limp and some arthritis, but he would still be around to create havoc for years to come, just a bit slower maybe.

"Hey Taryn, how's Tacoma?"

"Mia, come on in. He's doing great, but we are sporting matching limps now."

She looks down at Taryn's foot and frowns.

"What on earth did you do?"

"I stepped on one of Jessie's stupid little princess figurines and the crown got imbedded in my foot. I actually needed ten stitches on the bottom of my foot, so it's in a boot with crutches for a while."

"Dang girl, I thought Legos were bad."

"Nope, those are nothing compared to water beads," Corina adds, walking in and catching the tail end of their conversation.

The two ladies look at her like she might be crazy, since those are super soft.

Corina waves off their looks and dives into her story. "I had to pee in the middle of the night one night and walked into the bathroom and swore to god I stepped on a slug. It squished all between my toes, so I screamed to holy hell, waking all four kids and my husband." They laugh and she gets a little embarrassed.

"Turned out it was just some water beads that Max had left over from his bath. But let me tell you, they feel exactly like squished slugs."

"I love you crazy ladies, you know that, right?" Taryn says as Liz walks in with several bottles of wine.

"I'm pretty sure we are the sane ones, but we love you too," she adds.

They just finished the first draft of their guidebook, and Taryn wanted all the ladies to be here when she sent the first draft over to the beta readers. Liz pours the wine and they all raise their glasses.

"To the amazing women who inspired this guidebook," Taryn toasts.

"And to the amazing women who will read it, finding strength and community in its words," Mia adds.

"To mamas in the trenches!" Corina adds, as they all clink glasses and chant, "To warrior moms."

Epilog

Warrior Moms

Mia never would have thought that all of their struggles, battles and personal heartaches, would have gotten them to this point.

She looks around the couch at each of her fellow warrior mamas. Because that's what they are. They fought their own battles, stood by each other, and helped fight each other's as well.

She looks at each of her amazing friends and thinks of all the things they have conquered. Cancer, taking on an entire school board, homeschooling, and a grand adventure.

Not to mention her own life. A failed marriage leaving her hurt and finally letting herself love again. Her eyes automatically shoot over to Hudson in the audience, where she sees only love and admiration shining back at her.

One of Taryn's crazy idea actually turned out to be the best idea of their life. Just a short year later, and here they are, on *Mornings with Moria*. They are here to discuss their new best seller *The Girlfriend's Guide Through Autism*. Mia's had to pinch herself many times throughout this process to make sure this is actually happening.

"So ladies, tell me why you think this book is selling like gangbusters? Is it because self-help books are in an uptrend?"

"I'm not sure about trends, Moria, but I think what makes the book so popular is that it's relatable. We aren't hiding behind theories or degrees, or big words and outdated concepts," Taryn states in her much too blunt manner.

"Not that those types of books aren't valid or super helpful," Liz is quick to add in, causing the audience, as well as host, to chuckle.

"We are just a bunch of moms who have lived your life, experienced your struggles, and who break it down in a way that you can relate to," Mia chimes in.

"Along with quite a bit of humor as well," Moira adds and they all chuckle.

"Our group motto is if you don't laugh, you will cry," Corina says.

"Sometimes you have to find the humor and small blessings in life. When your life is a constant barrage of little battles, it's easy to let yourself get overcome by them. I know I did, before these amazing women came into my life," Mia gestures to her three friends on the couch next to her.

"I felt like I was failing at life. It wasn't until they showed me the beauty in it, that I was able to take control of my power again," She says, dabbing her eyes with a tissue.

"Tell me, does having autistic children change you as a person?" She asks the group, and they all just look at one another.

366

"I think it absolutely does," Taryn finally answers. "I'm going to be straight up honest with you. This isn't clinical or backed up by anything just so you know, but I'm pretty sure autism wears off on people." All three of the friends groan and Liz smacks her head, causing more chuckles from the audience.

"Just hear me out. When your kid is so thrown off by change, you find yourself doing everything you can to avoid it. It actually becomes a fear that manifests itself, because you know if change happens, your kid is gonna flip. You avoid change at all cost, and now I find myself with these tendencies I never had before."

"Oh, my gosh, that's so true," Corina pipes in, "before Max, I never thought about things in a tactile way. But since he is so sensory sensitive with colors and smells, it's how I see everything now. I view people in bright vivid colors or muted tones. My memories now all have scents. Like when I think of my grandma's house, I instantly smell cinnamon."

"That's one of the greatest things I've learned from not just my kids, but from all of our kids, is that autism isn't bad. It doesn't have to be a life sentence. It sometimes has this stigma attached to it that it's this scary thing, but it's not. It can be beautiful, and eye opening." Liz looks over at Taryn for a moment who winks at her.

"Our kids see the world in ways I wish I could. When I experience things through their eyes, I feel like I'm really experiencing life, and not just walking through it," Liz says as she reaches out and squeezes Taryn's hand.

"I love that about you guys, and this book," the host holds up a copy of the book, "and everyone in the audience today is going home with your own signed copy." Cheers are heard all around and the women fight to blink back the tears.

"But before we go, there's one person in the audience who has been changed significantly, not only by this book, but by one of its authors."

The four women all exchange confused looks, trying to figure out what she's talking about when Hudson stands up and starts to walk on the stage.

Mia's heart feels like it literally stopped. Like, she's not even sure she's breathing. Until he smiles that slow grin that takes over her entire body, and it feels like it can beat again.

Hudson walks over to Mia and grabs her left hand. Not saying a word, he drops to one knee. The girls start to shriek and Mia is back to feeling like she can't breathe again.

The man who is never out of words, who always knows the right thing to say, is speechless as tears stream down his face. All he does is raise his eyebrows in question and holds up the ring.

Something about that one small nonverbal communication speaks such high volume to Mia. He asks her in the same way her son asks for things. Without words, but with all heart. So, of course she answers back in the same way, by placing his ring on her finger and kissing him fiercely.

Has anyone ever refused Hudson anything? She's not going to start now.

THE END.

Glossary

Stimming – is short for self-stimulatory behavior and is sometimes also called "stereotypic" behavior in a person with autism. Stimming usually refers to specific behaviors that include hand-flapping, rocking, spinning, or repetition of words and phrases.

Chewies – Is a chew-safe soft silicone designed for the needs of children with sensory processing disorder and autism. Many children with unique sensory needs mouth and chew objects for oral motor input.

ABA – Applied behavior analysis is a scientific discipline concerned with applying techniques based upon the principles of learning to change behavior of social significance.

IEP – The individualized education program is a document that is developed for each public school child in the United States who needs special education. The IEP is created through a team effort, reviewed periodically.

The Spectrum – Also known as **autism spectrum disorder** or **ASD**, is a range of mental disorders of the neurodevelopmental type. It includes autism and Asperger syndrome. Individuals on the spectrum often experience problems with social communication and interaction, and restricted, repetitive patterns of behavior, interests or activities. Symptoms are typically recognized between one and two years of age. Long-term problems may include difficulties in performing daily tasks, creating and keeping relationships, and maintaining a job.

Parent Advocate – Advocacy is taking action to help people say what they want, secure their rights, represent their interests and obtain services they need.

FAPE – The Individuals with Disabilities Education Act (IDEA) guarantees the right to a free and appropriate public education for kids with disabilities. That can include kids with learning and attention issues.

BCBA – Board certified behavior analyst is a graduate-level certification in behavior analysis. Professionals who are certified at the BCBA level are independent practitioners who provide behavior-analytic services.

PECS – Stands for **Picture Exchange Communication System**. It is an alternative communication system developed in 1985 by Andy Bondy and Lori Frost, to help children affected by autism convey their thoughts and needs.

Letter to the Readers

Thank you so much for taking the time to read this book. I've always used humor as a coping mechanism, so I tend to make inappropriate jokes at the worst times. I like to laugh at myself and my crazy life, and I know that my dark humor can sometimes turn people off. I'm sorry if it offended you while reading in anyway. That was certainly not my intention.

This is the first time I've put all of me into a single book. My kids and their crazy antics. Our therapy dog turned instigator. Amazing friendships and heart-breaking hardships. A lot of the stories come from my very own life with enough humor and fiction added in for enjoyment.

I wanted a book that other autism moms could relate to, and something people who know nothing about the spectrum could learn from. But if you are wanting to learn more about autism and services near you, please reach out to your local regional center.

I'm always more than happy to connect with other parents with kids on or off the spectrum, so please feel free to go to my website www.jaciwheeler.com and click on connect.

One of the topics I touch on in the book is ABA. I know ABA isn't for everyone and can be controversial in the autism community (Especially in other countries). It has worked wonders for my son, which is why I wanted to add it, but I know it isn't the only form of therapy out there to help people on the spectrum.

Having my kids has changed my life. They have made me a better mother and a better writer. Looking at the world from their eyes has brought me more joy than I've ever found anywhere else.

I hope you were able to take something positive away from this story. Keep in mind that even though the circumstances and stories are close to my own, it is still very much fiction. Thank you for taking the time to read. Make sure to show love to all people and remember that normal is just the setting on your washing machine.

Much love!

xoxo

*Jaci

Acknowledgments

There are so many people to thank that I'm sure I'll forget a few of you. (But I still love you all to the moon and back.)

Starting with my amazing husband who is in the trenches with me daily. He's never missed a single IEP or doctor appointment, he is right there during meltdowns, and rushes home to help me when I fall off the roof trying to rescue one of my kid's toys. I love you more than words can say, Willis.

To all the amazing warrior mamas in my corner. I have a fabulous group of fellow autism moms who are only a click away. Rebecca, thank you for your amazing insight into support groups. Rebecca is also the brilliant mind behind the title.

Taryn, Kathryn, Bek and Mindy. Thank you for being my tribe. Thank you for always having my back and understanding my crazy life, even though you don't live it yourselves. Thank you for all the talks off the ledge, for the morning coffees when I haven't slept in weeks, and the meals that would miraculously show up on my doorstep. I love and miss you girls more than words can express.

To my beta readers on this book. Carissa, Jodi, Jenn, Liz, Bec and Elizabeth. You are worth more than gold. You guys got this book in the worst of conditions and were able to look past all of that.

I also have the best proofers! Mrs. Q, you have such a great eye, thank you for all your hard work. Cindy, thank you for your sharp eyes...even in the middle of construction.

To my family and friends. Thank you for always being there and understanding our insane life. You've loved and accepted my kids without hesitation and that means the world to us.

Emily, Carissa, Kathryn, Katt, Kaitlyn, Daysi, Kale'a and the Bridges staff, and all the amazing teachers and staff who have worked with my kids. The only people outside of my family crazy enough to take on both of my kids and live to tell the tale. You guys are beyond wonderful. Thank you for loving my babies and seeing so much good in them. You have hearts of pure gold.

To my editor Shannan, thank you for taking this book and me on.

Thank you to my writing tribe: Jodi, Jenny, Tara, Heather, Meg, Amy, Cathi, Bridgette and Katy. You girls help get me through the hard times and keep me focused on the goals ahead. Thank you to Jenny, Tara and Nicole, for being my sprinter buddies for this book. Your encouragement and whip cracking are very appreciated.

Thank you to my street team of amazing ladies. You guys keep me going, and cheer me on unlike no others. Thank you for taking the time to read, love and share my books. It means the world me.

Teshia, you made magic happen with the cover! You took the image directly out of my head and put it on paper.

Lyda, thank you for all your hard work and research you put into PR for this book.

Lastly, to the amazing teachers, therapists, specialists, bus drivers, doctors and dentists that have made my journey as a mother just a little bit easier. Thank you for choosing to give of yourselves when you don't have to. You are a special breed of human, and I will never have enough words to express what you mean to the parents of the kids you bless.

To my mom, thank you for teaching me that people are people. I've never seen disability as a bad thing, and that's all because of you and your love of all people.

Most importantly, thank each and every one of you who read this book. I know it's not your typical fiction book. I'm just a sleep deprived mother who wanted to share her crazy life, hoping that another sleep deprived and emotionally spent mother might read it and feel heard. Thank you for taking the ride with me.

Made in the USA
Coppell, TX
02 December 2020

42775019R00213